EDITORIAL REVIEW

Dragoria: The Lost Dragon Realm
Book Two

DRAGON HEART

"As Samara struggles to tell friend from foe, her life with the Sacred Flame coterie grows increasingly dangerous. Readers will eagerly turn the pages to find out who the bad guys are and whether Samara and her allies can save the dragons." Susie D., Line Editor, Red Adept Editing

DRAGON HEART

DRAGORIA: THE LOST DRAGON REALM

KATRINA COPE

COSY BURROW BOOKS

DRAGORIA: THE LOST DRAGON REALM BOOKS

DRAGON MOON

Dragon Moon

Dragon Heart

Dragon Breeze

Dragon Heart

Ebook first published in USA in June 2023 by Cosy Burrow
Books

Ebook first published in Great Britain in June 2023 by Cosy
Burrow Books

www.katrinacopebooks.com

Published by Cosy Burrow Books
All rights reserved

Paperback ISBN: 978-0645510263

❊ Created with Vellum

Michael ~ your support means the world to me

BLURB

Weeding out your enemies from your friends can be dangerous.

After Samara makes a shocking discovery, something must be done. She can't leave the coterie, or her family will again face poverty. If she stays, she must discover who is committing these horrendous acts.

Two senior commanders who patrol the borders of the human and elven kingdoms visit. The young apprentices soon discover that these two aren't as friendly as their instructors. They employ all kinds of sadistic mind games and revel in inflicting pain. In the trials the apprentices face, lives are lost, and many more are on the line.

Friendship is found in the most unexpected places, and secrets of the coven are uncovered, creating danger for those involved—especially Samara, as she works to save Ulrieg's cousin, a special elf, and the dragons.

CHAPTER ONE

Early-morning light streamed through the windows edging one side of the stone room, casting thick shadows on the ceiling from the wooden rafters. Every part of Samara's body shook. No matter how much she tried, she couldn't calm her nerves. Not only had they discovered a great secret of the Sacred Flame coterie, but when they had gotten up that morning, Callista's magic had called the apprentices to the meeting hall. The head sorceress's early return was a surprise. She had also brought two intimidating men with her. Their brightly colored hair marked them as members of the Sacred Flame coterie.

Gray sat on Samara's shoulder. The owl's protests over being forced to stay with her were rare lately. He was closer to becoming trained as a loyal friend, but to be sure, she had spelled him to stay. He had been playing the part of a familiar well and often didn't need Ulrieg's coaxing to stay on her shoulder. To ensure that no one accidentally ran into Ulrieg, he turned invisible and lurked in vacant spaces or hung from the rafters.

The apprentices sat in rows, while Devi, Zofia, Artemise, and Eliphas stood against the walls, their familiars close by. All eyes turned to Callista and the two strange men standing at the front.

Trying to conceal her trembling, Samara sat at the back of the room next to Rehan, one of the younger apprentices. He was only three years younger than Samara, although his thin frame hadn't filled out, making him look much younger. His orange hair had grown straggly, covering his rounded ears and hanging over his green eyes.

Samara whispered, "Who are they?"

He shrugged. "I don't know. They were here when we arrived." When he looked at Samara's pretend familiar, he smiled broadly and pushed the strands of hair out of his face, exposing more of his pale, freckly skin. "I hope I get a familiar like yours. That would be a dream come true."

Samara gave him a small smile and wondered if he would feel the same way when he found out her real familiar was a dragon.

Her legs crossed and covered with her long leaf-patterned gown, Callista sat at the front of the room. The enchanted throne-shaped chair made from intertwined branches framed the sorceress with a display of fresh flowers lining the chair's back. The floral display differed daily. Her lilac hair reached her upper arms and was pulled back at the sides and top, revealing her pointed elven ears. An elegant golden diadem laced across her forehead and dipped toward her nose. Her striking blue eyes scanned the room, only softening when they landed on Mystique, her black jaguar, who was sauntering her way down the aisle to be by Callista's side.

Mist marched past Samara, her crow, Okak, perched on her shoulder. She had been proud to be the first of the current apprentices to receive her familiar. The stocky swordswoman made her way through the small aisle and sat next to Kaine in the front row. Ginger, his fox, was curled up at his feet.

Kaine peered over his shoulder at Samara, a questioning expression on his face. He indicated the seat Mist had just sat in, and guilt washed over Samara. The seat must have been meant for Samara, but in her nervousness and distraction from the discovery made the previous night, she had opted for the closest one to the door. She mouthed, "Sorry."

Samara didn't know if the visitors had come before, much less recently, but they definitely hadn't been publicly announced to the apprentices since Samara had started there.

Kaine turned back to the front and draped his arm around the top of Mist's chair. On the other side, Luna's long golden hair draped over the back of her wooden chair, and Kaine circled his other arm around her shoulders. Samara didn't know if he was trying to make her jealous. Even so, her stomach always stirred every time he showed other females affection. Mist and Luna shifted closer to him, almost pressing against him, making the feeling worse. Samara and Kaine's relationship was new and not yet common knowledge, leading many of the female apprentices to think he was still available.

Peadar, sitting behind Luna, wore a distraught expression on his face as he watched her snuggle closer to Kaine, which made her emotions feel slightly more justified. She wasn't the only one who didn't like Kaine's and Luna's getting too cozy. Though Samara couldn't see her clearly, she was confident that the beautiful elf was wearing a plunging neckline to show off her bountiful breasts.

Stop staring at your foxy love interest. He's honestly not that special. He's alluring because he's the bad boy you wouldn't bring home to your parents. If you acted like him around the other males, you'd have as many, if not more, falling all over you, but you've got better character than that. Ulrieg's chiding pulled Samara's attention back into the room. *I don't know why you're worried about his interests when the real threat is standing at the front of the room.*

Samara's eyes narrowed. *Oh, I haven't forgotten about our real threat. Trust me. Besides, Kaine is probably just tormenting me because I didn't sit next to him.*

Huh! Probably. He loves to be the center of attention, that one. I still think that quiet one would be a better love interest. He's loyal and wouldn't play with your heart like Pretty Boy.

At Ulrieg's words, Samara surveyed the room, taking in the students and spotting Paxton at the front, discreetly tucked in the left-hand corner. Jojo sat on his hand, and Paxton's other hand was cupped protectively above him, far enough away so he wouldn't burn the frog's skin.

Samara liked frogs, but she was glad her familiar wasn't one she would have to protect from all the other familiars. Although after what she and Ulrieg discovered the previous night, her familiar could be in danger and also dangerous to her in many ways. She swallowed and focused on the two sorcerers and the head sorceress at the front of the room.

Satisfied that all the apprentices were in the hall,

Callista raised her hands, drawing everyone's attention to her. "As you can see, we have two honored guests. These two sorcerers are the top commanders of the coterie and serve to protect the kingdoms. On my left, we have Vexx Shadowend, the commander and protector of Clialarion, the elven realm, who is based at the Specter Region."

The sorcerer on the left looked to be in his forties. A long dark-brown cloak draped over his tall, thin form, and when he pulled his hood back, it exposed short, spiky hair the color of blood. Surprisingly, since he patrolled the elven border, he was human. The expression in the sorcerer's dark-brown eyes was chilling as he surveyed the room. Something shifted under the sorcerer's cloak at the neck, and the thin, pointy head of a yellow snake slid out and circled Vexx's shoulders, showing off its muscular body.

Now, there's a slithery creature if I've ever seen one. No surprise there.

Out of habit, Samara was tempted to chastise Ulrieg for being negative and critical, but after what they'd seen, he could be right. Eyeing the three-foot yellow snake, she cringed. She didn't like snakes.

Callista continued, "On my other side is Kellam Mallor, the commander and protector of Slosiaran, the human realm, who is based in the Nebula Yonder."

Pointy elven ears poked out of his deep-orange hair when he pulled back the hood of his cloak. He looked young, but being an elf, he was probably at least a hundred summers or older. With a face set in disapproval, he didn't appear approachable, even less so when a monkey baring his long fangs circled the front of his long brown cloak. The monkey stood on his hind paws and was approximately two feet tall. He scratched his long golden fur then sat next to his sorcerer.

That one there is screaming that he wants to kill. Look at the kind of people your so-called incredible sorceress is surrounding herself with.

They don't look friendly, I admit. But that still doesn't make Callista guilty of hurting your cousin. Samara clasped the hem of her tunic, her knuckles turning white. *Maybe the two figures we saw last night were these men.*

Ulrieg answered her with a grunt.

He probably thought she was standing up for Callista again, but she didn't like accusing someone, especially someone who had looked after her family, when they hadn't been proven guilty. If the two sorcerers had come, then any past apprentices could return and harm the dragon. The coterie's building wouldn't be hidden from them, as they were current coterie members.

The sorcerers stood with their hands behind their backs, scowling as they surveyed the students. Samara struggled to keep an open mind. As for keeping her nerves in check, that had failed a long time ago.

Callista clasped her hands in front of her and paced the front of the room between the apprentices and the two strangers. "On my recent trip to the borders, I informed Vexx and Kellam about the coterie's senior apprentices and how they had bonded with their familiars. This piqued their interest, and they insisted on returning with me to meet you." The head sorceress gazed at the two men, and they reinforced her words with nods. "These commanders worked hard to prove their strength and worth for their roles, and they take pride in testing the apprentices who have bonded with their familiars." Her gaze landed on the four older apprentices who'd recently bonded with their familiars then veered to Peadar and Luna.

Confusion washed over Samara until she peered past Kaine, barely catching a glimpse of a furry white snout and the long, pointed ears of a rabbit peering over Luna's shoulder. Then she looked at

Peadar, who was sitting not far behind Luna. Resting at his feet was a raccoon.

Callista's voice pulled her attention back to the front. "It was a lovely surprise to return and find two other students had found their familiars. I'm pleased to announce that Peadar and Luna bonded with their familiars last night, and even though their bond is new, their strength will also be tested with the others'." She adjusted her diadem. "Kanara, Paxton, Samara, Kaine, plus Peadar and Luna, come to the front, and bring your familiars."

CHAPTER TWO

Samara froze. She wasn't ready for the challenge. Not only was she new to the familiar bond, but all evidence pointed to the possibility that her familiar was an enemy to either the entire Sacred Flame coterie or certain members of the elite inner circle. The two commanders' status would indicate strongly that they were members of the inner circle, perhaps even the figures she saw entering the catacombs and persecuting Ulrieg's cousin. She glanced at Gray. He was being the perfect pet, portraying the lie that he was her familiar. However, he was an ordinary animal, and if asked to execute anything a familiar should be able to do, he wouldn't understand or be able to do it. Samara couldn't communicate with him like she could with Ulrieg.

Paxton, Mist, Kaine, Luna, and Peadar moved to the front, their familiars either on them or following them.

What am I going to do, Ulrieg?

Unfortunately, you're going to have to go to the front. If you do anything else, it will make you look suspicious before the sorcerers even start testing.

Samara remained fixed to the spot.

Samara! You have to move! Ulrieg shouted through their bond. *I'll be with you in a moment. We'll work it out as we go along.*

Hesitantly, Samara made her way to the front between Paxton and Kaine. Her boots clicked softly on the stone floor, increasing her nerves. Kaine flashed her a charismatic smile, and she reciprocated with what must look like a grimace. His smile faltered, and his blue eyes flashed from her to Gray in confusion. She ignored it. Like everyone else in the coterie, he didn't know Gray wasn't her familiar.

Luna stood next to Kaine, with Mist on the other side, and Peadar stood beside Paxton.

All eyes turned to the front.

A lump resided in Samara's throat, and she resisted the temptation to swallow repeatedly to get rid of it. Callista's steel-blue eyes followed her, and Samara tried not to let panic show.

Gray beat his wings, clobbering Samara in the

head, and she wondered if her tension was affecting him. But then a heavy weight landed on her back, and something sharp dragged down the skin of her arm and back.

Ulrieg, is that you?

Yes. I figured it would be better if we were together. At least then, I can direct Gray to do as instructed as much as possible.

Do you honestly think this will work? Hearing the tension in her voice sent another jolt of sickness to her stomach, which roiled.

I don't know. Like you, I'm still determining what they have planned.

Something brushed against Samara's leg, and she looked down to find Ginger, Kaine's fox familiar, staring up at her, her nose twitching. Knowing that foxes have an acute sense of smell, her cheeks turned clammy. Apprehensive, she looked toward the front of the room, only to confirm her fear. Mystique sat a couple of feet behind Callista, her yellow eyes fixed on Samara.

Her heart quickened. *Ulrieg, I think Ginger and Mystique can smell you.*

Dragon moon! Ulrieg grumbled. *Stupid meddling animals. Good luck to them in trying to find me.*

I'm not comfortable with that. Samara stopped

wringing her hands, realizing it was gathering attention from the senior sorcerers.

I should shove cloves up their nose.

Ulrieg! That's not nice.

Yeah, well. That's what they get for sticking their noses in places they're not welcome.

Do you have any useful suggestions?

Sure. Tell them Gray ate a lizard or something if Callista or Kaine asks questions.

Do they smell the same as you?

How should I know? Sense of smell isn't my strong suit. They have scales similar to ours, so they may smell like us.

Samara blinked, trying not to let her panic show. To take her mind off being watched, she looked at Gray. The owl had settled again, although something about his stance had Samara thinking that Ulrieg had his talons around his feet.

Boots clicked on the stone floor, bringing her attention back to the front. Kellam paced in front of the older apprentices, scrutinizing each one, his monkey following close behind with a scowl that mimicked his bonded elf's. After passing Mist and Luna, he stopped in front of Kaine, eyeing his rounded human ears. His nose scrunched with what looked like distaste before the sorcerer paced in front of Samara, Paxton, then Peadar. The creases in his nose decreased slightly as he investigated their semipointed ears.

I don't know about you, but to me, it looks like this guy has something against humans.

Samara barely refrained from jumping at the sound of Ulrieg's voice. *I have to agree with you. But he's the one who governs the border of Slosiaran. If he hates humans, that's not good for keeping the peace. It would only cause more disruption.*

Exactly!

Samara glanced at Callista. The sorceress's face was set in her usual unreadable expression. *Maybe Callista doesn't know he hates humans.*

Dragon moon! Honestly! You're going to try to say she's innocent again. This guy clearly wears his hatred.

I'm doing no such thing. It took all of Samara's effort not to cross her arms. *Argh! You know where I stand. Now shush before I do something that'll grab their attention.*

Kellam stopped in front of Paxton, glancing over his body. "Where's your familiar?"

Calmly, Paxton reached into his jerkin, and when he pulled his hand out, Jojo sat on his raised palm. After a nod from Kellam, he placed the frog back in his jerkin. "I often keep him covered for his protection. There are too many predators among the other familiars."

Kellam snorted. "Is that the best familiar you could get?"

Paxton frowned. "What do you mean?"

"Well. What can a frog do? It seems like a useless familiar, if you ask me." Kellam glanced at Vexx, and the other senior sorcerer nodded.

Callista's calm, authoritative voice cut through their mockery. "Sorcerers, control yourselves. Paxton is very knowledgeable and spends a lot of time studying plants in the library. Never underestimate a scholar. They may not have the brawn, but they have other ways they could easily defeat you. A frog is a perfect familiar for him."

Paxton's chin lifted higher as the men halted their taunting, put in their place by the senior sorceress.

Callista stroked the top of Mystique's head. "However, Kellam and Vexx have permission to test your magical strength while they are here. Every time they visit, they will want to see how far you have progressed. One day, they may be in charge of you."

Kellam's sneer grew, and Vexx's was almost as taunting. For men who were supposedly there to keep the peace of the kingdoms, they seemed to revel in making others uncomfortable. The two sorcerers stood side by side in front of the apprentices.

Vexx straightened his back, and his expression hardened. "What challenge do you want to set for these apprentices, Kellam?"

A sneer passed over Kellam's face, and he shifted slightly away from Vexx, his posture betraying his distaste for humans. He looked Kaine up and down, and his monkey bared his fangs. "I think it should be a battle of the fittest."

Vexx stretched his arms in front and cracked his knuckles. "Yes. That's the best way to tell who is the strongest for now."

Mist cleared her throat.

Kellam focused on her, eyeing her muscular arms. "Yes, young elf?"

"What are the rules for this challenge?" She shifted her weight to one leg.

An evil glint came to Kellam's eye. "There is only one rule. Don't kill your fellow apprentices."

"And what kind of combat will be used?" Mist's face filled with enthusiasm, and she stood tall with her feet together.

Vexx moved toward her, the yellow snake slithering over his shoulders. "All kinds. Whatever you're comfortable with."

CHAPTER THREE

As Samara commando crawled, her bow in hand and her quiver on her back, she passed over dried leaves and avoided twigs on the forest floor. The large cloak draped over her like a blanket with a hood. Ulrieg was nowhere to be found, though he was probably up a tree somewhere, invisible, or perhaps he was keeping an eye on Gray, making sure he was safe from the other apprentices and their familiars' attacks.

Something yellow slithered a few yards away, and when she turned, she spotted Vexx's snake familiar winding its way through the leaves in the opposite direction. The sorcerers had told them they wouldn't join them on the field but would send their familiars to watch instead.

The caw of a crow cut through the forest air in

the near distance. Okak sounded wounded. Mist's empathetic scream followed shortly behind, and a thick fog shrouded the forest.

Samara froze, her eyes wide as she scanned the area around her. The hood of her cloak acted like blinkers. *Do you know what happened, Ulrieg?*

Ginger caught him on one of his wings. I think she broke it.

Empathy flooded through Samara, and she worked hard to push it away, reminding herself that she was in a fight to the end. Mist probably wouldn't worry about her or her familiar if she were in the same situation.

Honing her focus, Samara tried to find a clearing through the fog. Boot steps sounded lightly ahead, and she pulled out an arrow and fixed it with an incantation before shooting it into the leg. Lying on her belly was a difficult position to shoot from, but hours of practice had paid off. A wail of pain cut through the fog before Peadar fell to the ground, stunned, with his eyes wide, his machete dropping to his side.

Samara swallowed. She felt terrible for Peadar. However, it was probably for the best. He was so clumsy that it was surprising that he hadn't cut himself with his own weapon. At least one person was out of the competition, but that left Luna, Mist, Kaine, and Paxton.

Scanning the area again, she looked for signs of the others. She hadn't seen any of them since they split.

Peadar's raccoon caught Samara's eye as he checked on his bonded. She charmed another arrow, which nicked the familiar's skin before it sank into the tree behind him. The raccoon fell next to his apprentice, already asleep.

Having the option of charming her weapon instead of severely harming others was a gift Samara would never grow tired of. She hadn't even met the raccoon yet, but she was already working against him.

Quietly, she crawled to a nearby shrub, continually scanning under the fog for any signs of the others. Moving to a sitting position, she pressed her back against the foliage only to jump when something moved behind her. She spun to find the golden snub-nosed monkey that belonged to Kellam. The monkey hissed, and Samara darted away, letting the fog envelop her. The monkey should be neutral in the fight, but she couldn't risk it. It wouldn't be surprising if the sorcerers didn't play fair and sent their familiars to injure the apprentices. When the monkey didn't follow her, she breathed a sigh of relief and continued her search for the others. Mist's fog had utterly changed the game to become more like hide-and-seek.

She edged around the shrubs, the branches rubbing against her bare arms. A noise overhead caught her attention, and she looked up to find Gray moving out of her limited line of sight within the fog to a higher branch. It wasn't his fight, so she hoped he would find a secluded place to rest for the day.

Suddenly, just before he could disappear, a flash of orange cut through the fog and careened toward him, knocking him to the ground. Samara gasped in horror as Gray and the orange flash landed not far from where she was hiding. The creature's head spun, and the pale face of the monkey pointed toward her as he hissed, exposing his large fangs. Samara reeled back and fired an arrow, barely getting out *"Manictium"* before it left her string. The monkey leaped, but it was too late. The arrow hit him in the leg, and he squealed before running in the opposite direction, yanking at his fur.

Samara scooted forward to find Gray's still form.

"I knew I liked you for a reason," someone whispered behind her. "There's nothing more alluring than a female who knows how to use her weapon."

Samara turned to find Kaine squatting behind her, his hood over his head. She sprang to her feet, preparing to defend herself as mixed emotions whirled through her. It didn't seem right to fight fellow apprentices, especially ones who were romantic interests, but the sorcerers had left them no choice.

A sly smile spread across his handsome face, showing off his straight teeth and causing Samara's heart to skip a beat. "Relax. I'm not here to attack you."

Though she should know better, it was as though Kaine's charm was driven by magic. No matter what her head told her, her emotions took over. She frowned, another battle occurring inside her. After all, they were more than friends.

Slowly, Kaine touched her, his fingers trailing the edge of her face. "I was hoping we could work together to find the others. I haven't seen them for quite some time."

Tut, tut. Don't you dare be stupid enough to work with him. He's pulling one over on you. You should be working with Paxton against him.

Samara glanced above, looking for Ulrieg, but was unable to find him because of either the thick fog or his invisibility.

"Looking for your owl?"

Sadness washed over her as she shook her head. She squatted and scooped the still bird off the forest floor. His gray-and-white wings fell limp at his sides. None of the contestants or their familiars were supposed to be killed, but she didn't trust the sorcerers or their familiars.

"Oh. I didn't see Gray. I thought you were just chasing the monkey away." He placed a hand on her arm. "Is he all right?"

Samara held the bird's chest up to her ear. The soft thudding of his heart was a welcome sound. She tucked his wings by his sides, cradling him in her hands. "His heart is beating, so I hope he's only stunned." She searched for a safe place to put him and opted to hide him in the shrubs where she'd hidden before. She balked, concerned for his safety around the familiars with a keen sense of smell. "Ginger won't eat him, will she?"

Kaine paused, his face blank as he communicated with his fox. "All the familiars are supposed to play nice and not permanently hurt the others. I've told her to leave Gray alone."

Nodding, Samara brushed off dried leaves stuck to her cloak and reached out to Ulrieg with her mind. *Do you know where I am?*

Of course I do. I'll watch over Gray as much as I can. I wouldn't trust anything Sweet Talker or his fox says. I'm kicking myself that I didn't see that conniving monkey. This fog made it difficult to protect him.

Samara hooked a loose strand of her pink hair behind her ear, trying to dull the urge to search the trees for him in front of Kaine. *Make sure you look after yourself also.*

You're one to talk. You look like you're about to make a bad decision and hang out with a sly charmer. Though you may think he's on your side, remember that this is a competition. Make sure you remain alert, even with him. You know what they say—keep your friends close and your enemies closer.

"Do you feel any different?" Kaine was studying her, and she wondered if she had been wearing a strange expression while she communicated with Ulrieg.

Samara frowned. "What do you mean?"

Kaine fiddled with his knife holster. "You know, because your familiar is unconscious. They said if they die, we'll grow weaker."

"Oh." Samara's frown deepened. "No. At this point, I can't say I do. Maybe if they're still alive, then the bond is still current, strengthening the magic."

His eyes clouded with thought. "I guess that makes sense."

Samara crept farther through the fog, and Kaine followed, even though she hadn't agreed for him to join her. She was unsure how she felt about him following her. Ulrieg could be correct in what he'd said about not trusting Kaine for the competition. But she wouldn't attack him without being provoked. It might work out better if they worked together.

The sound of sliding metal rang through the air, and Samara turned in time to see Mist only a couple of feet away, swinging her sword. She scooted back, and the sword tip skimmed her chest.

Metal clanged as Kaine blocked the swing with the blades of two of his knives. Mist withdrew her attack, then her hood fell back as she abruptly swung her sword in the opposite direction. Kaine twisted in time to block the attack with one of his knives and swiped at Mist's abdomen with the other. She recoiled then held her sword ready for another attack.

Whistling caught Samara's attention, and she turned to see Luna sneaking up behind Kaine, bo staff swinging. At the same time, Mist's strike swung down at him. Instinctively, Samara pushed her hands forward, firing at Mist with a blast of magic, knocking her backward. Kaine ducked, narrowly missing Luna's strike, and the bo staff skimmed over the top of him. Luna swung the bo staff with expertise, twirling it around her body and blocking any counterattack from Kaine's knives. She hadn't

trained with Kaine and Samara before, and her effi-
ciency was surprising. A little white form, Luna's
rabbit, crept into the view behind her, her nose
twitching.

Samara darted behind a bush as Mist rose to her
feet and marched toward Kaine. He threw a knife at
her, and she narrowly dodged it by leaning to the
side as Ginger darted toward Luna's familiar. The
rabbit hopped away, and when Luna spotted the fox,
she whacked her with her twirling bo staff. The
sound of bones snapping accompanied Ginger flying
to the side. Kaine roared, charging at Luna, only to
receive a cut from Mist's sword across his side.
Blood dampened his cloak as he shot a spell at Mist.
The blast threw her against a tree.

Samara aimed an arrow at Luna, her mind
ticking over the different spell options too slowly.
Right as she thought of one she wanted to use,
Luna's bo staff knocked the bow, and the arrow flew
past Luna and into her rabbit, who was lurking not
far from where Ginger had fallen. With the arrow
protruding from her leg, the rabbit fell to the
ground, her flesh wobbling as though she lacked
bones.

Luna shrieked and came at Samara with force,
her bo staff twirling faster than before.

CHAPTER FOUR

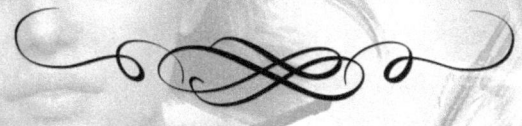

With her bow lying on the ground, Samara struggled to retreat to keep out of the bo staff's reach.

I've got this.

A large stick poked out of the trees above Luna, blocking the bo staff and giving Samara time to throw a spell at her.

Thanks, Ulrieg. Samara grinned at the vacant branch above Luna.

Luna's face turned red and twitched. She let go of the bo staff and scratched under her cloak, the motion becoming more and more frantic. Amused that her spell was working, Samara scooped up her bow and straightened in time to see Mist lunging again at Kaine. He blasted her with another spell, and within moments, Mist was writhing on the

26

ground, her face distorted in pain as she looked to be having a seizure.

That's nasty! Ulrieg's disgust couldn't be misunderstood.

Samara was thinking the same thing, and she frowned, sick to the stomach over the pain that Mist was experiencing. With a flick of the wrist, she whispered, *"Childora,"* calming Mist's anguish in an instant, before knocking her unconscious with another spell. The witch's body slumped, unmoving.

With Mist unconscious, the fog dissipated, giving them a clear view of the area. Samara turned to assess the damage.

Something dark jumped out of a nearby tree and landed on Kaine, knocking him to the ground. His hood fell from his head, exposing his long dark-green low ponytail. Paxton raised his flail and struck Kaine on the arm with its spiked head. With a cry of pain, Kaine thrashed on the ground, twisting and piercing Paxton in the leg with one of his knives. Paxton cried out, and Jojo leaped out of Paxton's jerkin and landed on Kaine's eyes, blocking his vision.

Though Samara shifted to help, she didn't know which one to choose. Both were her friends, and either would be her only opponent if she took down the other. Kaine was the stronger fighter and more challenging for her to defeat physically, but Paxton knew how to use his brain and probably knew some spell or trick she hadn't thought of. Kaine was pulled from under Paxton and thrown against a tree as she remained fixated. An invisible force pinned him, and unopposed, Paxton fell to his backside.

A cloaked figure stomped out of the thicket, his arm outstretched as though clasping Kaine around the throat, knocking his hood from his head and exposing his blue hair. Ginger snarled, and the figure waved a hand, throwing the fox against a tree and knocking her unconscious. The masculine cloaked figure pressed forward with determination and stopped when his hand was wrapped around Kaine's throat.

Paxton scrambled backward, climbing to his feet, his eyes fixed on the newcomer, and Jojo leaped away into the cover of the forest.

Kaine smirked and managed to get words past his constricted throat. "Revered sorcerer."

The figure twisted, exposing his face to Samara. It was Kellam. She had been the one who stilled his monkey familiar, yet he was going after Kaine. Only one explanation made sense. Kellam hated humans, and Kaine was the only pure human in the competition.

"Quit trying to lay on the charm, human. I've

cloaked myself with protection against it," the sorcerer sneered. The veins in his throat bulged. "You may be able to charm the others, but I know better."

Seemingly struggling to remain upbeat, Kaine choked out, "I didn't think you were part of this competition."

"If I choose to be part of this challenge, then I'll be part of this challenge. I've made the rules, and I can change them. Especially when it comes to taking down a human."

Paxton and Samara moved, ready to defend their fellow apprentice, when another shadow shifted from the cover of the shrubs.

"Kellam, don't play with the apprentices. Either finish them or fight them." Vexx stood facing them, his yellow snake slithering out of the leaves on the forest floor.

Paxton shifted farther forward, only to be thrown through the branches by an invisible force. Silence followed, indicating that Paxton was no longer conscious.

As Vexx focused on Samara, something ripped the snake from the forest floor. It hissed as it flew in the opposite direction. Vexx stared after it momentarily, though the confusion plastered over his face disappeared when Samara raised a hand, pretending she was the one who'd sent the snake flying. At the same time, she raised the other hand to strike him with a spell.

Suddenly, Samara's body rose in the air and hovered, her arms limp by her sides, leaving her at the mercy of the senior human sorcerer.

Vexx screamed in pain and lurched forward. The claw marks trailing down his back oozed blood. With Samara released from his spell, she dropped to the ground.

The sorcerer spun, searching for the perpetrator, to find no one. "Where is your owl?" he bellowed. "Is he still functioning?"

Shrugging, Samara sent a spell at the sorcerer, but Vexx dodged it. He quickly retaliated by sending a spell of his own. When Samara sidestepped it, she caught sight of Kaine fighting off Kellam. Kaine threw a knife at his opponent, and Kellam shifted. The blade sliced through his cloak and landed in Vexx's leg.

Vexx roared, *"Petra!"* and used both hands to cast the spell at Kaine.

Simultaneously, Kellam yelled, *"Needleprenora!"* thrusting out his palm.

Kaine dropped to the ground, twitching despite being unconscious, his face distorted in pain.

A branch cracked to Samara's right, and she

turned to find Vexx with his hands raised in her direction. She moved aside and felt the magic barely slide past her.

The sorcerer roared in pain as more scratch marks showed through his sleeve, and blood oozed onto his cloak. Frantically, he searched the trees. "Where's your familiar?"

"*Childora.*" While Vexx was distracted, Samara sent the spell at Kaine, satisfaction washing over her when his body rested and the pain melted from his face. She lunged for her bow then spelled and fired an arrow at Kellam as he still leered over Kaine. The arrow hit the sorcerer in the leg, and he growled in pain before he froze.

A movement caught her eye just in time for her to discover Vexx returning his attention to her. She twisted while grabbing another arrow and aimed it at him, only to have it knocked out of her hands by a magical force he'd sent. With a hand push, she was lifted into the air, her arms pinned to her sides. Suddenly, the sorcerer cried in pain then searched the trees. "Where's your familiar?" he asked again.

As Vexx was looking in one direction, Ulrieg attacked him from the other, leaving more claw marks on his arm.

His eyes wild, the sorcerer screamed, *"Where's your familiar?"*

Samara stared down at him, slightly shaking her head in answer to both the sorcerer and Ulrieg. The sorcerer magically gripped her neck, and she struggled to breathe. Still, she forced the words through her bond. *Leave it, Ulrieg.*

The dragon growled. *What? Are you mad? I'm not leaving you defenseless!*

It's not worth your getting caught. He's not going to harm me permanently. But it would be different for you. I don't want you to end up like your cousin. Fake an owl leaving, and look after yourself. She grunted as the hold around her neck tightened, and she saw stars.

Ulrieg's growl reverberated through their bond right as Vexx threw a blasting spell aimlessly into the branches. A moment later, leaves rustled, as though something had flown through the tops of the forest. Samara was certain that Ulrieg had done as she asked. That meant she was on her own.

CHAPTER FIVE

Samara attempted to reach for her magic. It lingered within, but she was unable to use its power with her hands pinned to her sides.

"Your owl is rather vicious." Vexx pressed forward, still holding her high with force around her throat. He peered at the scratches on his arm. "The claws are larger than I expected."

Samara held her tongue. No matter what Vexx put her through, she wouldn't tell him about Ulrieg.

The sorcerer's vise grip around her throat tightened. "Why is your owl so strong?"

Trying to keep the pride over Ulrieg from her face, Samara shrugged. "I guess I'm just lucky." She hoped the sorcerer wouldn't find the unconscious owl stashed in the shrubs not far from here. That would be hard to explain.

Vexx growled before he threw her against a tree trunk, and all went dark.

SAMARA'S HEAD THROBBED. She fingered the large lump at the back. Something moist coated her fingertips, and when she pulled her hand away, they were smeared with blood. Grimacing, she took in her surroundings. The room's walls were made of stone, making her assume she was back in the coterie's building. A couple of beds with crisp white sheets stood on either side of her, and a bench sat by the far wall, stacked with bowls and medical equipment. The setup looked like the caves underneath the building, except for the extra beds in the room and minus the restraints and torture utensils.

"Ah, you're awake."

Slowly, Samara turned to find Artemise entering the room, her feet in moccasins as she smashed a concoction in a bowl with a pestle. Her tabby cat familiar followed her slowly. "I've just mixed up a paste to put on that wound. You took quite a hit." Though she was short, the elderly human towered over Samara as she lay on the low bed. Her orange hair puffed around her head like an aura. Pointy paws dug into Samara's feet as Tabatha jumped onto the end of her bed. "I was wondering when you would wake."

Samara croaked, "How long have I been here?"

"Overnight."

"*Overnight?* That long?"

The teacher nodded. She helped Samara sit and applied the poultice on her head. Tabatha sat, eyeing Samara.

Samara hadn't been under Artemise's care before and found her astoundingly tender. A behavior completely different to her classes. It made her feel guilty that Ulrieg had stolen her key to get into the cave in the catacombs under the building. Something swung from her neck, and Samara spotted the key dangling from a leather necklace. Ulrieg must've replaced it after their visit. That was surprisingly clever. Pride surged through her, even more than when he had attempted to protect her from Vexx.

"Where's everyone else?" Samara croaked.

Artemise carefully pushed her back against her pillows and passed her a cup of water. "The others weren't as physically injured as you. It looks like you annoyed Vexx a little too much." She took the cup from Samara after she drank. "What did you do?"

Samara shook her head only to have it spin wildly, and she grimaced, placing a palm against her forehead. "Nothing, really. Although he seemed to get angry when I wouldn't tell him where my familiar was."

The teacher raised her eyebrows. "They didn't find your familiar?"

Samara shook her head slightly, avoiding the spinning sensation. "Not as far as I know."

"Then that means you won the challenge. You should have won it, anyway, because you were the last apprentice conscious. But if your familiar was the last one functioning, then you definitely won." Artemise took the bowl from the bench, her long black cloak swaying with her movements. "I'm going to clean these up and organize a meal for you. Then I'll be back to check on you." Tabatha jumped from the bed and followed her human as Artemise shuffled out the door, the pestle clanking against the bowl in time with her footsteps.

With her pillows piled high to keep her upright, Samara leaned back, her thoughts whirling. Gray had been taken out of the challenge by Kellam's monkey familiar, but she didn't know if the owl had been functioning before she passed out. She doubted it. Kaine was the only person who knew he'd been taken out of the competition. Either way, no one knew about Ulrieg, and he was her true familiar. So it was true that her familiar was the last one standing, but the owl wasn't the animal they were thinking of.

I grabbed Gray right after I left you. As though he'd read her thoughts, Ulrieg's voice entered her head.

She looked around.

I'm invisible. You're not going to find me, he said snarkily.

I know that. Samara kept their conversation through their bond. *I was so excited to hear your voice that I looked forward to seeing your grumpy face again.*

You'll see it soon enough but not here. His tone softened. *I took Gray back to your room. He's still unconscious, but I hope you can heal him when you return, if he hasn't already woken up.*

Thank you, Ulrieg. The poor thing had no idea what was going on.

Of course I'd look after him, he snapped. *He's our cover.* His voice softened. *Besides, I'm growing quite fond of the owl. How are you feeling? I didn't want to leave you there alone with the nasty sorcerer, but you're right. I can't get caught, or there's no way to help my cousin.*

I wouldn't want anything to happen to you, either. But if it did, I'd still try to help your cousin, although it'll be easier if you help me. Something touched Samara's leg, and talons scratched the floor, shifting closer to the head of her bed.

It looks like she's healed most of your bruises.

Were they bad? Samara glanced over her bare arms. They were free of all markings. Her tunic was dirty and ruffled but still in reasonably good condition.

He threw you hard against that tree a couple of times. That's how he knocked you out. It was tough to watch. Concern laced the dragon's voice. He was getting better at showing affection. *I'm glad you're all right.*

Her heart warmed.

Whistling echoed through the room, and Ulrieg's talons clicked away from her bed and toward the corner.

A moment later, Forgrac entered the room, carrying a bowl filled with stew and a large hunk of freshly baked bread on a side plate. When he saw she was awake, he smiled, his teeth barely visible between his dark-brown bushy mustache and square-cut beard. He placed the plate on her lap and scratched his large hooked nose. "Ya sure know how to get y'self into trouble, don't ya?"

Samara's mouth watered as she inhaled deeply. The food smelled delicious. She picked up the spoon embedded in the stew and filled it. "I was only doing what I was supposed to do. I think all the apprentices took a bashing." She blew on the stew, watching the overflow drop back into the bowl before putting the spoon in her mouth.

Forgrac's beard twitched, and disbelief washed over his face. "I think ya copped the worst of it, love. You're the only one that ended up 'ere. All the others were treated while sittin' in a chair. Wha' 'appened?"

"Kellam and Vexx joined the competition, and the last few apprentices left in the fight faced their attacks. I didn't think they'd be able to take part."

The dwarf ran a hand through his short brown hair and gazed at the ground. Lowering his voice, he said, "It's not like 'em to play fair. If I was ya, I'd stay as far away from 'em two as possible."

Samara tore off a piece of bread. "What makes you say that?"

"Them's the ones that won't let me pass through the borders to see me family. They won't even let me go be with other dwarfs."

Dunking the piece of bread into the stew's juices, Samara frowned. "Did you tell Callista that?"

Forgrac nodded. "Yep. It made no difference. 'Cept the head sorceress at least said I could earn me way. The two sorcerers didn't care at all."

Images of what she and Ulrieg had encountered the previous night flashed through her mind. She stirred the chunk of bread through the stew and studied the dwarf from the corner of her eye, weighing up her decision. She decided to go with her gut. "What do you think of the strong sorcerers?" She popped the soaked piece of bread into her mouth.

Forgrac scrunched his nose. "I thought 'at would be pretty self-explanatory. Seein' as they won't let me see me family, I don't like them."

Samara asked quietly, "What about Callista? Do you trust her to keep her word and let you go through the borders when you've finished your time here?"

"She should. So far, she's kept every promise she's made me." A deep scowl lowered over the dwarf's brow. "She betta get 'em to let me through. I'm not gettin' paid to work here. I get food an' lodgin's in a simple room. That's it."

Samara lowered her spoon and found it hard to keep her voice quiet. "You're not getting paid anything?"

Forgrac shook his head.

"Dragon moon! Then she treats you as badly as the Vallenses were treating my family."

The dwarf's jaw dropped. "What did you say?"

"I said she treats you as badly as my family was being treated. Like a slave," Samara repeated, wondering if the kitchen work was starting to affect his hearing.

Forgrac raised an eyebrow. "No. The bit before 'at."

Frowning, Samara thought over her words.

You said "dragon moon." Ulrieg's agitated voice cut through her thoughts. *Not a very good way to keep your knowledge of dragons quiet.*

Her cheeks turned clammy, and she cursed herself.

CHAPTER SIX

Gradually, Samara made eye contact with Forgrac. She had no idea how she would explain what she'd said.

Just tell him it was a silly saying used in your village. Ulrieg's voice of reason slightly calmed her nerves.

She opened her mouth to explain, only for Forgrac to place his stubby hand over her mouth.

"By the look on your face, you know you've said something wrong." His hazel eyes turned shifty, and he glanced out the door as if looking for someone before he whispered, "If ya know any dragons or where the realm of Dragoria is, you'd best keep ya mouth shut 'round 'ere." He removed his hand from her mouth.

Keeping her face straight, Samara asked, "What do you mean?"

With an incredulous look, the dwarf replied, "Don't insult me, love. I know ya know more than ya makin' out. An' from what I know about ya, you're not the kind to be biased 'gainst any creature or bein'."

Huh! What do you know? This guy looks like he's on our side. Ulrieg's voice cut through Samara's confusion. *But don't give away anything just yet, in case he's playing you.*

Forgrac rubbed a hand through his bushy beard and lowered his voice further. "I'm not certain, but from what I've seen, especially from them two commanders, if ya a friend of the dragons, ya an enemy of the sorcerers."

Samara frowned and lowered her voice to match his, her eagerness making her words come out with a hiss. "What do you know about dragons? Have you seen any? I haven't heard anything about dragons around here, for or against."

The dwarf pulled back and studied her, many expressions passing over his face. "Ya not playin' me, are ya?"

"No!" She shook her head. "No. Not at all. I'm curious."

He laughed. "Oh, I'm jus' goin' by feelin's. I don't know anythin' as fact."

Balancing her bowl on her lap, Samara held up her hands. "Like I said, I'm just curious. I haven't heard anyone mention dragons around here."

"Yet you're the one that looked guilty after sayin' the word."

"It was how you acted when you asked me about it," she protested. "It's an old saying from my village."

"Uh-huh." He lifted his chin and peered at her with disbelief. "I bet." Slyness filled his eyes as he looked over his shoulder again before turning back to her. "Oh, why not? I got less to lose then ya. So I'll tell ya wha' I know."

Samara's grip on the bowl tightened with anticipation. "I won't tell anyone."

Forgrac lifted his hands in defense. "I'm just going by hearsay."

Hesitantly, Samara said, "All right."

"There's a rumor that this coterie houses the great magician who took down the realm of Dragoria."

Ulrieg coughed, sounding as though he was choking on something. The sound was primarily through their bond, but some noise projected externally and caught Forgrac's attention. He spun to face the door.

Samara laid a hand on him. "I'll let you know if someone is coming."

He wobbled to the door and peered out, checking for anyone approaching. When satisfied that no one was out there, he came back. "Did ya hear that noise?"

"I think it was the wind knocking something over." She reached for him. "Tell me more. What about this Dragoria? What is this place?"

Forgrac frowned. "Haven't ya heard of it?"

She shook her head.

"But you've heard of dragons?"

"Only from the saying my village used. I heard it was a bad cuss word, so that's why I looked guilty when you brought it to my attention."

Ha! Good save.

Samara tried not to let her smugness show from Ulrieg's praise.

Confusion flooded Forgrac's face. Still, he continued, "From the tales, dragons used to be everywhere, governin' the kingdoms an' protectin' them from a great magical evil. A special kind of li'l dragon, called the guardian dragon, bonded with an elf an' created dragon elves. Their bond was more special than ya bond is with ya familiar." As if suddenly remembering, he glanced around the room. "Where is your owl? Is he all right?"

Samara waved a hand dismissively. "Oh, he's fine. He's recovering in my room. I've been told he's sleeping it off."

"Ah. That's good. I got worried when I didn't see him."

"So, how was their bond more special?"

Forgrac sat with his hands clasped between his knees. "From wha' I've been told, when they was together, the little dragons was able to shift into large dragons, and the elves were able to shapeshift into dragons. The magic the elves held also grew in strength when they was together. When they was apart, their magic was a catastrophe."

"What do you mean?"

"Their magic would hardly ever do what it was supposed to, unless they were near the guardian dragons."

Samara frowned. "That sounds rather cumbersome."

Forgrac huffed. "I believe it would be." He shrugged. "I don't 'ave magic, so I wouldn't know for sure. I can only imagine it would be annoyin' and stinkin' impractical."

She ran her hand down her arm. Nearly everything he had told her so far was close to matching what Ulrieg had told her not long after they met. "So you're saying these dragon elves and their dragons protected the kingdoms from the great evil."

Forgrac nodded.

"Were they kind to the kingdoms?"

"Much more than the current leadership."

"Were they fighting against the same evil as Callista and her Sacred Flame coterie members?" Samara rubbed at a small scratch on her forearm.

Forgrac shook his head. "I don't believe so."

Samara's brow pinched. "How do you know so much about this?"

"I worked as an actor in a roamin' stage show. I was on tour when I was separated permanently from me family, and the two sorcerers took over patrollin' the borders. They blocked me access home to me family or even me kind in the other kingdom."

"Vexx and Kellam have been controlling the borders for *one hundred years*?" Samara exclaimed.

He nodded unenthusiastically. "Well, Kellam has, but Vexx is human, so he's fairly new, but he's no betta than the sorcerer before 'im. Believe me. I've tried."

"Have you seen a dragon?" Samara asked. "I thought they were just made-up creatures in stories."

The dwarf's eyes turned wistful. "I did once."

"When?"

I'm keen to hear this story. Ulrieg cut through

Samara's thoughts. He had been so quiet that she had almost forgotten he was there.

"While I was travelin' with me acting crew. We stumbled across three dragons. I think they may've been a small family, as one of them was half the size of the other two and seemed to want to hide behind the bigger ones."

"Were they scary?"

He screwed up his nose. "They looked scary—they 'ad horns all over the place—but they were only about 'alf the size of a human. Though that's pretty big for a dwarf."

That sounds like it was some of my distant relatives.

"I'm sure it is. Did they attack?"

He shook his head. "Far from it. They simply wanted to live their lives. They showed us their extensive teeth, but I think that was only to scare us away, not because they wanted to attack. They've been hunted since Dragoria disappeared. They couldn't go home either. I thought 'at was sad for them. Not long after, I was stuck in the same situation."

Samara had learned most of that from Ulrieg, but Forgrac was confirming his story—not that she doubted her familiar. "So if this is all true and actual history, why are you whispering it?"

Forgrac glanced at the door again. "'Cause I get

the feeling that this coterie is against the dragons, what's left of 'em—especially the two sorcerers controlling the borders of Clialarion and Slossiaran. I don't know if Callista realizes how evil they are. She's a very powerful sorceress, and I think she means well. If so, then she has chosen the wrong commanders. So be very mindful around those two and also Callista, just in case. In fact, don't trust any of the teachers and probably many of the students here."

Sounds like words out of my own mouth.

Samara pursed her lips.

"What?"

"You sound like someone I know."

"Oh."

Before he could continue, Samara asked, "So, are you for the dragons? If they still exist?" She added at the last moment.

He eyed her cautiously, silence filling the room. "Oh, they exist. I 'ope me gut is right over you. Otherwise, ya could get me in a lot of trouble." He screwed up his nose as though in thought then took a deep breath. "Please, don't tell anyone, but I'm for the dragons if there is any left. They haven't been treated well." He held up a stubby finger. "Although if someone finds Dragoria, I believe there will be plenty of dragons. I jus' wish someone was strong enough to not only find the realm but also break the curse cutting it off from the rest of the kingdoms. From what I've heard, the kingdoms were in a much better place when the dragons held the peace." He sighed loudly. "If we had some dragon elves left, the realm would still have a possibility. And from what I've been told, they were the ones protecting the kingdoms before their realm was segregated."

"Do you think there are still some left?"

Forgrac shrugged. "I hope so. Although they've been hunted down also."

Samara gasped. "By whom?"

"Probably Vexx. Maybe even Kellam." He gave her a solemn look. "You were lucky to come out of your encounter fairly unscathed, even if it was only for play."

Someone's coming!

Heeding Ulrieg's words, Samara indicated the door right as footsteps sounded outside.

Forgrac stood away from the bed and grumbled loudly, "Come on. Hurry up and finish your stew. I don't want to make another trip to get ya bowl."

Samara had been so distracted by Forgrac's story that she had forgotten about her food. She spooned some more into her mouth as Artemise charged into the room.

"What are you still doing here?" the teacher barked at the dwarf.

Tabatha pounced onto the end of Samara's bed.

Samara swallowed. "It's my fault. I'm taking too long to eat my stew. She clutched at her neck. I guess it's still a little bruised on the inside. Although the food's delicious."

Artemise grunted. "Good-for-nothing dwarf. At least he can cook."

She nodded enthusiastically. "Very well at that. We're lucky to have him." She spooned the last of the stew into her mouth and passed the bowl to Forgrac.

The dwarf grabbed the bowl and exited the room.

When his footsteps quietened, Artemise said, "The dwarf holds no magic, yet he resides in our sacred coterie building. I don't know what was going on in Callista's head when she let him stay." She pulled Samara forward and checked the back of her head.

"He seems harmless." Samara braced her hands against her knees. "He does a lot of work around here that others don't want to do. At the same time, he's earning his way across the borders to be with his family."

Artemise grunted, her creased face showing her

displeasure. "Who told you that?" She dabbed a cloth on the spot of the injury as Tabatha curled into a ball on the bed.

"Forgrac told me that's the agreement he and Callista came up with."

Artemise directed her back against her pillow. "Is that what he told you?"

Samara met her eyes. "Isn't it true?"

"Hmm." Artemise turned and packed away a few items on the bench. "You're all healed. You can go."

"Really?" Samara asked, absently feeling the back of her head. The lump had vanished. The poultice and magic had done their job.

Artemise turned to face her, bundling the few items in her arms. "You'll be fine as long as you don't overdo it for the next day. As soon as you're ready, you can leave."

Tabatha jumped off the bed and fell in behind Artemise.

The teacher called over her shoulder, "I can't hang around. I've got another potion to make." She exited the room, leaving Samara alone.

Samara felt glad that Ulrieg was lurking, ready to help her. Her head didn't feel normal yet. She slowly moved into a sitting position and felt the mattress shift under Ulrieg's weight.

Take your time. Just because your teacher couldn't

care less doesn't mean you don't need more attention or time to recover.

She reached for him, and a light scratching ran up her arm as it brushed against his horns. *Thanks for being here for me when no one else is.*

Pfft. Of course I'll be here for you. You're my bonded.

Is that the only reason? she teased.

She could almost hear him struggling with the words. *And because I've grown fond of you and would miss you if something happened to you.*

Samara shoved him softly. *There you go. That wasn't so bad, was it?*

CHAPTER SEVEN

With Ulrieg's help, Samara returned to her room, the invisible dragon stabilizing her every time she swayed. She was a little surprised by how Artemise could be so gentle and caring one moment then distant and cold the next. Perhaps it was because Samara had stood up for Forgrac. Although as far as she was concerned, he deserved the praise, especially if he wasn't getting paid.

Their conversation ran through her mind. *It's nice to know someone in the Sacred Flame coterie is for dragons.*

Ulrieg grunted. *Ah. I have to correct you there. He's not part of the coterie. He isn't a wizard and doesn't have magic.*

Leaning against the wall, Samara rolled her

eyes. *Okay, technically, he's not part of the coterie. But he does live here, and Callista brought him here, so she must trust him.*

I don't know about trusting him. Using him is more like it. Ulrieg pressed against her, giving her extra support.

She sighed and continued her journey. *My point is if someone here supports the dragons, then others may also support them.*

Ulrieg harrumphed. *We'll see. They may be like you and completely unaware of them.*

Then there is room for hope that the bias isn't implanted, and their minds are open. She swayed, and Ulrieg grabbed her hips.

"Samara, are you all right?" Paxton was jogging toward her, Jojo balancing on his shoulder, mainly hiding under his low green ponytail.

Ah. Look, a coterie member with a heart.

She attempted to look healthier. "I'm fine. Thank you. I'm just a little weak after the battle. I thought I was strong, but I was brought down several notches in a few moments."

Paxton huffed, amusement washing over his plain face. "At least you lasted until the end. I was knocked out in a matter of moments. It's quite embarrassing, really." He looked at the ground.

"Nonsense! They ambushed you. No one would have had a chance if they were in your shoes."

"It's nice of you to say so." He leaned in closer, his voice slightly lowering. "I've been wanting to talk to you."

"Oh?"

"Yeah. Since we met in the library, we haven't had a chance to catch up."

When she remembered how Paxton had covered for her in Artemise's class by asking questions she wanted to know. Guilt swept over her. "Thanks for asking Artemise about the symbol and not giving away that it was my interest."

His pale skin turned even paler, and he grabbed her arm lightly, a strange look flashing through his brown eyes. "I'll be in the library after dinner. If you're up to going out, meet me there."

"All right," Samara said hesitantly. She couldn't think of why he wanted to meet her later instead of discussing it right then, and she hoped he hadn't discovered her secret.

Noticing her leaning against the wall, he asked, "Are you sure you don't need help to get to your room?"

She nodded. "I'll be fine."

He frowned with concern. "Didn't someone tend to your wounds?"

"Artemise tended to me."

"Figures," he grunted.

"She was actually quite tender and caring until I stood up for Forgrac."

"Forgrac?" Paxton looked confused.

"The dwarf you met on the stairs the other day."

"Oh." He nodded. "That makes sense. She is a little racist, even with us. So I can imagine she's worse with someone who doesn't have any human in them."

"But she gets along with Callista."

He gave a small smile. "Callista's in charge of her. Plus, she's part of the coterie and is a powerful sorceress."

"That's true."

He turned to leave. "So, will I see you later if you're up to it?"

"I'll try."

"If you can't make it, then try after dinner tomorrow. I'm usually in the library after dinner. It's the only time I don't have to worry about being elsewhere."

Samara nodded. "All right." She watched him leave, confused.

Now, that was curious. Are you going to meet him?

Samara pushed herself off the wall and started

toward the stairs. *I certainly want to. He's piqued my interest. Let's get back to my room so I can sleep.*

"Hello, beautiful!"

Wingless flight! Here we go again, Ulrieg grumbled.

Samara ignored him and turned to find Kaine standing behind her, grinning. Her cheeks heated as he gazed over her. She must look a mess, especially since she was still wearing the same clothes from the challenge. "I thought you would be off charming Luna and Mist. You seemed cozy in the meeting before the challenge."

"Are you jealous?" He studied her face as Ginger shifted to stand behind him, her nose raised and twitching as though she was picking up a strange scent. "We've been through this before. You're the only one I care for."

Samara huffed. "You have a funny way of showing it."

"It's you and only you."

Oh, I want to be sick! You should have just left with Paxton, and we would've avoided this whole cringy scene.

Concern filled his eyes. "You look like you should be sleeping." He hooked his arm around her shoulder and steadied her with his other hand. "Come on. I'll help you to your room."

Ginger whimpered.

Kaine peered down at her. "What is it, Ginger?"

The fox's head tilted in one direction then the next, her eyes fixed on Kaine.

"I've told you before. It's probably because she hasn't been able to clean up and has been rolling around in the forest. There are all kinds of weird smells out there."

The fox's eyes narrowed, and she snorted as Kaine turned his attention back to Samara.

"I'm sorry. She keeps complaining that there is a strange smell around you." He ran a hand through his brilliant blue hair.

"Oh. So she's telling you I stink. How embarrassing!" She gazed down and kicked the toes of her boots against the stone floor. Her mind raced with worry. She could probably smell Ulrieg.

I want to stick a horn in her nose. That'll stop her sniffing where she shouldn't.

Don't be nasty to her, Ulrieg. She's just doing her job.

Ulrieg grunted.

Kaine lifted her chin. "She's just being obnoxious. Most of the time, she says it when you're outside and probably dirty and sweaty. Or you've just come in from outside. She could be smelling a mixture of animals on you."

Samara gently turned away and tried not to get too close to him as he helped her up the stairs. "I'm so glad your nose isn't as efficient as hers."

He chuckled. "No, I can't smell as well as her, which is a good thing." He searched around her. "Where's Gray?"

"I've been told someone put him safely in my room."

"Is he all right after the challenge?"

She hooked a strand of pink hair behind her semipointed ear. "I've been told his wounds have been healed, and he's sleeping it off." She looked him over. He had been attacked badly by Kellam. "What about you? Are all your wounds taken care of?" She glanced at his neck, unable to see any strangulation marks.

Kaine rubbed the spot self-consciously. "Everything has been healed. I think because you were the last one standing, you were hurt the worst."

He helped her up the last step, down the corridor to her door, and led her inside. Gray sat on his perch. A rat and a lizard lay unmoving in his food dish. The owl untucked his beak from his wing to peek at what had made noise, and when he saw there was no threat, he snuggled in and went back to sleep.

Samara's heart thrummed a happy beat when she saw he was all right. She knew Ulrieg would look after him, but it was lovely to see him uninjured.

After telling Ginger to remain by the door, away from Gray, Kaine directed Samara to her bed, helping her sit. "Now, would the lovely lady like some help bathing?"

Samara's cheeks burned.

Kaine chuckled and raised his eyebrows in question as he lowered his face to hers, stopping a few inches away.

She shoved him lightly. "We don't have that kind of relationship."

He grinned. "We could." When she didn't budge, he shrugged. "Can't blame a guy for trying." He kissed her on the lips softly and slowly and cupped her chin between his thumb and forefinger. "I'll let you rest. But the offer stands."

Oh, please! Can I escape out the window? Wingless flight! I didn't sign up for this.

Samara looked away and glared at the spot where she assumed Ulrieg was sitting before turning back to Kaine. "I don't need your assistance. Thank you. I'll take it from here."

Kaine knelt at her feet and set to work, untying her bootlaces.

Samara took over and gave him a warning look. "I don't need help undressing, either."

Kaine pouted then kissed her on the forehead, filling her with warmth and the urge to give in.

Samara opened her mouth to speak, a strange feeling stirring through her body.

Don't you dare let him stay!

Kaine gazed at her curiously. "Were you going to say something?"

She shook her head.

"All right. I'll leave you be so you can recover." He exited the room, Ginger following close behind, her nose raised and her nostrils flaring.

CHAPTER EIGHT

Darkness surrounded Samara as she cracked open an eye and looked around. After taking off her boots, she had collapsed onto her unmade bed and slept. Shifting slightly, she could feel that much of her energy had returned. Something moved near her leg, and she gently probed the area only to knock one of Ulrieg's horns. Her hand felt cut, and she set to work healing it before it bled everywhere.

Gray flapped on his stand, and Samara slowly sat up, trying not to disturb Ulrieg.

The dragon yawned. *You're finally awake. Do you feel better?*

Yes, I do. I guess the sleep helped the magic work quicker. She climbed to her feet and peered out the window. *Any idea what time it is?*

A plume of fire ignited the torch on the wall.

Ulrieg's horned black form clung to the rocks halfway up the wall, not far from the light. His red eyes focused on her. *I don't know exactly. But I believe it is after your dinnertime.*

Samara cursed. *I wanted to bathe before I met with Paxton.* She grabbed her long black boots, slid them on, and worked at their laces. *I'll just have to meet him first then bathe.*

She stood, and Ulrieg lowered to the ground, ready to go with her.

Gray hooted, and Samara went to him and stroked him lightly on the chest. The owl raised a leg, and she lowered her hand, allowing him to climb on.

"Did you want to come with me?" Samara stroked his back feathers, and the owl didn't protest. Her touch must be becoming familiar to him. She placed her hand in front of her shoulder, and he climbed on. "It's probably best if I take you, just in case people get suspicious of why I don't take my familiar everywhere." She glanced down at the black, aggressive-looking dragon. "Even though you do come pretty much everywhere with me."

His red eyes seemed to soften. "All right. Let's find out what Paxton wants to talk to me about."

Ulrieg turned invisible, and they headed out the door, the hinges groaning when she pulled it shut.

As she made her way through the corridors and rooms, she found them close to empty. *I hope I'm not too late.*

It's not looking good. It seems too quiet to be just after dinner. But Paxton didn't say how long he would be there for. Ulrieg's talons clicked lightly on the stone floor.

They weaved their way to the library and entered the lower level. A light glowed dimly, showing a room centered with reading tables, surrounded with rows of bookshelves. The room seemed empty. From the few times Samara had been there, that wasn't unusual. She took the stairs at the back of the room and entered the upper level, which was a U-shaped balcony overlooking the desks below. They checked between the shelves.

"Paxton! Are you here?" she called softly.

Silence was her answer.

She checked between more shelves, jumping when something moved on the stone floor. Glancing down, she spotted Vexx's yellow snake familiar. She shivered. The two sorcerers must still be there or at least Vexx.

She checked the last few rows of shelves, finding them empty as well. *He isn't here. I don't know how late we are, but I wouldn't blame him if he left because he spotted Vexx's familiar.*

From the way he acted, I wouldn't be surprised if what

he wanted to talk about was something he didn't want anyone else to hear.

Samara's stomach grumbled, reminding her that she hadn't eaten for a long time. *Maybe I'll catch him another time. I need to eat.*

Isn't the kitchen closed?

Yes.

Then you're not going to get any food from there. Do you want me to catch you something?

Picturing Ulrieg bringing her rats and lizards like he'd often caught for Gray made her stomach turn. *Ah, thanks, but I'll try my luck in the kitchen first.*

Suit yourself. If you don't find anything, I'll catch something for you, and we can cook it over a fire.

They made their way through the dimly lit corridors. Darkness engulfed the empty dining area and also the kitchen. Samara grabbed a torch from the wall and pushed through the kitchen doors. The benches were clean, with the majority of the food put away. A few items lay on the bench, and she moved closer to have a better look at her options. Holding the torch over them, she found remnants of the day's bread and a fruit bowl. *I'm happy with this. Did you need me to find you something?*

His talons clicked on the bench top beside her. Remaining cautious, Ulrieg stayed in his invisible form whenever they traveled within the building's walls. *Pfft! I'm not going to eat that.*

Samara cast an annoyed glance toward the spot she suspected he stood. *I know that. That's why I asked you if you wanted me to find anything else.*

Ulrieg cleared his throat and sounded humbler. *Of course you know that. Sorry. What I meant to say is I'd rather catch something. Fresh raw meat is always tastier, and there's an abundance in the forest surrounding the building.*

Samara tore off a large portion of bread and gathered a few pieces of fruit. As she turned to leave, a movement caught her eye, and she worried that Vexx's snake had found her again. Instead, she spotted the golden snub-nosed monkey that was Kellam's familiar. Protectively, she blocked the monkey's access to Gray with a slight shift of the body. The monkey scowled, making its tiny pale face look smaller.

The look made Samara feel as though she had to explain herself. She held up the fruit and bread. "I'm just grabbing some food. I missed out on dinner because I was sleeping off my injuries."

The monkey snorted.

Ulrieg carefully climbed onto Samara's back. He was too close to the monkey to let his talons click on the hard surfaces, and his wing beats would be heard in the small room. Slowly, she sidestepped away from the monkey and out of the kitchen.

What is it with the sorcerers' familiars tonight? Are they following me, or do I just have bad luck? Samara whispered through their bond.

Or they're watching the building maliciously during the night to spy on all the apprentices or perhaps even the teachers, Ulrieg grumbled.

Surveying every dark spot, Samara headed back to her bedroom to eat in peace.

Ulrieg jumped from her back. *I'm going to do a little discovering while you eat.*

What? With the sorcerers' familiars stalking the building?

I'll be fine. I'll be careful and remain invisible. I'm more worried about Ginger than those two familiars discovering me. The others haven't shown any sign of suspecting my being around.

Samara quirked her mouth. *Be careful. Those two familiars give me the creeps just as much as the sorcerers.*

Ulrieg's wings beat swiftly as he flew down the corridor, then he glided down the stairs.

When she returned to her room, she placed Gray on his perch, where he immediately began devouring the last of his lizard. Unable to watch him tear the animal apart, she sat at her desk and gazed out the window onto the moonlit plain. As she ate, she observed the shadows the trees at the edge cast over the field of flowers. The night was beautiful and clear. She took her time eating through the bread and the few pieces of fruit. It wasn't as good as one of Forgrac's cooked meals, but the bread was still crusty and fresh, and she had always enjoyed fruit.

When she finished, she opened the window and peered down. She tried to imagine what it would be like if she weren't a coterie member and couldn't see the building.

A rush of wind passed over her through the window, and she shrieked. She spun, pressing her back against the wall as she faced the inside of the room.

Wingless flight! It's only me, Ulrieg said as he turned visible. *You're jumpy after seeing those two familiars.* His red eyes shone with amusement.

"I wasn't expecting you back so quickly, either." Samara held a hand over her heart. "Usually, when you go discovering, you take all night."

The dragon stood on his hind legs and held a looped leather necklace in his talons. *Well, I found what I wanted more quickly than I thought I would.*

Samara bent to have a closer look. Swinging from the end of the necklace was the charm that sent chills down her spine. She spoke through her bond to ensure no one else would hear through the open window. *That's the key to the secret rooms.*

Exactly.

Her heart raced. *Where did you find that?*

I borrowed it from Artemise again. She sleeps like a log.

What about Tabatha?

He waved a claw at her. *She was out hunting in the hallways.*

In the hallways?

Yes. There's a bit of a mice infestation in this building at the moment.

Samara screwed up her nose. *I thought Mystique was supposed to deal with that.*

No. Mystique has more refined tastes, like animals in the forest. He rounded his back, making his horns look larger. *Anyway, are you up for a little trip tonight? I'd like to see if we have a chance to help Byzarid.*

CHAPTER NINE

S amara closed the window. "Are you sure that's wise with the familiars stalking the building?"

Ulrieg exposed his teeth in what looked like a vicious smile. *I can always rip their heads off if they become too troublesome.*

"Ulrieg. You're supposed to respect other familiars," Samara chastised.

Hmph! He frowned, making the horns on his head bunch. *I'm sure they wouldn't respect any of the apprentices' familiars if they chose not to.*

Samara screwed up her face. "That's not making me want to walk through the building."

There's no other way, unless you can climb out your window. If they spotted you doing that, you would be under more suspicion. We can take Gray and say he needs to hunt. Tell them he was locked in your room all day while you slept. It's not far from the truth, so they shouldn't detect a lie.

Samara expelled a breath and pushed a strand of hair behind her ear. "I want to help Byzarid if we can. It's upsetting me to think he could still be getting tortured under the building." She glanced at Gray, worry creasing her brow. "Let's go. It's not like I haven't had to get past Mystique before." She held her hand under Gray's chest, and he climbed on. "It's time for you to have a little flight and fun in the forest." She placed him on her shoulder, and he stayed. She then took the necklace from Ulrieg and hung it around her neck, tucking it under her tunic. She glanced at her bed. "I should take a sheet, just in case." Ignoring Ulrieg's curious expression, she pulled off her top sheet, folded it, and placed it in her quiver beside her arrows.

She grabbed her bow and quiver from the wall and slung them over her shoulders before exiting the room with an invisible Ulrieg following her. Passing through the building made her jumpy. She was still unsure what to make of Vexx, Kellam, and their familiars. Having to deal with Mystique was terrible enough.

The coast was clear down the corridor, and she progressed down the stairs, almost jumping every time she thought she saw a shadow move. They made it as far as the front door when the shadow morphed into Mystique. Her yellow eyes were critical and full of suspicion. Samara still hadn't gotten over the time the trolls had attempted to slaughter her and Kaine while the black jaguar watched.

"Oh. Hello, Mystique." Despite feeling deep resentment, Samara tried to sound friendly and respectful to the head sorceress's familiar.

The large cat blinked, unmoving.

"I can't sleep, so I thought I'd take Gray out for a hunt. He's been trapped in my room all day while I've been sleeping off my injury."

Mystique's eyes narrowed.

As if on cue, Gray hooted, somehow managing to sound displeased.

Samara's heart swelled with pride. Ulrieg had caught the perfect owl to act as her familiar. He had been tamed so quickly that it was hard sometimes to remember he was a wild bird.

The cat shifted out of the entrance, allowing them to pass.

I'm right beside you, Ulrieg said as she shifted to close the door behind them.

They descended the stairs at a regular pace, trying not to raise suspicions if anyone saw them. The waxing gibbous moon illuminated the area enough to be able to see several feet ahead.

Make sure you keep your ears open, Samara told Ulrieg.

Already on it.

Samara encouraged Gray to take off and watched him as he gracefully flew into the forest. Then she and Ulrieg moved down the side of the building, ducking behind bushes every time they approached a window.

How late do you think it is? She glanced up at the moon, but she hadn't spent enough time outside to tell the time that way.

I'd say it's closer to the middle of the night. We must've slept a lot longer than we thought.

One good thing is that everyone should be asleep.

Let's hope that means whoever is torturing Byzarid is also asleep.

They reached the hidden entrance to the cata-combs. After a long, careful look around the area, checking to see if they were being watched, they pushed aside the bush and climbed down the hole. Samara's boots clomped on the stone stairs, and she occasionally slipped on the damp rocks. She clung to the stones in the wall until she reached the bottom. The sconce on the wall still shone dimly, as though it had been charmed to remain on at all times. She pulled the torch from the holder and took it with her down the dank-smelling corridors. Visible again,

Ulrieg led the way. The first time they had traveled down there, it had seemed a long way past the many doors until they reached the one at the end. Her nerves still made it seem distant, especially when she slipped in several places. It was hard not to make unnecessary noises when she struggled to remain upright. The floor seemed slipperier than the previous time.

Ulrieg noticed her struggle. *I forgot. It rained last night when you were sleeping off your injuries.*

That would definitely explain the slipperiness.

When they reached the door with the glow shining underneath, Samara placed the torch in a holder and dug for the key. She lined the emblem on the key up with the one on the door, paused, and looked at Ulrieg. *Are you ready?*

His red eyes seemed to catch the glow, making him look menacing. *As ready as I'll ever be.*

With her heart thumping against her chest, Samara took a deep breath, turned the key, and cracked open the door. The bright-orange-and-yellow light pulsed into the dark corridor. They peeked into the room, and Samara caught sight of the pulsing orb trapped in the magical dome. Its large size still surprised her. The orb sank halfway into a chasm several feet deep. The half above the floor filled the room with its light.

Together, they searched the cave, making sure they were alone before pressing into the large room, leaving the door open a crack.

Ulrieg shivered. *That orb is giving me the creeps. It's getting closer to the full moon, and my senses are heightened. It's only going to get worse.*

If that is the power from the malevolent sorcerer you and Forgrac talk about, I'm not surprised. Samara moved toward the room where they'd found Byzarid.

Ulrieg scurried past her, his black wings slightly unfurled. Before he reached the door, he turned invisible. *The room is clear of sorcerers. It's only Byzarid.* He groaned. *And he's in bad shape.*

Samara quickened her footsteps and entered the room. The brown dragon was unconscious and chained to the gurney in the middle of the small cave. He had cuts on almost every part of his body. Blood stained the table and trickled down the sides. It looked fresh, like his torturer had left not long before they arrived. She glanced at his right claw to find a talon had been removed. Quickly, she checked his other ones to find him missing a talon on each back foot. Not only that, but some horns had been cut from his back, leaving gaping wounds. The blood drained from her face. *Whoever captured him has put him through a tremendous amount of pain.* She pumped him with a healing incantation and checked his wounds. Several had been infected the previous time, and more had started to puff up and turn red. The dragon had seemed half dead the previous time, but he looked even worse now. She wanted to heal his wounds as much as possible, but she would need a lot more time, energy, potions, and most likely, stronger magic than hers.

She started on the locks. "*Aperti,*" she whispered over one around his wrist. It clicked open. "Good. They haven't been magically enchanted not to open. I guess they weren't expecting someone to break in and set him free." She worked on the other claw then the back legs, and a satisfied grin spread across her face when the final lock clicked. "All right. I'm not going to be able to carry him, and I doubt you could either. I can't even lay him over your back because you're a walking pincushion."

Ulrieg gave her a strange look.

"In other words, you have horns everywhere, and they would pierce his underbelly if I laid him over you."

Then what do you suggest we do?

"That's what the sheet is for." She pulled off her quiver, laid the sheet on the floor, and unfolded it. Then she grabbed the dragon's legs, the front ones in one hand and the back ones in the other. "This is going to be heavy." She took a deep breath and heaved the dragon off the table and onto the middle of the sheet. Panting, she released his legs. "I would've threaded the sheet underneath him, but I didn't want to get it covered in blood and leave a trail."

Smart thinking. Now what?

Samara grabbed the edges of the sheet at Byzarid's head and put them together. "I'll get this end, and you take that end to help lift him out of here without leaving a trail. Our first step is getting him out of this orb-filled cave before someone returns."

Ulrieg put together the ends of the sheet, and they walked toward the entrance they'd come through.

Dragon moon! I didn't think my cousin would weigh this much. It feels like we're carrying a large boulder.

"What did you expect? He's the same size as you, if not slightly bigger."

The orb pulsed and spun continually on its axis. The force felt angry, as though it were upset with them for dragging the dragon away.

Grunting under the weight, Ulrieg said, *I can't wait to get out of here. My heightened senses are picking up bad sensations from that thing. Its anger is pulsing so hard that it almost feels as though it's speaking to me.*

Samara quickened her pace as much as she could without tearing the sheet or causing injury. They had a long way to go before they were out of the catacombs. Ulrieg's talons clacked on the floor as he tried to keep up with her pace.

As they reached the door, a noise sounded from the far side of the cave. Samara froze, and her eyes widened with fear as she searched for the cause. Ulrieg disappeared, and his side of the sheet dropped to the floor.

CHAPTER TEN

S amara tugged open the door and slowly dragged Byzarid through the entrance. She had no idea where Ulrieg had gone, but she didn't want to risk her or the brown dragon being caught. She pulled Ulrieg's cousin to a dark corner outside the room and dropped the sheet then headed back to the door and peeked through the gap wide enough for her head, hoping to find Ulrieg and that whatever had made the noise wasn't one of the cloaked magic wielders. They needed more time to get Byzarid out of there.

Ulrieg, where are you?

The silence that followed tore at her nerves. She didn't know if he had been caught, found something more disturbing, or left her alone in the catacombs. Although she didn't think he would leave her on her own on purpose. But it would be almost impossible for her to drag the brown dragon up the stairs and to safety.

Ulrieg, are you all right? Images of her trying to save her familiar ran through her head, and her body turned numb.

I'm all right. Argh! You won't believe what I found, Ulrieg said sadly.

Where are you? What is it? She stuck her head farther through the door and searched the larger room but couldn't find him.

I'm in one of the other smaller rooms. I think it's the second from the left. The sadness in his voice seemed to accentuate. *I think you need to see this.*

She entered the big room and cautiously made her way to the one Ulrieg had mentioned, the hairs on the back of her neck rising. Standing outside the door, she inhaled deeply, then she entered. When she saw what he was talking about, the air blew out of her lungs.

A tiny form was lying on the gurney, the animal still and lifeless. The reptilian scales were dull gray-brown and covered in blood.

Samara studied the creature, which couldn't be any bigger than an owl. "Is that a dragon?"

Ulrieg nodded, his red eyes serene. *It's one of the guardian dragons both Forgrac and I mentioned. I've never seen one in real life, but this is precisely how they have been described.* He circled the table, surveying every part of the dragon. *I don't even know how they found him. I didn't know any were out of Dragoria. I thought they were all trapped in the dragon realm.*

Samara followed him around the table, studying the intricate details of the tiny creature, and gasped. "Is that..." The thought devastated her so much, she was unable to finish saying the words out loud.

Yes. They have cut out his heart.

Samara wanted to retch. "That's barbaric. I mean, it's all brutal, but seriously!"

Ulrieg stopped circling and sat on his haunches, his dark face clouded with anger and sadness. *They probably took it for a potion or even sacrificed it to the orb —stupid evil, magical abomination.*

With the image planted in Samara's mind, she glared at the orange-and-yellow pulsating orb. Suddenly, she remembered. "Hang on. Didn't you come back in here because we heard a noise?"

Ulrieg frowned and nodded. *Yes. I did.*

"Well, it couldn't have come from the dragon. Maybe there's something else in these rooms."

Instantly, Ulrieg was on his feet, heading for the nearest room, and Samara followed. Dread stirred in her stomach. Finding the two dragons had been gruesome enough. She quickly checked the first room on the left and found it empty. Then she hurried to catch up to Ulrieg. He promptly checked several rooms until he came to the tenth one and stopped in the doorway. Concerned red eyes met with hers before he disappeared through the opening.

She hurried to the door and charged inside then stopped at the end of the table. On it lay an unconscious elven female, golden-blond hair fanning around her head and blood saturating the sheet beneath her. Samara's cheeks turned numb. The elf's simple brown cotton pants and loose beige tunic had been destroyed by incisions seeping with blood. Deep cuts marred her body, and patches of gray scales formed on her skin before disappearing and moving to another part of her body.

Samara moved closer, her legs feeling almost boneless. The elf's legs and arms were chained to the table, precisely like Byzarid's had been. "Ulrieg, what am I looking at?"

If Ulrieg's face weren't black, color would have drained from it. His eyes wouldn't leave the elf. *By the way her flesh changes, I'm pretty sure this is a dragon elf. I heard that if they are away from their bonded guardian dragon, their skin will manifest scales when their emotions are heightened. But they can't change into a dragon.* He hissed. *Wingless flight! I wonder if she was bonded to the guardian dragon in the other room, and they were discovered. I didn't think, with Dragoria being hidden, that any guardian dragons were on this side, let alone had a chance to meet with their dragon elf. Stupid blood-sucking coterie! How were they able to find probably the only matching of a dragon elf and guardian in existence?*

Moving closer, Samara started to work on the elf's wounds, glad they didn't seem infected. The elf probably hadn't been there long enough for the infection to set in. Still, whoever had captured her had managed to cause her a great deal of pain and distress. They probably even broke her bond and her heart.

It pained Samara that they didn't have the resources to take her with them in an unconscious state, but she couldn't leave her there. She glanced at Ulrieg. "I'm going to be here a while, and I may also draw most of my strength and maybe yours through our bond. I don't know if I can do it, but I'm going to try to heal her enough that she will regain consciousness. Her wounds are deep but still clean. Maybe then we can get her out of here."

Ulrieg headed toward the door and turned briefly to face her. *I'll go and stand watch at the entrance into this area.*

Samara nodded. "Thanks."

She continued healing the elf's wounds, pushing healing energy into her head every so often, hoping to slowly bring her out of the coma. More minor flesh wounds knitted together in front of her eyes, each one draining her energy. If it were only a few, it wouldn't be a problem, but so many would rob her of a lot of energy. Even so, each wound she watched mend together made her feel satisfied. She didn't know who was responsible for taking the captives, but with Ulrieg's help, she was determined to at least release as many as possible if not stop the perpetrators.

She pumped more healing energy into the elf's head and stopped the bleeding in a couple of deep wounds then paused to take a deep breath. Her power was fading fast. Then she pumped more healing energy into the elf's brain before turning to heal a couple more wounds. When she noticed the elf's eyes fluttering, she stopped. Terrified crystal-blue eyes met hers. The elf screamed, and Samara held up her hands in defense.

"Shh. I'm here to help you, and I don't need you to tell your captors I'm here."

The elf stopped, but her eyes never left Samara's face, as if she were judging whether she was telling the truth. The dragon elf slowly sat up.

Are you all right back there? Ulrieg called.

Yes. The dragon elf just woke up and spotted me. I think she's worked out I'm here to help her.

As Samara continued to work on the more minor wounds, the elf watched the skin meld back together. The dragon elf seemed to relax until she clutched at her chest and groaned with pain.

Samara stopped healing her, trying to see what was hurting her. "Are you all right?"

The dragon elf shook her head. "It's my heart."

"Are you having a heart attack?" Samara watched her with concern.

She shook her head. "I think it's my dragon. Have you seen a dragon? He may be in his small form, as we hadn't been together long."

Samara's stomach turned, and again, she wanted to be sick. "Is he tiny with gray scales?"

The dragon elf nodded.

Closing her eyes, Samara pulled from all the inner strength she had. "There's a tiny gray dragon a few rooms away."

The dragon elf's face lit with excitement.

Samara laid a hand softly on her leg and slowly shook her head. "I'm afraid the dragon is no longer with us."

"*What?*" The dragon elf's face twisted with anger and disbelief.

"I'm so sorry. He had passed before we found him."

The dragon elf wailed, and again, though Samara didn't want to, she had to beg her to be quiet.

With tears streaming down her face, the dragon elf nodded. "I guess that's what my heart was trying to tell me. We only found each other two days before we were captured."

"Who caught you?"

She shook her head. "I didn't get a chance to see them properly, but the leader had a yellow snake following him, and he had strong magic."

"The snake would have been his familiar."

Frowning, she asked, "What's a familiar?"

"An animal guide for powerful magic wielders, usually ones who are part of the Sacred Flame coterie. That is one of their markings along with brilliant-colored hair."

"Now I think of it, I did spot something bright under his hood."

"Probably bright red."

She looked baffled. "Yes. How did you know?"

"I guessed. I met a strong sorcerer recently called Vexx, and he had spiky red hair and a yellow snake for a familiar." Samara healed a couple more of her wounds.

The elf's eyes were on her the whole time. "You

have bright hair and appear to have strong magic. Are you part of the Sacred Flame coterie also?" A distrusting look crossed the dragon-elf's face.

"Yes. But as you can see, I'm helping you, not him."

"Why?"

"Because less than a month ago, they basically kicked me out because I didn't have a familiar. Well, in truth, they made me fight a bunch of trolls to prove my worth and stripped me of my magic before the fight."

The dragon elf gasped.

"I was captured, and I bonded with my familiar during that time." She stopped healing her for a moment and looked her in the eyes. "He's a dragon."

The dragon elf grunted a laugh. "Really?"

"He was the first dragon I had heard of, let alone seen."

"How did you stumble into Vexx's lair? I hope you realize it's dangerous if you have a dragon."

"I do now. I wasn't sure who was hurting these dragons and now you too. But this isn't his lair. This is the bottom level of the coterie's building."

"Then how did it go when you returned to the coterie? Are they all like Vexx?"

Samara looked at the ground. "I don't know. The thing is, there may be some who like dragons. It's not something that's been talked about in my time here. I'm fortunate that my dragon can turn invisible. And he's the one who planted the seed that this coterie isn't what I thought it was. I hope I'll have time to sort out the good from the bad."

The sound of clacking talons approached the door, and Samara turned to find Ulrieg in the doorway. *Come on. We have to go. It's approaching morning, and I'm worried the perpetrators will try to get their fun before the day starts.*

"Oh. Is this your dragon? He's adorable!"

Ulrieg's horns bunched together. *Wingless flight! Dragon forbid you insult me like that. I'm not some cute toy or animal. Here we are, saving your butt, and you hurl insults at me.*

The dragon elf's face dropped. Ulrieg must have directed his voice so that she could hear him.

Samara chuckled. "Yes. This is my dragon familiar, Ulrieg. He's also a sarcastic, rude partner, but we've grown on each other."

CHAPTER ELEVEN

Ulrieg growled. *Is she all right to walk? We must go. I'm honestly worried about them coming back.*

"We haven't tried. How do you feel?" she asked the dragon elf.

"I'll find the energy. Don't worry." She pulled her wrists up, and the chains rattled.

Haven't you taken them off yet? Ulrieg grumbled.

"I'm sorry. I was so busy healing you that I forgot about your restraints," Samara said, quickly unlocking them.

Rubbing her wrists while Samara worked on the chains around her ankles, the dragon elf said, "We haven't introduced ourselves yet. I'm Daena Wynstone."

"Samara Wren. I'm glad we found you."

The last lock clicked open, and Daena climbed off the table. Her back was drenched in blood. "Trust me—me too."

She staggered a few paces, and Samara hooked her arm under hers as Ulrieg led the way to the door. They quickly filed through, and Samara closed the door behind them, glad to shut off the room with the pulsating orb. They stopped by the still form of Byzarid. Ulrieg approached the dragon and sniffed, and Samara could almost feel his heart breaking.

Squinting in the dull light from the torch, Daena gasped. "Who's this?"

Samara squatted by the dragon, feeling for breath. "This is Byzarid, Ulrieg's cousin. It's only by Ulrieg's investigation of the property that we found him and you. If I didn't have Ulrieg as my familiar, I wouldn't have a clue that this existed." She felt a hot breath against her hand and breathed a sigh of relief. "We found him a couple of days ago, but two cloaked figures came into the cave before we could rescue him. This was our first chance to go back, and we found more than we expected."

"What's your plan for him?" Daena squatted next to Samara as Ulrieg stood back.

"We're trying to carry him out of here to safety— or at least as much safety as we can offer—and I'll work on his wounds. Some of them are badly infected, and I'm afraid I'll need to find some help to heal him. Either by potions or stronger magic than what I hold. I'm only an apprentice in this coterie and haven't mastered advanced healing, among other things."

Daena stood and looked down the passageway. "I should be able to help you carry him."

Samara stood next to her. "I'd appreciate it. Ulrieg is slightly smaller than him and struggles with the weight."

I'm right here, you know, Ulrieg snapped, his eyes glowing eerily under the torchlight.

Samara dropped to his level and held a hand along his jaw. "I know that. It's not a criticism. It's pointing out the obvious. Daena is bigger, and if she has enough energy, her help would be useful."

"Exactly! No criticism here. Did you see the size of my guardian? He only got to shift into his enormous size twice before Vexx took us." Her face distorted with pain.

Sorry, Ulrieg grumbled. *Your loss is more significant than my qualm. I was being a sook.*

Samara's jaw dropped. "Wow! He likes you. He apologized within a few moments of meeting you."

Daena shrugged. "We're all friends now. Okay, let's get out of here."

She moved to grab the sheet at Byzarid's feet, and

Samara pulled the torch from the wall and grasped the sheet at the dragon's head. Slowly, they made their way down the corridor, past the other doors. Daena occasionally used the walls for support. After a slow trip, they made it to the stairs.

"We have to go up these to get out of here. I know you're still struggling, so I'll take the bottom if you can carry the top with less weight."

"All right." Daena lowered her side to the floor and moved around to the front and took the sheet from Samara. Samara placed the torch back into the sconce and moved to the lower half of the sheet.

Ulrieg bounded up the stairs. *I'll check to see if the coast is clear.* His black form disappeared into the darkness as he turned invisible and pushed through the branches blocking the hole.

On unsteady feet, Daena worked her way up the stairs, Samara following her, struggling with the heavy weight. She felt glad that it was unlikely that anyone would discover them in that part of the catacombs. Yet their mission was far from over. After much struggling, they made it to the top, and Daena climbed through the hole, her grip on the sheet slipping. With Ulrieg's help, they pushed aside the bush, and Daena hunkered down and yanked the sheet up. Samara pushed from below, her legs almost buckling, until the dragon was finally hoisted through the gap and into the open air.

Samara climbed into the night, and they all paused, catching their breath. The dragon might be half their size, but he was still a significant weight for two females to carry.

Samara instantly set to work surveying the area for threats. If Ulrieg was correct, and it was the early-morning hours, then the possibility of their being caught by another coterie member was slim. Still, it was best to be on guard.

"Now what?" Daena sat on the ground and leaned back onto her hands, struggling to regain her breath as blood ran down her arm. The struggle had put too much pressure on a deep cut there.

Noticing it in the dull moonlight, Samara lethargically leaned forward, placed a hand on the hole, and whispered an incantation to seal the artery. "We don't know. We're working it out as we go. But we can't take him inside the building."

"What building?" Daena asked, searching the plain.

"Oh, right. I just thought you'd be able to see it since you were in there." She indicated the building, which sat only a few feet away. "Believe it or not, there is a huge building made of stone right there. It's the base for the Sacred Flame coterie. Only coterie members and their familiars or people invited through the front door can see it."

A grin spread across Daena's face. "You're joking with me, aren't you?"

Well, I can't say she's stupid because I've seen it with my own eyes, Ulrieg chimed in.

Daena glanced at him then back at Samara.

"It's true. You can't see it. But I wonder if you can still feel it." She looked at Ulrieg for confirmation.

He shrugged. *I didn't try to feel for it when I found the plain.*

"Curious. Daena, why don't you walk several feet that way and see if you run into it? Take it slowly. I don't want you to knock yourself out on the stone walls."

Daena climbed to her feet and did as Samara asked, running into a solid wall only a few feet away. "Interesting!" She glanced back. "I wouldn't have believed you if I didn't feel it for myself." She felt farther along the wall. "How big is it?"

"Pretty big. I wouldn't keep going that way. Eventually, you'll pass some windows and may be spotted," Samara warned.

Daena immediately stopped and returned to the group. She had a slight limp, and Samara knew she had more wounds to heal.

"Where are you going to take him?" Daena sat next to Samara.

Samara shook her head. "I don't know. We can't take him inside. I guess our only option is somewhere in the forest."

Ulrieg sat on his haunches, his dark form eerie in the moonlight. *There is a place I've seen a little way from here that might be safe. I haven't seen any coterie members go out that way.*

The strength leaked from Samara's muscles at the thought of carrying the dragon a long way after all the healing she had done and still had to do. "How far is it?"

Ulrieg screwed up his pointy nose. *It's quite a distance. I mean, it's not far if you're walking normally, but carrying a heavy load, it will probably feel like several miles.*

Samara groaned.

Daena placed a hand on her shoulder. "We'll take it slowly."

"I'm also worried about returning to the coterie before morning and acting like I've had a restful night's sleep." Samara's shoulders slumped.

"I understand that. I'll take as much weight as I can." Daena reached down for the sheet at the dragon's legs.

Ulrieg pressed against Samara's leg. *Drain as*

much energy as you need from me. I won't be doing all the healing or the carrying, but I can lend you more strength.

"But I don't want to drain too much from you either."

Just do as you're told, Ulrieg grumbled. *You're the one who needs it more.*

Reluctantly, she placed a hand on his shoulder, avoiding his many horns, and pulled out some energy. Her muscles instantly felt more robust, and she released her hold on him. "That should be enough." She grabbed the other side of the sheet, and she and Daena hoisted it from the ground.

If you need more, I'm here. Make sure you use my strength. I'll lead the way. He headed toward the forest.

They followed him, sometimes stumbling over the forest floor or tree roots.

Ulrieg had been right. The trip did seem to take forever under the weight of a dragon, but eventually, they arrived at a gathering of boulders. One of the rocks towered over the others and leaned on two below, creating a semiopen cave. Dried leaves were piled in the corner, and Ulrieg hurried in and swept them away with his wings.

Samara and Daena staggered into the shelter, the toll of the trip weighing heavily on them, and they placed Byzarid in the most sheltered corner.

Ulrieg hovered around his cousin, the worry over his well-being clear on his features. *It's not the best place for you, cousin, but it's the best we have for now. I hope we can help you heal and send you on your way.*

Daena moved in next to Ulrieg. "I'll stay with him. Samara must return to keep up pretenses, and she needs your help. So I'll stay."

"Are you sure?" Samara asked, watching her familiar's rough edges almost crumble over her offer.

"Of course. It's the least I can do after what you've done for me." She held a hand over her stomach. "Although I am hungry, and I don't have any weapons to catch a meal or items to start a fire to cook it."

"Easily solved," Samara said, having spotted a rabbit only a few feet away. She quickly drew out an arrow and shot it.

Ulrieg scurried to the animal then brought it back and tossed the rabbit at Daena's feet. *Here you go. You start skinning it, and I'll build your fire.* He began gathering sticks for kindling.

Daena felt in her clothes for a knife, but when she came up empty, Samara handed her a small knife she'd recently started keeping on the side of her quiver, and the dragon elf set to work on the animal. Ulrieg lit the kindling he had gathered then searched for larger logs for Daena to keep it well stocked.

Samara worked on a couple more of Byzarid's wounds, her brow creasing with worry as she looked over the badly infected ones. "I'm going to need to get someone to help. I hope I can find someone to trust."

CHAPTER TWELVE

A dull glow had begun in the eastern sky, slowly pushing away the darkness, when Samara and Ulrieg found Gray and returned to the building.

Samara groaned as they climbed the front steps. *I was really hoping to get some sleep. I'm exhausted.*

Ulrieg was already invisible, and Samara only knew where he was by the occasional clacking of his talons on the stone stairs. *Can you afford to skip breakfast? That's a little time to have a rest.*

I could. I saved a little bread in my room last night. It'll be stale, but sleep is more important at the moment. She looked down at her clothes. *Dragon moon! I haven't even washed since the battle. I thought I'd have some time after our side trek.*

She pushed through the double doors and held

them open long enough for Ulrieg to follow. Mystique was no longer at her post, and Samara quickened her steps to get to her room before anyone saw her.

A figure suddenly darted out of a side corridor, scaring Gray from her shoulder, and pinned her to the cold stone wall by her shoulders.

Her gaze met hard brown eyes. "Vexx. You startled me." Her heart thumped rapidly, and her nerves fired on all ends. All sleepiness had been shoved away.

Gray perched on the stair railing, watching from above. Vexx's snake poked its head out from under his sleeve, and Samara shied away.

"What are you doing wandering the building this early in the morning? You should be asleep in your room." The lines pinched around his eyes, and with his fiery red hair, he looked as evil as Samara had heard he was.

She shifted under his arm, twisting out of his hold and giving herself space. "I couldn't sleep, so I took Gray out to hunt."

"Then you should have been back a long time ago."

From the way he scrutinized her, Samara wondered if he had found the empty catacombs. She pushed the thought aside to help calm her nerves.

"Normally, I wouldn't be out that long, but Gray decided to be mischievous and not come back when I called him."

"Do you not have control over your familiar?" He crossed his arms and circled her.

"I see it more as a mutual respect rather than my controlling him." She slightly raised her chin.

"Then you should have left the animal out in the wild." He stopped in front of her, his legs shoulder distance apart as though bracing for a battle.

"You see, I have a problem with that. As much as he annoyed me by not coming when called, I can't just leave him alone all night in the wild to defend himself. I'd be devastated if something happened to him." She mimicked his stance. "I'd rather miss a night's sleep protecting him than face a formidable opponent again without magic." She held her arm out to Gray, and the owl landed on her hand then migrated to her shoulder. "Now, if you don't mind, I'd like to get a little sleep before I have to start today's lessons."

She moved to follow Gray up the stairs only to find the path blocked by the sorcerer. His dark-brown eyes narrowed on her, and his brown cloak billowed as he placed his hands on his hips.

"What's going on here?" The cool voice of Callista broke the tension.

Vexx shifted slightly away as Callista moved closer, her long leaf-patterned gown flowing around her ankles. Mystique sauntered not far behind her. The head sorceress's blue eyes held the hardness of crystals as they turned to Vexx.

The sorcerer scowled, waving a finger at Samara. "She was wandering around the building in the early hours of the morning."

Callista straightened, and the light of the sconces glimmered off her headdress. "That is not a crime around here, Vexx. The apprentices are not under curfew."

Vexx eyed his snake before glaring at Samara then facing Callista. "But don't you find that suspicious behavior?"

The head sorceress glanced up at Gray before returning her gaze to Vexx. "She has an owl for a familiar. I don't find after-hours activity for a witch with a creature of the night for a familiar to be suspicious. Especially when the bond is new." She faced Samara. "Although I do hope you learn to get back into your human routine soon. A lack of sleep can mess with how your body functions."

Samara nodded, feeling confused. Callista's expressionless face made it impossible to tell where her loyalties lay. She hoped Callista wasn't against dragons or Dragoria, but she was still puzzled as to why there had been no mention of them for the whole time she had been with the coterie. "I am rather tired. Gray decided to spend the whole night flying around and hunting."

Callista nodded. "I can't blame him. That's what he's used to. He probably misses it." She placed a hand on Samara's shoulder, and warmth crept through her, bringing a slight feeling of revitalization. "Go get some sleep. I've transferred you some energy, but it won't replace a night of good sleep."

"Thank you." Samara inclined her head then climbed the stairs, feeling Vexx's eyes on the back of her head. She wondered if he suspected her of taking his captives as much as she suspected him of entrapping them.

That was close! Ulrieg's voice almost startled her, but she stopped her reaction before Vexx saw her.

Samara trudged down the corridor leading to her room. *You don't have to tell me. I mean, who wanders through the building at this hour of the morning?*

It wouldn't be any of us.

Samara didn't miss the sarcasm in Ulrieg's voice. *Fair point. I really need to go to bed.* Samara tossed her head back and let out a groan.

We're here now. You only need to open the door and lie down. Can you manage that?

I think so. She groaned again and opened the

door, and after throwing her stuff aside, she plopped facedown onto the bed. Gray flew to his perch, and she was asleep in moments.

A LOUD BANG WOKE SAMARA, and someone else's magic pulsed through her veins. She frowned. It wasn't Callista's magic, and a wave of underlying anger tainted the strand. Samara rubbed the sleep out of her eyes and glanced out the window, taking in the bright sky illuminating the treetops before she looked for Ulrieg. He lay next to her legs, positioned so his horns wouldn't accidentally pierce her.

He lifted his head to look at her.

"Can you feel that?" Samara asked.

It's almost full moon, he grumbled. *I can feel pretty much everything. This sensation has an underlying darkness that reminds me of the orb.*

"Do you think it's the orb?" Slowly, Samara shifted her legs to dangle over the edge of the bed. Her muscles ached from the ordeal the previous night and the lack of sleep.

Ulrieg shook his head. *No. It has a slightly different feel.* He yawned and climbed to his feet, stretching each leg individually.

Something didn't sit right with Samara. "I think

it's calling us to the hall. It feels like when Callista calls us for a gathering, but usually, her callings are authoritative but friendly."

It's probably because they have discovered two of their captives missing, Ulrieg sniped.

Samara froze as the previous night's activities flooded back to her. "Dragon moon! That probably *is* what it's about."

Ulrieg leveled his gaze at her, his red eyes serious. *I'm flattered that you have taken to my cursing, but you must stop before saying it in front of someone against dragons. You were lucky with Forgrac. That dwarf has seen more than he lets on.*

Samara sighed. "You're right. But I like your cursing. I haven't heard anyone else use intriguing curses like yours." She put on her house shoes.

Why don't you say something like "arrow sparks"?

"'Arrow sparks'?" Samara looked at him strangely.

Ulrieg spread his wings and shrugged. *I thought it suited you because you're good at incanting your arrows with explosive magic. You can always think of something else if you don't like it.* He jumped to the floor and headed to the door, turning to watch Samara as she coaxed Gray onto her hand. *Or you could use "wingless flight." That one would pass as something you picked up because Gray also has wings.* He tilted his head to one side as Samara flinched from Gray's claws digging into her skin. *Or how about "pointy talons"? Just don't use one with the word "dragon" in it.*

"They're all pretty good. I'll see what rolls off my tongue when I need it." She put her hand on the door handle.

Are you ready? Ulrieg turned invisible.

She shook her head. "No, but I have to be. It will be suspicious if we don't go." She opened the door, and they headed down the stairs to the hall, her nerves firing.

They rounded the corner to the hall to find the chairs cleared away and all the apprentices standing in a circle, casting her uncomfortable glances.

Kellam towered over one of the newer apprentices, an average-sized human male just past his sixteenth summer. Samara had heard his name was Blade, and he had a strange hairstyle she couldn't bring herself to like. The sides of his brilliant red hair were short, almost shaven, and the top and back were on the slightly longer side. Blade seemed to cower under the elf's scrutiny.

The monkey patrolled the floor, circling in front of the apprentices as though keeping them in line.

Vexx's eyes narrowed on Samara, and he abruptly indicated for her to enter the circle.

Samara found a spot next to Kaine. Gray fidgeted

on her shoulder as Ginger stared at him. She wanted to ask Kaine what was going on, but with one look at his drawn face, she knew it wasn't a time to bring him to the attention of the human-hating elf.

The sneer on the elf's face turned savage as he raised his hand, clawed as if to cast a spell on Blade. "My comrade tells me that something was stolen from him last night. And you, human, are my first target."

CHAPTER THIRTEEN

Guilt filled Samara. She should be the one under Kellam's scrutiny. She shifted a foot forward.

Don't you dare. I realize that this is killing your conscience, but if you admit to it, you put Byzarid, Daena, and me at risk as well as yourself.

Samara halted and drew her foot back, catching a glance from Paxton a couple of apprentices down. She ignored him, not willing to spark any more suspicion.

Blade trembled under the sorcerer's scrutiny. "I didn't do anything. I swear. I have no idea what you're talking about."

"What were you doing last night?" Kellam asked, raising his voice.

Henriette stood beside Blade, her arms shaking by her sides.

As though sensing a friendship between the two teens, Kellam turned his attention to her. He grabbed a clump of her long turquoise hair and yanked it back to expose her rounded human ears. "Ah. That would make sense. The two of you were working together. Weren't you?"

The young female's body trembled violently, making her head shake jerkily.

Seeing the attention turned toward Henriette, Blade steeled his spine and puffed out his chest, looking to be physically bracing himself as he drew Kellam's attention back to him. "After talking with Henriette until late, I saw her to her room then went straight to mine and slept the whole night."

Kellam's eyes narrowed. "Prove it."

His chest caved slightly. "I-I can't."

"Then I shall force it out of you." Kellam twisted his raised wrist.

Sickening amusement filled Vexx's face. He leaned to one side and crossed his arms, waiting for a satisfying outcome.

"What is going on here?"

At the same time, Vexx and Kellam turned to the door.

Standing at the entrance, Callista fixed the

sorcerers with a hard stare. "You're not here to mistreat my apprentices. You had your chance to test their skills the other day in the challenge. What you are doing now is not approved."

Vexx stood tall, his chest puffed out. "But someone broke into the catacombs last night and took important items."

Ulrieg growled. *My cousin and Daena aren't items.*

Honestly, Ulrieg. Did you expect anything else to come out of that sorcerer's mouth?

I guess not. They seem to be made from the same mold. At the moment, it looks like Kellam is the other cloaked figure.

As much as I dislike him, he is saying Vexx is the one who had something stolen. So we can't just assume.

Yeah, right.

Slowly, Callista entered the room, the golden diadem glimmering under the light from the windows. The way she walked reminded Samara of a cat surveying her prey. Mystique followed, her long black tail flicking.

"Whatever important items you claim were stolen are not my concern. For one, none of the apprentices have access to the catacombs."

"You're wrong! There was definitely someone in there last night."

Her face expressionless, the head sorceress rolled

something in her hand, and the ground and walls shook. Kellam lowered his hand from Blade, creating distance between him and the apprentice.

Vexx stood defiant, his snake familiar sticking its head out of his sleeve. The vibration of the floor seemed to increase in intensity until the sorcerer bent his knees to keep his balance, knocking the arrogance from his face.

"Leave my apprentices alone." Callista's voice was cold, a deep threat resonating through it.

Vexx whipped his cloak around him and stormed out of the room, Kellam and his monkey following him.

The floor instantly stopped vibrating, and calmness swept through the air. Callista's fingers still worked the crystals. "I apologize for the behavior of my commanders. They can forget their place at times."

The chairs, which had been shoved against the walls, shifted and magically lined back up as Callista's woven-branch chair filled with a fresh array of flowers. As though expecting to be addressed by the head sorceress, the apprentices sat on the lined chairs as Callista strolled to the front of the room.

Callista spread her arms. "Please, go eat your

breakfast. The cook has complained that it's getting ruined while he waits for you to turn up."

In stunned silence, the apprentices filed out of the room. A sullen ambiance followed them to the dining hall as each one acted almost as though in a trance.

Only Ulrieg's voice broke Samara out of it. *All right. Now I'm confused.*

Samara blinked, her vision clearing and her mind whirling. *About what?*

Callista just stopped her commanding sorcerers from hurting the apprentices because Vexx's things *were missing from the catacombs. She clearly knows about that room and didn't seem to care about the missing items.*

Of course she knows about the catacombs. That's where the tremendous magical power that she consults is.

But what about the missing things she didn't seem to care about? I'm a hundred percent sure he was talking about my cousin and the dragon elf.

Samara sighed. *Like I've said from the start, you can't just assume Callista is guilty. If anything, today has proved the opposite. Maybe she last went down there a few days ago and didn't know what Vexx and possibly Kellam were up to.*

Samara put some freshly baked bread, boiled eggs, and fruit on a plate and took it to a table.

Moments after she sat down, someone sat opposite her.

"Paxton! Morning!"

Her greeting seemed to pull him out of the trance. "Morning."

Samara leaned forward a little and whispered, "If you waited for me last night, I'm sorry I missed you. I did look for you after I woke, but you were already gone. It seemed to be pretty late when I went, though."

His face filled with panic, he replied, "I wasn't the one who took Vexx's stuff."

Samara leaned back and raised her hands. "That's not at all what I meant. I was just saying I'm sorry I missed you."

"Oh." He ran a hand over his dark-green hair. "Actually, I left the library early, as Vexx's and Kellam's familiars were hanging around."

"They were still there when I arrived. I thought they might have been spying on me or something."

Paxton huffed. "I thought the same thing."

"What did you want to meet with me about?" She bit off a piece of bread.

Paxton was suddenly distracted, and Samara turned to find Kaine on his way to the table. Paxton leaned forward and whispered, "If you can, meet me in the library later tonight. Providing the sorcerers' familiars aren't there."

Samara nodded. Although the way Paxton was acting, she didn't want to wait to find out what it was.

"There's my favorite girl." Kaine placed his plate next to Samara's and sat close enough to touch her.

Samara's side warmed, and her heart fluttered.

Oh, that is still sickening every time I see it. The dragon huffed. *Ha! Did you see that?*

Samara groaned through their bond. *I wish you'd lay off. It's off-putting.*

That's the point. Amusement laced the dragon's voice. *But did you see it?*

Her shoulders sagged. *See what?*

The kind one rolled his eyes when Kaine spoke. Even he's sickened by that charmer's efforts.

Samara couldn't help glancing at Paxton, only to find him pulling his eyes away. After that, it was an effort not to show her annoyance. She bit into her apple. "What's our next lesson again?"

Paxton gave her a curious look.

She shrugged. "I think I'm still recovering from my head injury."

Kaine placed a hand on her thigh, and heat pulsed through her. "It's herbology with the lovely people-awkward Eliphas Heliot."

"Oh, that's right. Thanks." She smiled coyly at him.

Ha. He did it again.

Instantly, any pleasant heat was forced away by anger. *Who did what?*

Paxton rolled his eyes again.

Samara closed her eyes, trying to gain control of her anger.

"Are you all right, beautiful?"

Samara opened her eyes in time to see Paxton's face distorted. Ignoring him, she smiled at Kaine. "Yes, I'm fine. Thanks. As I said, my head isn't back to normal yet. I must have taken a massive hit."

He rubbed her leg. "As soon as we're finished eating, I'll escort you on my muscular arm to our next class."

Samara chuckled. "Modest, aren't we?"

Kaine looked hurt. "Me? Never!"

Paxton took the last of his bread from his plate and stood. "I'll see you at the next lesson."

"Bye," Samara called.

Kaine watched him walk away. "What's wrong with him?"

Samara shrugged. "He seemed all right to me." She picked up the second apple and a large chunk of bread and hid them under the hem of her tunic. Daena would need more than just game to eat.

Shrugging, Kaine eyed Samara's empty plate. "Wow! You finished that quickly."

"I was hungry."

He looked at his plate, taking in the two eggs and a large clump of bread. "I guess I need to get to work and finish this."

Samara placed her free hand on his arm. "Take your time. Actually, I need to wash up. I must reek by now."

"Now I really have to eat quickly." He grinned mischievously.

She blushed but regained her composure quickly, thanks to Ulrieg's gagging. "Like I said before. We don't have one of those relationships."

"Not yet."

CHAPTER FOURTEEN

Eliphas Heliot foraged through the potted plants lined up on a bench. The sixty-summers-old instructor continued his usual teaching method of ignoring the students. Phobae, his long stick insect familiar, leaned over his shoulder, watching everything he did. The students might think he was losing his mind if it weren't for the stick insect turning his head, looking interested, every time the teacher muttered.

Every so often, the wizard inserted his fingers into the pot of a struggling plant, and not long later, the leaves flourished, turning brilliant green.

"Eliphas?" Peadar asked. His raccoon familiar, Ziggy, sat near his feet. "Do you mutter incantations to help the plant heal?"

"Hm?" Eliphas spun to face the apprentices,

looking surprised to see them. "Oh, right. You lot are here." He rubbed his large hooked nose, leaving a patch of soil on the tip. "What was the question again?"

"Do you mutter incantations to help the plant heal?" Henriette repeated, her usually mischievous face reflecting some of Peadar's annoyance over a poorly run class.

"Ah. No." Eliphas's eyes crossed as he spotted the dirt on his nose and brushed it off.

"What?" Although Peadar had been with the coterie for a couple of months, he struggled with Eliphas's teaching method.

The teacher stood straight yet still had to look up to meet the tall male's eyes. "I'm a green wizard. My power resides in plants and healing, hence my green hair."

Peadar frowned and ran a hand through his bright-yellow hair. "Then how are we supposed to learn the gift?"

"Oh, right. Um, many of you won't learn how to heal plants. Some may, by learning incantations, and some may also be a green witch or wizard." His eyes landed on Paxton, and he raised an overly hairy eyebrow.

Paxton looked at the plants, his face filled with confusion.

Unfazed that he hadn't answered the question properly, the instructor returned to fiddling with the plants.

After a few moments of awkward silence, Paxton said, "But I haven't shown any sign of being a plant healer."

As though he had forgotten the class again, Eliphas turned to face Paxton, surprise on his face. Phobae seemed to fill him in on the conversation. "The hair color doesn't mean the magic wielder will have the gift. You're a bright young lad. I'm sure you'll work it out."

Paxton leaned against a bench and crossed his arms, looking as annoyed as Peadar.

We need someone like your absentminded teacher here to help heal Byzarid.

Ulrieg had a point. Samara worried her lip. *I know. But it's not like I can tell Eliphas about him. I don't know if he's for or against dragons.*

Well, we certainly can't tell Artemise.

No. I don't trust her at the best of times, Samara agreed. "Eliphas, what about healing humans? Like, say, wound infections?"

"Can't you heal them by magic?" the teacher asked.

"I don't think any of us are at the stage where we can heal infections." Samara looked around, looking for someone to dispute her claim. The apprentices she connected eyes with shook their heads. "It would be nice to know how to heal infections. I ask because when we were captured by the trolls, Kaine's wounds became badly infected, and no matter how hard I tried, I couldn't heal them. He was lucky we could get him back here in time to be healed by our teachers."

"All right. All right. I get the point." Eliphas looked awkward talking to an apprentice for so long, and his words came out rushed. "A couple of things that help fight infection are rosemary and ground cinnamon. Aloe vera is also good for some infections but better for burns or rashes." As though finished with talking to people, he spun back around and continued fiddling with his plants.

"Thank you," Samara said, studying him. Sometimes, his mannerisms were just as hard for others to deal with as it was for him to socialize with people. "That's very helpful. You've told us about aloe vera and comfrey before, and we've seen the plants. Do we have cinnamon or rosemary here to see what they look like? I've seen small branches of dried rosemary in Artemise's class, but I haven't seen a flourishing plant."

Eliphas grabbed a pot with many branches and thin leaves almost an inch long and put it on the empty bench. "This is rosemary. It can grow to a couple of feet tall." He brushed the leaves, and a pungent scent filled the room.

"What about cinnamon? Is that plant in here?" Samara asked, stopping him before he turned back to his bench full of plants.

A surprising sound came out of the wizard, and it took Samara a few moments to realize that he was laughing. "That's wouldn't fit in here. It's a huge tree from which you harvest the bark."

"Oh. Does the coterie have a cinnamon tree?" She gazed out the greenhouse window.

"Of course. Artemise would boil me up in one of her potions if I didn't have one growing."

The image of Artemise cutting him into pieces for her potions ran through her mind. It sounded like something the potions teacher would do. "We don't want that. Where is it?"

"It's the large tree that lies between the pine forest and the typical forest. It's easy to distinguish, as it has large chunks of bark cut from its trunk."

"Can you take us to it?" Peadar asked as though sensing Samara's frustration at only receiving small amounts of information at a time.

"Oh, no. Once you know what to look for, it's obvious." He turned back to his plants, and Samara groaned.

"I know where it is," Henriette said. "I can show you later if you can't find it."

Samara attempted to read her face but came up blank. "As long as it isn't one of your tricks."

Henriette grinned. "I guess you'll just have to find out."

Resting on one of the beams supplied for the flying familiars, Gray flapped above Samara, and she wondered if Ulrieg was with him. The owl still hadn't gotten used to the dragon being invisible and sneaking up on him.

Samara called to him, and he landed on her hand before hopping onto her shoulder. She shifted closer to the rosemary and attempted to break off some while no one was looking, only to find the stems tougher than they looked. She pulled at the leaves, stripping off a long branch, certain Eliphas would notice the damage later. She stripped off another branch on the other side and tried to hide it in her hands. The amount she had taken didn't seem enough.

You're making a mess of that plant, Ulrieg sniped.

I know, but it's tough to break off.

Leave it, and I'll grab more later. I'm sure my talons or teeth will cut through the branches.

Thanks. She shifted away from the plant, hoping no one would notice, only to turn and find Paxton's brown eyes fixed on her. *Arrow sparks! Why is it always the quiet ones who notice everything?*

At least Eliphas didn't see.

I hope. Samara moved farther away from Paxton.

He shifted his gaze away from her, but the hairs on her neck rose, and she cringed, uncertain how she would deal with him later when they met at the library.

CHAPTER FIFTEEN

Turning the corner into the defense class, Samara was hit with a jolt of lightning, and her body convulsed. The power was strong enough to give her pain, but she wasn't singed like in a hit from an actual bolt of lightning. Stunned, she glanced into the room to find Mist grinning, her crow familiar hovering near her.

"Ha! Got you!" the swordswoman called with excitement.

Samara's mind had been elsewhere, and she'd forgotten to be on her guard when she walked into the room. "Where did you learn that?" It wasn't a defense spell she had been taught.

Devi approached Samara. The instructor's long brown gown was fitted around her thin torso and flowed around her ankles. "You're usually on guard when you enter this class. What's wrong?"

"I'm just tired. After I slept off my injury, it was hard to sleep last night." She hated lying to the nicest instructor they had, but it was necessary when she didn't know who to trust.

Devi's young elven face filled with concern. It seemed hard to believe that she was approximately a hundred summers old. She looked over Samara's shoulder. "Where's your familiar?"

Dread filled Samara. She had left Gray in her room. Smacking a palm to her forehead, she said, "I must have forgotten him. I was letting him sleep, then I thought I would be late for this class, so I rushed here." She knew Ulrieg was close, either climbing the walls or slipping into some corner.

Ulrieg, how did we forget Gray?

I thought you were letting him sleep. After all, he is a night creature.

The instructor ran a hand through her short salmon-colored hair. "Are you going to have enough energy to do this class without him?"

"I should. He's only in my room. It's not that far."

Devi placed a hand on her shoulder. "Of course it isn't. I guess it was how pale you looked that made me think that."

Samara turned back to Mist. "Seriously, how did you do that?"

"It's my special gift." Mist pulled at a clump of short white hair at the back of her neck before dropping it and pulling her shoulders back.

Devi walked to the circle of apprentices in the middle of the room to begin class. "Since Mist has been with her familiar longer, she learned to use her power differently."

Samara joined them, wondering if her gift would grow as strong as Mist's. Not that she wanted to hurt people, but wielding power like that would make her ability to enchant arrows to do different things not seem as spectacular.

Blade entered the room, and Henriette hit him with a spell the second he turned the corner. His red hair stretched high and wide, and at the same time, his tunic ripped open, exposing his chest.

"Henriette! I hope you knew that was a male coming and not a female," Devi chided her.

The young witch grinned. "They should be on alert so it won't happen to them."

Devi shook her head. "You are mischievous, aren't you? A move like that on a female would put you in a horrible position, especially if you did it to one of the ones with a familiar. For instance, if you did it to Mist, you might find yourself semifried."

Henriette's pale face turned ghostly, and she brushed her waist-length turquoise hair to drape at the front on one side. Nervously, she glanced at Mist to find her glaring at her. "All right. Next time, I'll be more careful." She turned her attention to Blade's bare chest. "Although he has nothing to worry about. I didn't know he was so muscular underneath." Her pale-blue eyes shone with appreciation, and Blade seemed to enjoy the attention of a female his age, letting the torn fabric separate as he patted down his hair.

Devi cleared her throat. "Today, we're going to learn something different. We're not going to attack each other randomly. I heard a couple of you were forced to levitate during the competition set by the two commanding sorcerers. They used magic above your level, leaving you defenseless." She gazed at Samara and Kaine before turning her attention toward the rest of the class. "I will teach you how to conduct that spell and counter it. But please be aware that the counterspell must be spoken, or it won't work. So if the person is holding your throat magically so you can't speak, you're not going to be able to get down."

She paced in front of the circle of students then stopped in front of Rehan. "Are you willing to be my guinea pig?"

His eyes lit with enthusiasm at first, then his face paled, highlighting his freckles. "Only if you don't choke me." His not-quite-adult voice cracked.

Devi smiled reassuringly. "Like I would hurt you." She tousled his hair then stood farther back. Suddenly, she thrust out a hand and said, *"Elevorto."*

Rehan rose, hovering above head height, his face bright with excitement. "This is spectacular!"

"It's all fun if it's not being used to throw you around. Now, remember this word—*liborte.*"

He nodded and muttered the word softly. Then he dropped to the ground, thinking quickly enough to land on his feet.

"Very good." Devi pushed her sleeves up to her elbows. "You can use this one while you can still speak if they magically have their hands around your throat. But if you can't speak, you're most likely stuck and at their mercy."

"Like this."

Suddenly, Rehan was lifted by a force not simulated by Devi. His eyes widened, and he grabbed at his throat as Devi shifted back.

Soft footsteps padded on the floor as Callista entered the circle, her arm raised, face blank and her eyes shining. Mystique sat just inside the door, looking unimpressed. "The more powerful you are, the better the chance to make the spells work with only a whisper. This can make it dangerous for the unsuspecting."

"You're hurting him, Callista!" Devi looked horrified as Rehan continued to clutch at his throat, his face red and his legs kicking.

Watching him struggle, Callista tilted her head to the side. "Rehan doesn't have a familiar and therefore hasn't grown with the strength given by a familiar." She twisted her hand, turning him upside down.

"Callista," Devi protested. "I was trying to help them defend themselves against the older sorcerers' mistreatment."

"I know." She shifted her hand slightly, releasing the grip around Rehan's throat. "Vexx and Kellam went too far with the apprentices."

Relief washed over Rehan's face until he glanced at the ground. If he said the releasing spell, he would land on his head.

"I was giving him a taste of what it was like." With a twist of a hand, she shifted him back the right way. "Here. He isn't in danger. Although I wanted to give him a more realistic treatment than the soft one you were going to give them."

"*Liborte,*" Rehan muttered and dropped to the ground. He rubbed his throat.

Callista leveled her gaze at Devi. "You get too attached to these apprentices. They need to toughen up, not be instructed like they're toddlers." The head sorceress surveyed the apprentices then stopped in front of Peadar, her eyes dropping to the raccoon familiar by his side. Peadar's Adam's apple bobbed, and Ziggy grimaced as Peadar was magically lifted and clutched at his throat.

Callista's hand had hardly moved. "Work for it. You should be stronger than Rehan, even if your bond with your familiar is new."

Peadar kicked while grasping his throat. His eyes bulged as he fought to regain control. Ziggy chittered, catching Peadar's attention, which seemed to calm him. He gasped out, "*Liborte.*" The grip on his throat loosened.

More clearly, he said, "*Liborte.*" His thin frame dropped to the floor, and he landed awkwardly on his feet. He cried out in pain and held his right ankle.

Devi hurried to him and felt the ankle. "*Mendamora.*" She turned to Callista. "His ankle was sprained."

"I assure you he has been through much worse in Zofia's class. They need to learn by pain." Callista knelt and observed Peadar's ankle. "You've healed it nicely." Rising, she looked down at Peadar. "Did you learn anything from this?"

He nodded, leaving Samara unsure whether he

agreed or was doing it to keep her from doing it again.

"As much as I disagree with Vexx and Kellam taking over the challenge, you will only learn properly if you deal with the pain. My two commanders are brutal, but they have some limitations placed on them in how they treat you because you are apprentices of the coterie. But outside the protection of this building, there are no restrictions. I'm being rough for your own good."

CHAPTER SIXTEEN

Samara gathered the bread, some salted meat, an apple, and the rosemary she had collected as soon as she could. Ulrieg had cut off a couple of large rosemary branches, and she hoped it wasn't the coterie's only rosemary plant. She grabbed her bow and quiver, leaving Gray on his stand. The owl tucked his beak under his wing feathers to get some sleep.

Ulrieg circled between the pine forest and the general forest area to find a tree that looked as Eliphas had described, directing Samara to it. Once she was there, it didn't take her long to confirm that it was the cinnamon tree by the way the bark had been peeled off in large sections.

After gathering several clumps of cinnamon bark, they made their way to see Daena and Byzarid.

She hoped Byzarid's infection hadn't gotten worse. She didn't want the dragon to die. Even worse, she didn't want to face Ulrieg if she couldn't save him.

It was late afternoon, and it had almost been a day since they rescued the two from the catacombs. Invisible, Ulrieg circled back regularly to check for anyone in the woods. If someone did spot her, at least she could use the excuse that she was going for target practice.

She picked up her pace when she was sure no one was near. They had left Daena and Byzarid quite a distance from the building, minimizing the chance that an apprentice or teacher would run into them. The boulder cave sheltered them, but it didn't have enough walls to hide behind if someone did pass by.

They arrived to find Byzarid's head resting in Daena's lap, the dragon elf stroking him along the chin and humming a soft tune.

Ulrieg turned visible and scurried up to his cousin. *What's going on? Is he all right?*

Daena's eyes filled with sadness, and many patches of gray flashed on her skin. "The infections are setting in. He's struggling. I can't even put healing magic into him, as it's so erratic without my dragon. I could end up hurting him more."

Ulrieg grunted. *I've heard about that.*

Samara set to work immediately, finding a large

stone on the ground and a smaller rock to crush the rosemary. The smell was pungent, even in the forest. She scooped up large quantities of the paste and spread it on Byzarid's wounds, using fresh leaves as an applicator. At the same time, she tried to fix the injuries with healing incantations, only to pull away, frustrated. "I hope the rosemary helps. Only time will tell. Unfortunately, herbs don't work as fast as magic does."

Daena worked her bottom lip. "I wish I could take him back to my village. There were some good healers there. Probably not as good as the ones from the Sacred Flame coterie, but they certainly saved many lives."

"Where are you from?" Samara smoothed over some uneven rosemary paste on one of Byzarid's wounds.

"Clialarion."

Now, there's an obvious answer for you.

"Ulrieg!" Samara chastised him.

Ulrieg plunked down next to his cousin's head. *All right, all right! I'm grumpy. It's just that her pointy ears kind of gave away the fact that she's from the land of the elves.*

Daena held up her hands. "You're right. I'm from a village called Astrye. Not many have heard of it."

"I haven't. But then, I've been to very few places."

Samara grabbed her quiver and pulled out pieces of cinnamon bark. "Were there other dragon elves living there?"

Daena picked up a stick and poked at some leaves. "I don't know. My skin didn't start doing these weird things until I passed puberty. Then, every time I felt emotional, I'd get these strange gray patches. I thought it was a weird rash, and I was getting sick." Her face clouded. "It was only after I met Kaida that I realized it was something else entirely."

Samara started grinding the cinnamon bark into powder. It was tough, and blisters grew on her hands, but she pushed through. "How did you meet Kaida?"

"I was a traveling merchant. My village makes woolen blankets. They're beautiful and warm, and I used to travel as far as possible to sell them. One day, a group of ogres pursued me, and my skin was rapidly flashing the gray patches." She looked down at her hand. "Like it is now. I hid in a large clump of thick bushes, and a small animal about the size of an owl wandered up and sat with me. I didn't know what to do. I didn't know what it was or if it was dangerous. Something about the creature felt sooth- ing, but I was still unsure. Before I could decide how to act, she spoke to me."

"Hadn't you heard of dragons either?" Samara pulled out another piece of cinnamon and continued grinding.

"No. And I'd never heard of animals talking before, let alone being intelligent beyond normal animal capabilities. Kaida was extremely knowledgeable about many different things. We talked for a while, then she touched my hand with her nose." The dragon elf lifted a hand to show a diamond shape on her palm.

Samara showed her the small tattoo-like mark in the shape of talons on her hand where Ulrieg had first touched her. "The members of the Sacred Flame coterie get a mark when we bond with our familiars. Although ours represent the animal we bond with." She looked at Ulrieg, whose eyes were fixed on Byzarid, and she gathered handfuls of cinnamon and started covering more infected wounds on the brown dragon. "Did anything else happen to you after Kaida touched you?"

Daena nodded. "It would have only been moments later that my body was completely covered in gray scales, and I started to change form."

Into a dragon? Ulrieg looked away from his cousin long enough to ask.

"Yes. I grew massive, exposing my new form and

whereabouts to the ogres. They came at me with spears and morning stars."

Couldn't you fly away? Ulrieg spread his wings like it would be an obvious choice.

"I tried, but I'd never flown before and was terrible at it, careening out of control and crashing into large trees. I ran and eventually found a place to hide and calm down, and it gave me enough time to work out how to shift back to elven form."

Didn't Kaida help you?

Daena worked her bottom lip. "She constantly talked to me and tried to help me through it, but at first, I was too worked up and scared to listen. When I did calm down, I learned that my magic was no longer a danger in my elven form. It worked well, not misfiring like before I bonded with Kaida. It didn't distort things, almost doing the opposite of what I wanted."

"I imagine that would have been a relief for you." Samara was almost finished covering the last few infected wounds with cinnamon.

Daena brushed her hands down her pants.

Samara realized they were full of holes and crusted with dried blood, and so was her long-sleeved tunic. She cringed. It must be horrible, wearing the evidence from what she'd experienced in the catacombs. She made a mental note to bring Daena some new clothes the next time she visited.

The dragon elf's face saddened. "It was a relief, but it only lasted two days, so it's not like I had a chance to use it much, let alone perfect it. It turns out the ogres I ran into worked for the sorcerer who hurt me and probably killed Kaida." She wiped her eyes, and her hand came back damp. "I wouldn't have thought I'd miss someone that much after only knowing them for such a short time. I guess it's a deep bond."

"I'm sorry." Samara placed a hand on Daena's shoulder. "They say it would deeply affect us if our familiar passed away." She gazed at Ulrieg. "I believe that would be true. They are a part of us."

The dragon elf nodded and let a tear trickle down her face.

What about the powers that come with that bond? Ulrieg asked.

She shook her head. "They're gone. I can no longer shapeshift, and my magic misfires again. I tried to make a pile of leaves for a bed using my magic." She pointed at a hole on the other side of the boulder's shelter. "Instead, it made that crater."

Samara rubbed her shoulder, not knowing what to say. Byzarid moaned, and she pulled her attention back to him to inspect his wounds. She hoped it was a sign that they were starting to mend. Her optimism died when she saw the redness of his infections. She hadn't expected instant healing, but she had hoped for some improvement, especially since she had also used magic.

Ulrieg paced, his eyes turning a deeper red as his worries for his cousin intensified.

Watching him going through the turmoil increased her worry. She wrapped her arms around her knees and rocked on her toes, watching over Byzarid, racking her brain for something else she could do. She was starting to question whether he would pull through. It was looking more like she would need outside help, but she didn't know who to trust.

Daena's stomach growled, reminding Samara that she was there.

"Oh. I'm so sorry. I was so caught up trying to help Byzarid that I forgot about the food I brought you."

The dragon elf's eyes lit up with enthusiasm.

Dragon moon! Ulrieg cursed before springing into flight.

After watching him curiously, Samara turned back to the dragon elf. "It's not a banquet, but it'll stop that growling." She went to her quiver, glad to have something productive to do, and pulled out the bread, fruit, and meat she had snuck from the dining hall.

The dragon elf took the food from Samara. "This is perfect. Thank you."

When Daena was halfway through her chunk of bread, Ulrieg returned with a hawk dangling from his talons. He tossed it at the dragon elf's feet. *Same as before. If you remove the feathers, I'll build a fire.*

Daena caught his worried glance at Byzarid. "I'll feed some to him, too, if he will eat."

Thank you. Ulrieg quickly gathered kindling and larger sticks. When he'd arranged them, he breathed out a small plume of fire, just enough to set the leaves alight. He tossed a long stick at Daena, and she sharpened it with Samara's knife and threaded the bird onto it.

CHAPTER SEVENTEEN

B y the time they had finished making sure Daena was fed, darkness filled the sky. The moon shone brightly, and as Ulrieg had said, it wasn't quite full. They stayed in the darkness under the trees' shadows. If they hurried, Samara would be able to make dinner. Though worry was stripping her of her appetite, she hoped to be able to get some more food for Daena. Ulrieg clung to her back. She didn't mind, even though he was heavy. It almost seemed like an emotional attachment he needed to fill after hearing Daena and Kaida's story and seeing his cousin in a bad way.

"I'm going to need some help healing Byzarid."

Ulrieg didn't respond, and her stomach churned.

"The rosemary and cinnamon may be helping him, but his infections are bad. I'm not confident they will work quickly enough. But I don't have a clue who to trust. Artemise would probably have some potions that would work better. Although I wouldn't trust her for even a moment."

There's no way I'm letting her near him. She'd probably torture him, or if she did heal him, she'd betray him to the others so they could do it all again.

"There's Eliphas and his healing gift."

I can't tell if he's harmless or not. His strangeness is hard to see through.

"Zofia and Devi don't specialize in healing. They focus on combat and defense."

Zofia is iffy. Devi is nice, but I can't trust any of your instructors, to be honest.

They reached the pine forest. The dried needles crunched under Samara's boots, and their scent gave the air a different kind of freshness. "Then the only other thing I know to do is try to learn some healing potions."

Ulrieg rested his chin on her shoulder, and his heat radiated through her body. *I'll think it over. If I think of someone I trust who may be able to help, I'll let you know. Otherwise, that may be our only option.*

"I guess I have to hit the library tonight."

Don't you have to go to the library anyway to see Paxton?

Remembering Paxton spotting her stealing the

rosemary made a lump form in her throat. She swallowed, trying to push it down. "After what he saw me do in herbology, I'm not sure how that meeting will go."

Ulrieg shrugged, and his talons shifted, digging into Samara's shoulders. *I'm not sure either. Although he's acting a little strange over this meeting he wants to have with you.*

Samara touched his front talons lightly, and he fixed his position. "True. Somehow, though, I don't think it'll be as big as our secret. Our bonding would get me kicked out of the coterie and cut off my family's assistance."

Under the shadow of a large tree, something black moved from behind the trunk.

Wingless flight! Ulrieg tensed, digging his talons into her shoulders again. *I was so distracted by my worry for Byzarid that I wasn't keeping an eye out.* He pushed off her shoulder and took flight.

Samara pulled her bow off her shoulder and nocked an arrow. She directed it at the shadow and noticed just in time that it was Zofia's sun bear familiar. She lowered the arrow. "Jet. You startled me."

The bear growled and gazed at where Samara imagined Ulrieg was perched.

Ulrieg, did he see you?

He shouldn't have. I changed a while back just in case someone was out here.

Then why is he looking for you?

I don't know. Maybe he can smell me.

Argh! Why do some animals have to have such great senses of smell? It's not like I can use Gray as an excuse to be out here.

A stick cracked several feet away. Zofia had a dark cape covering most of her body, and the hood was raised. She was hard enough to see because of her size, let alone in the dark, covered with dark fabric.

The instructor studied the area. "Samara, you're out late."

Samara placed her arrow back in her quiver and returned the bow to her shoulder. "Yes. I was out practicing my archery when I lost track of time."

"Where's your owl?"

"I left him in my room because he needed some sleep, and it was still midafternoon when I left. He's probably stuck there, cursing me." She huffed a laugh to try and lighten Zofia's mood. Zofia had always been levelheaded and, because of that, was probably one of the harder ones to lie to. She was a no-nonsense type.

"I guess you'd better hurry up and let him get out, or you might find your room destroyed."

"Really?"

Zofia nodded. "I've heard about it happening before. The night animals are happy to be kept in a small enclosure during the day but will let you know it if you leave them there during the night."

"Then I'd better get back to him. I'm rather attached to my room." Samara turned to jog away. "I'll see you tomorrow for training," she called over her shoulder.

Zofia lifted a hand in acknowledgment, and Jet made a low groaning sound.

That was close.

Do you think she believed me?

I don't know. She acted like she did, but there was an underlying current of tension.

We're going to have to be more careful.

Agreed. She hurried up the steps, grabbed Gray, and headed to the dining room to catch the last of dinner.

WHEN SHE FINISHED HER MEAL, she put the additional food she had taken in a sack and chose a long-sleeved tunic and long pants to take to Daena. The dragon elf seemed to be a similar size to her. She placed them in the bag she intended to take the next time she went and attached the bag to her quiver. While doing that, she fed Gray a little fowl from the kitchen. Forgrac had left her a small piece to give to him. The owl tore it to shreds, swallowing bits at a time.

He had finished his meal by the time Samara had put everything together, and she coaxed him onto her shoulder and headed for the library. Even if they didn't meet with Paxton, she needed to find books about potions. Artemise hadn't taught them any healing potions for infections yet. Samara frowned, realizing that the instructor hadn't taught them any potions for healing at all. She seemed to love focusing on ones that would cause discomfort, illness, or even death. But that wasn't surprising after seeing how the sorceress acted.

Weaving her way through the corridors, she spotted the monkey in the main room. She stopped short, peeking around the corner. Kellam's familiar marched through the room, holding his tail high and surveying the area from one side to the other. His golden head brightened every time he passed under a sconce.

Samara pressed farther back, hiding behind a large pot, and hoped the monkey hadn't seen her. Knowing the horrible sorcerer behind the familiar made Mystique seem tame. She flattened herself against the cold stone wall and held her breath, waiting for him to pass.

The monkey paused at the entrance to her corridor, surveying its length. The moment seemed to drag on forever. He fixed his eyes on something past Samara before he lifted his chin and pressed forward.

She released her breath, gazing down the far end of the corridor to find Mystique sitting with her back straight, watching her. Gray twitched. Seeing the yellow eyes still unsettled her, even if she and Callista were on their side. But that was unconfirmed. Nervous, Samara chuckled softly. "I hope you understand. After what his bonded did, I can't stand that familiar."

The jaguar merely stared back, blinking once.

Samara grimaced. She was trying to be open-minded about the cat and Callista, but Mystique still made her uneasy. Sensing that the monkey had passed, she pushed off the wall and continued, trying hard not to glance over her shoulder.

Once she arrived at the library, she checked the bottom level for Paxton before climbing the stairs to the upper level.

He's not here.

Samara cursed. *I was hoping to get this conversation over with. He has me on tenterhooks, wondering why he's being so secretive. I also hoped he could point me to the right books to learn healing potions.* Slowly, she weaved her way through the shelves, checking titles and any labeled shelves, looking for anything mentioning potions. *This is going to be a long night. You wouldn't happen to know how to read, would you?*

Sure. We dragons know how to read, Ulrieg said sarcastically.

Hey! I knew it was a long shot. I was hoping someone would be able to help. She found a section that looked like it would be about potions and pulled out a book to flick through the pages. There were so many potions, and she didn't know where she would find the ingredients.

If I find one I think will work, I might have to get you to break into Artemise's potions room to steal ingredients. Arrow sparks! I may have to use the room's equipment as well as her ingredients. She turned more pages. *If I can even work out which one to use. Some of them aren't even clear about what they're used for.* After passing over more pages, she groaned and tossed the book onto the shelf. Gray startled, flying to another shelf.

"Don't treat the books like that!" Paxton peeked around the corner, looking amused.

Relieved he had arrived yet also anxious, Samara said, "You're here."

He braced himself on one of the shelves. "Yes. It

took me a while to get past the monkey then the snake."

"I saw the monkey but not the snake." Samara picked up the book she'd manhandled and placed it neatly back in its spot, conscious that Paxton was watching her the whole time.

"What are you looking for?" he asked as Jojo peeked out of his blue tunic.

She looked at the book then at Paxton, trying to piece together what to tell him. "I was hoping to learn some healing potions."

He arched an eyebrow. "Something a little stronger than the rosemary you stole from Eliphas?"

She cleared her throat. "Ah, yes. I don't think rosemary or cinnamon will be strong enough."

His eyes quickly passed over her. "Are you injured?"

Her jaw dropped. "No! I just wanted to learn how to heal, you know, as I said in Eliphas's class."

Paxton's mouth thinned. "That's all right. If you don't want to tell me the real reason, I'll leave it that way."

He's clever, that one.

Thanks for your commentary, Ulrieg. I've already worked that out.

"What do you mean?" Samara attempted to look innocent.

"For a start, if you only want to learn how to heal infections, you wouldn't have pinched rosemary earlier. You'd just need the knowledge."

Samara expelled a long breath. She didn't know what to say.

He held up his hands. "As I said, if you don't want to tell me, you don't have to." His gaze flicked around the library, and he peered over the railing at the level below.

Dragon moon! He's being cautious and peculiar, Ulrieg grunted.

That, he is, Samara agreed.

CHAPTER EIGHTEEN

Looking satisfied that no one was in the library, Paxton turned back to Samara, uncertainty in his eyes.

"What did you want to talk to me about?" Samara asked, studying his face. "I won't tell anyone, unless you're a psychopath who's intentionally hurting people and things. Because I won't stand for that."

"What?" Paxton pulled back. "No. Where did that come from?"

Wingless flight! You have a way with words, Ulrieg grumbled.

Ignoring him, she chortled. "It was a bad attempt at a joke to try to ease your nerves. You can tell me."

"Jojo tells me I can."

Samara blinked. The comment surprised her. She didn't think a frog could be wise. Maybe it was something to do with the magic created when they bonded.

Huh! Look at that. He listens to his familiar. Smart lad.

Paxton moved closer, pushing his long green ponytail behind his shoulders. His face looked paler than normal. "I've been doing some more research since you asked about the emblem," he whispered.

"Do you mean the one of a triangle with softened corners and a five-pointed star in the middle?"

"Yes. The one that represents the exclusive circle of the Sacred Flame coterie."

"I don't think I thanked you for asking Artemise all those questions and not letting on it was me. I don't know why you did it, but thanks."

He waved a hand. "I was happy to. I'm always curious, especially about unusual things. And after questioning Artemise, I did some more digging through the books. It turns out more information about the emblem is here in the library. I had to ask Artemise because I didn't have time to find it before class."

Samara sat on a padded bench seat in front of the shelves, and Paxton sat on the opposite side.

"It turns out that this exclusive part of the coterie has members that were part of the last battle."

KATRINA COPE

"Do you mean the one Callista was in? The one where they defeated the great evil?"

"Yes." Paxton pushed off the chair and pulled a book from a shelf a few rows down. "It turns out that several of the teachers are part of this exclusive group either because they participated in the battle or are direct descendants of mages from the group."

Oh. This is getting interesting. He has *been digging.*

Samara ran a hand through her hair. "All right. That's not surprising. There would likely be a reason they were chosen to instruct us and live under the power that Callista consults."

"I understand that. It sounds interesting to me because when I found the book that displayed their emblem, it had pages of history written in it."

"All right," Samara said, holding back her enthusiasm.

Paxton flicked through the book then stopped at a page. He opened it wide and presented it to Samara. "But look." He pointed at the page. "So much of the history has been blotted out." He flicked through more pages, exposing the thick, black lines over many sentences and paragraphs.

Would you look at that? The coterie is covering its tracks. Trustworthy, are they?

Samara ignored Ulrieg's gripe, grabbed the book, and flicked through it at her own pace, passing the emblem, which was pictured precisely as she and Ulrieg had seen in the catacombs and also on Artemise's key. She met Paxton's enthusiastic eyes. "That's rather odd."

That's an understatement!

Ulrieg, your cynicism is distracting!

Just saying what I think.

Now, there's a shock! she sniped.

Paxton nodded, pulling Samara's attention back to their conversation. "Why would they delete so much of their history? Wouldn't they want us to be able to learn about their past?"

Samara quirked her mouth. "Lately, I've been rather untrusting, especially after what Kaine and I went through with the trolls. So my thought would be that this behavior is extremely suspicious."

His eyes clouded with confusion. "But we're supposed to be proud of this coterie and strive to serve them for the good of the realms."

Again, Ulrieg's voice cut through Samara's thoughts. *Honestly, there should have been warning bells when they said they'd cut your families' help off if you no longer served under them.*

Samara glowered at the spot where she thought Ulrieg was sitting. *Paxton's family was in just as bad a position as mine was when we joined. We had no other choice if we wanted to help our families survive.*

All right! Dragon moon! I'll take that back. I was only saying it as I saw it.

"Are you all right?"

Samara faced Paxton to realize he had been watching her when she was scolding Ulrieg. "Oh, yes. I was deep in thought." She focused on the book, trying to work out how much to say. "Have you ever thought about how brutal it is that they would cut off our families' help if we didn't bond with a familiar or failed to excel in the way they wanted us to?"

A frown creased his forehead, and he gazed toward the lower level. "It does seem rather callous, but they would've remained in that position if we didn't join the coterie. I'm sure the coterie's funds aren't unlimited."

"That's true." Samara inspected the book's pages, pointing at the blacked-out paragraphs. "Have you been able to read any of these?"

He pulled his shoulders back. "I've been able to read small parts but not enough to make sense of it."

"Do share." Samara nudged him playfully with her elbow.

"It's not much, but some parts mentioned dragons and something about a realm disappearing."

No wonder he's been acting so shifty.

Samara's heart raced. "Really? Have you found anything on these dragons or the realm?"

"Nothing about another realm so far. Although I have found a book that has an animal called a dragon." He went to another bookshelf and returned with a book, opening it to a page with pictures of different types of dragons. After he handed the book to Samara, he clenched his hands. "Is it me, or do these look like the creatures we've been taught are the great beasts and that we are to hunt down? The ones that certain elves can turn into."

Her jaw dropped, and she was glad to be able to focus on the book instead of Paxton's face. They even had a picture of dragons that looked like Ulrieg and tiny dragons that looked just like Kaida. Eventually, she nodded. "But why don't they call them by name when they mention them?"

Paxton shrugged. "At the risk of sounding like you, the more I find out, the more the Sacred Flame coterie's actions seem suspect."

Samara froze. *Ulrieg, what do I say? What does your moon sensitivity tell you?*

A strange silence filled their bond.

Ulrieg?

I don't know! he snapped. *It's such a big step. I believe my moon sensitivity is reinforcing that we can trust him, but my head is fighting it.*

Isn't your moon intuition usually correct?

Yes. But I still like to be cautious. I didn't tell you much the first day I met you either.

True.

"Are you all right?" Again, Paxton was watching Samara's face as she consulted with Ulrieg.

"Sorry, I was just talking with my familiar."

Good save, Ulrieg said. *See if you can dig a little about his healing abilities.*

"What does Gray have to say?" Paxton looked up at the owl, noticing that he was looking at his frog familiar. He tucked Jojo back into the safety of his tunic.

"Is it true that you may be able to heal?"

His eyebrows rose. "Why do you ask?"

Giving him a half smile, she said, "As you've already heard, I can't heal infected wounds. I can only heal a few cuts, bruises, et cetera, and that's very limiting."

Paxton pressed his palms together and slid them between his knees. "So you want me to spill more of my secrets?"

"Only if you're willing. I think it would be a fascinating and useful gift."

He rubbed his chin and pursed his lips. "As you know, I spend a lot of time in the library."

"Uh-huh."

"So that means I've learned all the healing spells I can find."

"Really?"

He nodded. "So I could help you with the potion you wanted to make."

"That would be fantastic!"

"But…"

Her heart plummeted as she thought about the lousy shape Byzarid was in.

Smiling slyly, he tugged at his emerald-green ponytail. "I can heal infected wounds. The hair color, in this case, is a sign."

Samara clasped her hands together as hope rushed through her. *Ulrieg, has this given you an answer?*

Tell him. Let's hope he's as trustworthy as my senses are saying.

CHAPTER NINETEEN

Samara's heart raced with apprehension as she leaned closer to Paxton and lowered her voice. "Can I trust you with *my* secret?"

His brow furrowed as he leaned back to look at her.

Worry niggled her. Still, she pressed on. "My familiar says I can."

He turned to the owl. "Gray?"

Samara grimaced through her teeth, hoping it could be mistaken as a smile that didn't hit the eyes. "Uh-huh."

"Of course. You keep my secret, and I'll keep yours."

"Perfect! Although I think mine might be bigger than yours." She rose and coaxed Gray off the top shelf then placed him on her shoulder. "Are you up for a trip?"

"Right now?" Paxton tilted his head to one side.

"Now is as good a time as any. Although can you bring your flail?"

"What for?" His frown deepened.

"As a cover. It's an excuse for being outside."

"All right," he said hesitantly.

"Great! I'll meet you outside, under the stairs."

AFTER FETCHING her bow and quiver with the extra bag for Daena from her room, Samara made it outside. The night was still young, and surprisingly, no familiars stopped her. With Gray on her shoulder, she waited under the stairs, night animals calling in the distance. A cool breeze rushed past, and she rubbed her bare arms.

Are we making the right choice, Ulrieg?

He had remained invisible. *I hope. If he exposes our secret, especially to Vexx and Kellam, we will all be in huge trouble.*

She fiddled with the hem of her tunic. *In the meantime, stay out of sight, just in case.*

Wild grass rustled behind her, and she spun to

see Paxton's silhouette in the moonlight. His flail was strapped to his back, the spiky end up in the air.

"That was a mission. The monkey and the snake were loitering down the corridor from my room." He surveyed the area, taking in the trees highlighted in the moonlight. "Besides the times I was trying to bond with my familiar, I've never left the building this late. It's kind of peaceful and eerie."

Samara pointed at Gray. "I've been out here a lot. I have to keep this one happy. You're right, though. Sometimes, the familiars make me feel like I'm doing the wrong thing. Even Mystique." She coaxed Gray onto her hand and tossed him into the air.

"Aren't you taking him with you?"

She shook her head. "He needs to spread his wings and eat. Come on." Samara led him through the pine forest and into the general forest. With each step, her nerves jangled. There was nothing they could do now. It would seem strange if they suddenly decided not to show him, and she was out of options for Byzarid.

After a while, Paxton asked, "How far are we going?"

"It's a bit of a walk, but it shouldn't be too long now." A breeze brushed her cheek, and she knew it was Ulrieg telling her where he was.

"Do you often travel so far without Gray?"

"I've done it several times over the last two days." Her answer was honest, although it wasn't the answer to his real question.

"I don't know if I could go that far from Jojo without feeling it."

They had walked a bit longer when Paxton suddenly grabbed her arm and yanked her to a stop.

"What is—"

He held his finger over his lips and pointed. A fire was flickering around the side of a boulder. She smiled and gently lowered his hand.

"It's all right. That's where we're going."

The confusion on his face was priceless.

"Who's there?" came a voice.

"It's just me, Daena," Samara called.

The dragon elf shifted from around the boulder's edge before she stopped short. "Who's that?"

"This is Paxton. He's a fellow apprentice. We can trust him."

Paxton followed close behind Samara, his expression just as uncertain as Daena's.

"How come he doesn't have brightly colored hair? I thought you said all the coterie members have it."

"He does. It's dark green, so it's hard to see in this light. He has the gift of healing and might be able to help us."

Paxton studied the dragon elf. "Is she injured?"

"Not anymore. Her wounds weren't infected."

A deep frown creased his forehead. "Then who's injured?"

Samara turned to face him and gently placed her hands on his upper arms. "I need you to remain calm."

"You're not making me feel comfortable here." He looked from her to the dragon elf several times.

"Do you remember how I said that my secret is probably bigger than yours?"

He nodded.

"Well, I lied. My secret is definitely bigger than yours."

He seemed even more uncertain as he pulled back slightly.

"Don't worry. You're not in any danger from us, although the knowledge may put you in danger from others." Samara clasped his hand.

"What's around the corner?" He gazed back at Daena.

Samara guided him around the boulder's edge to see what the firelight illuminated. Byzarid remained on his side, his breathing ragged. He was still covered in crushed rosemary and cinnamon.

Paxton froze. "Is... Is that a dragon?"

"Yes." Samara gently tugged him forward.

"Where did you find a dragon?" He moved with her, appearing keener to see more with every step.

Samara looked briefly to the ground. "Do you remember what Vexx and Kellam were harassing us about this morning?"

"About how someone had taken something of Vexx's from under the building?"

She nodded. "That was me and my familiar. We found these two chained up and being tortured along with a small guardian dragon with her heart cut out."

Paxton screwed up his nose in distaste. "Are you telling me Vexx did this?"

"From what Daena described of her captor and how Vexx acted this morning, I believe so." Byzarid's labored breath caught her attention. "The dragon was held captive for longer. I found him earlier but couldn't get him out then, as two cloaked figures entered the area. So his wounds are infected."

Paxton squatted next to the dragon, touched a smaller sore, and set to work healing it. "Isn't that area restricted and locked so that the apprentices can't enter?"

Samara dug the toe of her boot into the ground. "You know that emblem I asked you about?"

His eyebrows rose. "Yes."

"It was on a door I discovered in the underground cave and couldn't get past. After you asked Artemise about it, my familiar found a necklace she has with that emblem on it and borrowed it for the night. It acted as a key and let us into the restricted area."

He paused his healing, looking flabbergasted. "You're right. Your secret is bigger than mine."

Byzarid moaned, drawing his attention back to healing.

Something caught his eye, and he looked at Daena. "Is your skin suffering from a rash?"

Talking about the catacombs must have stirred up Daena's emotions, and gray scales flashed on her skin.

Daena shook her head. "I'm fine. This is normal."

Her answer only seemed to confuse him more.

Samara shifted closer to the dragon elf. "Daena was captured because she's one of the shifters they talk about being the enemy."

He faced her and pointed at Byzarid. "Is this your dragon?"

Daena shook her head, the patches appearing more rapidly. "My dragon was the one with her heart cut out."

Paxton wiped his brow with his sleeve. "That's horrible. I'm sorry."

She shook her head and stomped into the darkness.

Watch out for her, Ulrieg.

I will.

Watching her disappear, Paxton asked, "Is she changing into a dragon?"

"No." Samara poked the ground with a stick. "She can't anymore because her bonded dragon is dead."

His shoulders sagging, Paxton set back to work on Byzarid, and Samara watched in silence as he healed the wounds one by one. The infection drew out of the skin, almost making her stomach turn.

After a while, Ulrieg asked, *How's he doing? Is he succeeding?*

It looks to be working. Many of the external wounds are healed, although there were a lot. Paxton may run out of energy before Byzarid is fully healed.

Let's hope it'll be enough to stabilize him until another round.

Samara stoked the fire, remembering she had brought clothing and extra food for Daena. She untied the bag from her quiver and set it down near the boulder where the dragon elf had created her bed.

"Do you think Callista is in on the torture?" Paxton asked when she settled near him again.

She hooked a clump of hair behind her ear. "I

honestly don't know. She confuses me. But she did stop Vexx and Kellam harassing the apprentices this morning, claiming she didn't care what they had lost."

"What about the other instructors?" He started on another wound.

"I don't know. I'm certainly not going to ask them. It's why I couldn't ask Eliphas to come and heal the dragon."

He placed his hands on the dragon's head. "They're magnificent creatures."

"That's only a small one, apparently."

"Wow! I wonder what it's like seeing a big one." He pulled his hand away from the dragon, his face looking drained. "I hate to say it, but I think that's all I can do tonight. His wounds were quite bad."

"Thank you. It means a lot that you helped."

"I just hope it's enough." He studied her, and she focused on the flames. "You seem very invested in their well-being."

Samara glanced at him before returning her gaze to the fire, hoping her expression didn't give away too much.

"I'm not saying that's bad. I'm just saying that it's unusual to care so much for beings you don't know."

Samara stacked some more logs on the fire, causing sparks to rise in the air. She shrugged. "I guess I can't help it. They're a rare breed in need of help."

Silence cut the air between them, only broken by the crackling of the fire. A little while later, footsteps crunched in the leaves, and Samara turned to find Daena returning, her brow furrowed.

"Where's Ulrieg? I thought he was always by your side."

CHAPTER TWENTY

"Who's Ulrieg?" Paxton said the name slowly, like it was a foreign word.

Dragon moon! There's no hiding it now. Good job, Daena! I was staying invisible for a reason.

The dragon elf paled and met Samara's eyes with a wordless apology then sat down next to her.

Samara's heart jumped to her throat as she studied Paxton's exhausted, confused face. She took a deep breath, trying to calm her nerves. "How many surprises can you handle in one day?"

"You have more?"

"Unfortunately. This one, I've been keeping for longer. And it will explain a lot to you about tonight."

Jojo peeked out of Paxton's tunic, his black, beady eyes landing on Samara.

Paxton glanced down at him. "Jojo says he suspected as much."

"You have a very wise frog."

"All right. Fill me in, or trying to figure it out will drive me crazy." He crossed his legs, waiting expectantly.

"Ulrieg, please show yourself." Samara gazed at a spot between her and Paxton, where she had seen a leaf move unnaturally only moments before. Ulrieg's black, horn-covered body phased into view, his eyes set on the young wizard.

One look at the dragon's red eyes had Paxton scooting back. Then he stopped. "Hold on. He's exactly like one of the dragons in the book."

"Yes. I saw that picture."

Daena said to Ulrieg, "I'm sorry. I didn't know she hadn't told him about you before you came."

It's a bit late now. Ulrieg shot a look at her.

"The dragon talks?" Paxton's gaze bounced from Daena to Samara then to Ulrieg. "Do all dragons talk?"

Ulrieg leveled him with a stare. *I'm going to pretend I didn't hear that.*

"Ulrieg, be nice," Samara chided him. "He's had a big night."

That is *me being nice.*

"Remember, he's healing Byzarid." Samara frowned at him.

All right. Sorry. His voice held no regret, although his eyes softened when he lowered his head and sniffed Byzarid.

"Is that his name? Are you with this dragon?" Paxton asked while watching Ulrieg's tenderness toward the brown dragon.

Ulrieg moaned, expressing his grief for his cousin's pain.

"Please excuse Ulrieg. He's often sarcastic and appears grumpy, but I've learned it's usually for show." Samara watched her dragon and caressed the end of his tail.

"How do you know so much about him?"

"Ulrieg is my true familiar."

Paxton's eyes widened. "How did I miss this? I usually notice everything."

"It would have been hard. He's always invisible. Plus we had Gray as a cover."

His mouth formed a thin line as he looked from Samara to Ulrieg.

"And Byzarid, the dragon you've been healing, is his cousin."

Paxton studied Ulrieg. "I won't ask if I can pet you."

You'd better not! Ulrieg's eyes narrowed.

Paxton pulled his hands farther away from the dragon. "But your mark shows Gray as your familiar."

She held out her mark for him to study under the firelight. "It's a dragon's talon, although it could be mistaken for an owl's claw."

He studied the mark and nodded. "That's true. Then what's Gray?"

"He's a pet, caught for me by Ulrieg before we returned to the coterie when we escaped the trolls. Ulrieg doesn't trust any members of the Sacred Flame coterie and insisted on staying hidden." Samara placed her hands in her lap. "So far, it's proving a wise decision, especially after we found the two dragons and Daena under the building."

"Are you telling me Gray is a pet bird that would be interested in eating Jojo?"

Samara rubbed her ear, finding it hard to look Paxton in the eye. "I was doing my best not to let him."

"Wow! That's scary."

"You've always been very protective of him with all the familiars, so I didn't think it would make any difference. He's been well-behaved for a wild bird since I tamed him."

Paxton slapped a hand on his thigh. "That

explains why he was so unsettled when you first brought him back."

Samara brushed some leaves off her pants and nodded. "As you can see, I'm in a bit of a predicament. It appears as though my familiar is under threat by the coterie or at least some of its members. At the same time, I can't leave, because my family would no longer be looked after and could end up enslaved again, struggling to put food on their plates."

Paxton gazed at Ulrieg, his cousin, then at Daena. "Yes. You win. Your secret is bigger."

"I'm also making assumptions. I don't know if Callista or any instructors are opposed to dragons. But frankly, I'm not willing to risk it."

"Does Kaine know?"

She shook her head. "No one knows but the people here."

"So you traveled together all the way back from the trolls' lair with a new familiar and a wild bird, and Kaine didn't notice."

Samara nodded.

Paxton huffed. "I guess Kaine is too focused on himself and charming all the girls instead of noticing the important things."

Wow! Listen to him. He's nailed it on the head. I told you I liked him more.

"Ulrieg, please," Samara pleaded, noticing Paxton's reaction and realizing that the dragon had relayed his words, so everyone heard them.

Paxton gazed at the dragon with his head tilted to one side before turning back to Samara. "I will keep your secret. You're one of the best in this place. And you have a good heart."

Samara's cheeks warmed. "Thanks."

He threw some loose leaves onto the fire, and they crackled brightly. Then he turned to Daena. "Are you the only one of your kind?"

She shrugged. "I don't know. I didn't know what I was until I met Kaida. Then we were only together two days before we were captured and imprisoned under your building."

"Does anyone know about this realm that disappeared?"

Ulrieg lifted his gaze from his cousin, focusing on Paxton. *It's our homeland. We dragons can't find it to go home, but it's there somewhere. I can feel it. My family has been looking since we were cut off.*

"That's terrible! Can you tell me anything about it?" Paxton threw some more leaves onto the fire and watched them send sparks into the air.

Besides being our home, it is also the home of the guardian dragons.

"What are guardian dragons?"

Daena's skin pulsed with gray patches again. "They're the little dragons. Kaida was one of them, and when they bond with elves like me, we can turn into large dragons. While they're with us and we're in our elven form, our magic is powerful."

They become warriors and protectors. Before the realm was cut off, they used to protect the kingdoms from the dark magic threatening the lands. Ulrieg faced the fire, resting his head on his front talons.

"How long ago was this?" Paxton asked.

Four hundred years ago.

"Wow! Really? I know so little of any of this. I only knew about dragon elves for the two days I was bonded with Kaida." Daena played with a cut in her pants where a wound had been before she was healed.

"I forgot to mention." Samara pointed at the spot near the boulder. "I brought you some new clothes and some more food. I hope it'll be enough to last until I see you again."

"Thank you," Daena said. "You've been so kind."

"You're helping look after Byzarid. Of course I'll bring you what I can. I'm pretty sure Paxton is spent and can't do any more healing for tonight."

He nodded, his mouth turning down at the edges. "I hope it's been enough to stabilize him."

Ulrieg's misery passed through their bond, and

her heart wept when she looked into his red eyes. "It's late. We should be getting back before people get suspicious."

Ulrieg climbed to his feet, stretching his legs. We're coming back as soon as we can, though. Right?

"Of course," Paxton answered for her. "Like Samara, I can't stand it when creatures are being mistreated for no other reason than they exist."

Daena stood with them, squeezing Samara's and Paxton's hands. "Thank you for everything."

As they walked through the forest, back to the building, the calls from the animals surrounded them. They were peaceful sounds, owls hooting or raccoons chattering or crickets chirping mixed with many other animals and the gentle rustling of the leaves.

Paxton retrieved Jojo from his shoulder and cradled him in his hands, checking the trees for any threats to his familiar's life. "If Daena didn't know she was a dragon elf, let alone anything about dragon elves, I wonder how many others are out there."

Samara felt the breeze of Ulrieg's wings and was glad she didn't have to worry about his being eaten by nearly every animal. "I have no idea. But I hope there are more unsuspecting dragon elves with at least that many, if not more, guardian dragons in Dragoria."

"Does Ulrieg know any more?"

Samara shook her head. "I don't think so. I'll ask, but most of his knowledge has been handed down to him by dragons who've never seen a dragon elf and a guardian dragon."

Paxton brushed aside a low branch. "I'll have to go through that book with some history of the coterie and comb through the blotted pages. Hopefully, I'll find more information in there."

As they neared the building, they kept to the shadows cast by the almost-full moon.

Samara searched the trees. "You go back into the building, and I'll look for Gray. If anyone asks you where you've been, remember to say you were out practicing with your flail."

As he mounted the stairs, Paxton nodded and secured Jojo in his hand, protecting him from a potential attack from Gray or other creatures.

Samara called Gray, and the leaves rustled above her as Ulrieg settled in them with the owl in his talons and turned invisible. The owl struggled against the dragon's clasp but returned to Samara the moment Ulrieg let him go. He landed on her shoulder.

Be prepared, Ulrieg warned her.

"For what?" Samara asked then was startled when a branch cracked behind her. She turned and came face-to-face with Ginger and Kaine.

The fox sniffed the air as Kaine grinned. Her head swayed, leaving her puzzled. She'd never been so charmed by him.

"There's my favorite girl." He searched the area behind her. "Who were you speaking to?"

Samara's stomach twirled with nerves.

The owl, Ulrieg hissed when she took too long to respond.

She made a show of looking at her pet bird. "Gray, of course." She thought she saw the fox's eyes narrow. "Don't you talk to Ginger?"

Kaine chortled. "Of course. I guess I'm just on edge because I saw you out here with Paxton. Do you have something to tell me?"

CHAPTER TWENTY-ONE

Samara swallowed the lump in her throat as she tried to work out how much Kaine had seen or how long he had been watching them.

I don't think he saw us. There were no suspicious movements or noises out in the forest.

Then what is he on about? Samara frowned.

I don't know. Maybe he's just trying to make conversation. He's not the brightest.

Samara fought the urge to roll her eyes.

Kaine crossed his arms. "Are you tired of me already and moving on? Or are you wanting this to be an open relationship?"

Her jaw dropped. "Oh. You're talking about my being with Paxton." She huffed.

Hurt filled Kaine's face. "Naturally."

"Are you jealous?"

Kaine remained silent.

Look at that. The overconfident male has a weak spot. Ha. Let's see what that does to his pride.

Samara waved a hand, startling Gray and making him fly into the nearest tree. "You have nothing to worry about. We were only practicing with our weapons."

"And you didn't invite me?"

"We bumped into each other at the bottom of the stairs. I was letting Gray out to hunt, and since he ran into me, we decided to train while my owl caught his food. It wasn't prearranged."

He looked her over and pulled a leaf from her hair, dragging it down her pink strands. "Are you sure that's all you did?"

Samara blinked. "Yes. Of course. The leaf must have lodged itself in my hair when I passed through some bushes. What are you getting at?"

Kaine flicked the leaf aside, seeming pleased with her answer. Then he wrapped her in his arms and kissed her on the lips.

Argh! Where did that come from? Please don't tell me I have to put up with this every time he becomes jealous and realizes that you are, in this case, mistakenly loyal.

Samara tried hard to ignore Ulrieg, which was difficult, since his voice directly entered her head.

Kaine pushed a clump of hair behind her ear,

grazing the ends before stroking her cheek. "That's good to hear. You had me worried for a moment."

Samara leaned into him, hearing his rapid heartbeat through his tunic. Calmness washed over her as though she was enraptured, and she felt the urge to tell him everything. Pulling back, she gazed into his eyes and opened her mouth to speak.

Don't even think about telling Charmer Boy where we've been or what we've been up to. Ulrieg's voice broke the urge. *In fact, don't tell him anything.*

Kaine stroked her cheek again, messing with her senses. "Were you going to tell me something?"

Don't even!

She blinked rapidly, attempting to grasp hold of her emotions, unsure why they were volatile. "Paxton and I are friends. That's all."

She thought she saw a flash of annoyance in his eyes, but his face was tilted down, shadowed by the moonlight. Trying to push away the guilt of keeping secrets, she reminded herself of how she had seen him flirt with Luna earlier. That helped snap her out of it. She didn't know if her desire to trust him was because she was slowly letting him in or his charming power had grown after he'd bonded with Ginger. It didn't seem natural how much the females swooned over him. She shook her head. She was usually levelheaded and had never really fallen for charm before.

She tried a little charm of her own, smiling sweetly and hooking her arm through his. "Why don't you walk with me back to the building?" She called to Gray, and the owl landed on her opposite shoulder from Kaine.

Kaine fell into step, and Ginger followed, constantly watching Gray.

THE FOLLOWING DAY, Samara rose early after finding it hard to sleep. A lot had happened in one night. On one hand, she was glad to have someone to share things with. On the other, she was worried that she was putting Paxton and his family in danger. Even if Callista supported dragons, there was no telling what Vexx and Kellam would do to their families or anyone else who sided with them. It sounded like Paxton and his family had enough trouble from their village's racism because of his parents' mixed-race marriage. Samara felt glad her village wasn't like that.

Leaving Gray to sleep on his perch, she went to the dining hall with invisible Ulrieg in tow. None of the other apprentices seemed to be up, and the corridors were free from the sorcerers' familiars. As expected, the dining hall was empty. The only sign of life was banging in the kitchen. Samara pushed through the large doors and found Forgrac whacking a spoon on the top of a saucepan over the fire.

"Morning!" she called.

As soon as the dwarf looked up, the grumpy look left his face. "Mornin', love. You're up early."

"I couldn't sleep." She barely heard Ulrieg's talons clicking on the stone floor into the room, and she pulled the door closed. "Do you need a hand?"

"Sure. That'd be a nice change." Forgrac added some honey to the oatmeal brewing in the pot. "It'd be a great help if ya could stir this oatmeal to stop it from burnin'."

Samara took the wooden spoon from him and stirred, her mind churning over the things that had happened the day before.

Forgrac put some eggs into a pot filled with water and put it on the stove next to the porridge then tossed some bacon onto a hot plate and stood over it as it sizzled. Everything he did, he needed a stool to stand on to see his work.

After a period of silence, he asked, "Is somethin' botherin' ya?"

Samara needed to practice her indifferent face, or

more people would notice. "I'm fine. Do you want me to do anything with the eggs now that they're boiling?"

Forgrac flipped the bacon. "Give 'em a little while, and they should be done."

Nodding, Samara continued to stir the oatmeal, staring deep into its contents. "I've been thinking. How is it that so many apprentices don't know about dragons or Dragoria? It seems like we've all grown up being so naive. How does that happen?"

He pulled a serving tray from under the bench and began putting the bacon on it. "I put it down to the closin' of the borders."

She stopped stirring. "Oh? How?"

"Before the borders were closed, people like me who performed in roamin' plays used to travel through all the different realms. We used to learn what was happenin' in the different areas an' spread the stories to each village we visited. When the borders were closed, this could no longer happen. It's often difficult to travel within this realm. It appears as though they don't want people to mingle." He pointed at the pot. "Don't let 'at burn."

She set to work again. "But why would they stop people traveling within this realm?"

He shrugged. "Me *guess* is 'at they don't want people to find out what's happenin'. They can keep more secrets then. Naive people are easier to control."

Samara smirked.

"What?"

"You sound like someone I know."

"Then whoever this person is, I believe I will get along well with them." He stepped onto a stool to take the oatmeal off the stove and placed it on the bench then handed Samara a serrated knife and a loaf of bread.

She started slicing off large pieces without being asked, her movements slow, as she was distracted.

Forgrac lowered his voice. "Now, are ya goin' to tell me the truth?"

Samara sighed. *Ulrieg, should I say anything?*

He has shared things that could get him into trouble. It only seems fair that we share a little with him. Just be careful. I don't think he told you things to lure out your secrets, but it's still dangerous.

She looked at the dwarf. "Am I that readable?"

Forgrac rubbed his bushy beard thoughtfully. "Probably not to most. You forget I've been paying more attention to ya since ya were kind to me. I probably wouldn't 'ave a clue when any of the others were upset."

She cut off another slice of bread and placed it on

a tray. "I've found a book in the library with some history about the Sacred Flame coterie."

"Oh. And?" He took a large bowl to a box of fruit and filled it with apples and oranges.

"It had many parts blotted out."

"That's not at all fishy," he said sarcastically. "Could ya read any of it?"

"I could make out that they'd written about dragons and something about a missing realm."

He plunked the bowl onto the bench, giving her his full attention. "Sounds exactly like I was tellin' ya."

A loud noise sounded in the dining hall, and Forgrac held his stubby finger to his lips. "Best we be fillin' up the serving bench, or I'll be havin' some complaints."

Samara nodded and helped him gather items and carry them out of the kitchen, disappointed they couldn't continue the conversation. Since people were starting to enter the dining room, it would be too risky to say any more.

CHAPTER TWENTY-TWO

Leaves and twigs snapped under Samara's boots as she marched through the forest, a long cloak draped over her fighting leathers. With her bow and quiver slung over her back, the arrows clanked continuously. She pulled her hood over her head to conceal her pink hair. Why Callista insisted that the coven members have brilliantly colored hair, she would never know. Though she understood it was to mark them as an esteemed part of the coterie and strong magic wielder, the hair stood out like a beacon when they were trying to stay inconspicuous.

Gray was perched on her shoulder. As much as she enjoyed the owl's company, it was inconvenient to bring him along all of the time.

The flapping of wings sounded not far above her,

but when she looked up, she didn't spot anything.

It's only me, Ulrieg said.

The nearness of her familiar comforted her. Although she was only going to her next lesson with Zofia, she never knew what the weapons master's lessons would entail. They often ended with several students getting hurt.

A soft whistle headed in her direction, and she swerved, unsettling Gray, right before a thud sounded from a nearby tree trunk. One of Kaine's knives was embedded in the bark. Branches cracked off to the right, and she spun to see Kaine tromping her way, smirking.

"Good reflexes." He winked. "That's my girl."

She stood ready for more weapons or magic to be hurled her way. Instead, he wrapped his arms around her, scaring Gray from her shoulder, and pressed her back against the tree. He pulled his knife from the bark and placed it back in his holster. Her cheeks heated as his breath swirled over her face when he tilted her face up to meet his and stooped to kiss her lips. All strength melted from her body, making her grateful he was holding her up.

The sound of Ulrieg retching traveled through their bond, but she chose to ignore it, although it did help her regain some of her strength in time to stand on her own feet as Kaine pulled away.

A self-satisfied grin came to Kaine's face as he gazed down at her.

"What was that for?" Samara asked.

"What? I can't kiss my girl?" He ran a hand down the side of her face, igniting it.

Through the bond, Ulrieg's disapproval filled Samara, pulling her back to her senses.

She gave Kaine an incredulous look. "Don't you class all girls as your girl?"

His face distorted. "I've told you before. You're the only one I'm interested in."

Now, look what you've made me do. I wish you'd keep your opinions to yourself in times like this.

She placed a hand on Kaine's arm. "I'm sorry. It's just you're always so charming with the other women."

Kaine ran a hand through his brilliant blue hair. "It doesn't mean anything. If it helps, I was jealous when you returned from the forest with Paxton last night. I know what you mean now." Sheepish, he added, "Besides wanting to, I guess the kiss was also to prove that you're the one I want."

Samara's heart melted slightly. "As I said, Paxton and I were only training together and met by chance."

Something shifted behind Kaine, and Samara glanced past him to find Ginger, who was raising her nose and flaring her nostrils, as though trying to assess a scent. Samara cursed inwardly. If only Kaine didn't have a familiar with such a sensitive nose. She wouldn't be surprised if every time Ginger did that around her, she smelled Ulrieg.

A rustle of leaves sounded above Samara. *I'm scouting ahead. I need to find some pepper to shove up that fox's nose to put her off my scent.*

Good idea. Samara looped her arm through Kaine's. "Come on, or we're going to be late for the lesson. Zofia hates it when we're late." She called to Gray, and the owl obeyed, perching on her shoulder.

When they reached the training area, Paxton, Mist, and Luna had already arrived. Luna's height dwarfed the tiny human teacher as she stood beside her. Even though her large cloak draped over her figure-hugging fighter's uniform, Luna's plunging neckline emphasized her ample breasts. She smiled sweetly at Kaine, giving him a friendly wave.

Kaine raised his hand to return the wave then seemed to remember Samara was next to him, and after casting Luna a charming grin, he turned away.

Each apprentice held their weapons of choice, and their familiars were by their sides. A few months ago, the lessons had been conducted with the entire apprentice population, but the bonded apprentices had begun training without the unbonded ones, bringing the intensity of the training to a much higher level.

Mist swung her sword. Okak was sitting on one shoulder. "When are we starting?" Her muscles bulged even under her long leather sleeves.

"Patience, Mist. I know you're always keen to use your weapon, but we must wait until all the apprentices with familiars are here. We are still missing Peadar." Zofia fed Jet some berries, and the bear devoured them.

"What are we doing today?" Paxton's flail stuck out of its holster. The spikey end rested just above his head, and Jojo sat on his shoulder, in the weapon's shadow, as though it protected him from the other familiars.

"I should wait until everyone is here to keep it fair and ensure everyone gets the same information to help them through the next step." A long bright-purple ponytail tumbled out of the hood hanging over the instructor's shoulder, and impatience started to show on her face. "If he ever turns up." She clasped her hands behind her back. "Although I can tell you it will be your toughest lesson yet."

Expressions of confusion and dread passed through the group. They had been through some intense lessons under Zofia, with many getting severely hurt. Samara was starting to wonder if Ulrieg's theory about how the type of familiar a magic wielder bonded with influenced them. Zofia was bonded with a sun bear, and they were known for being vicious. She didn't know what to expect from being bonded to a dragon. He looked malicious and vindictive, but he was a big softy underneath.

Samara shook her head, trying to clear her thoughts. She would have to worry about that later.

The apprentices fell silent, and tension filled the air, except for Mist, who seemed to be preparing herself for her dream confrontation.

In an attempt to calm her nerves, Samara set to work charming some of her arrows. She didn't know how lethal to make the incantation, since they didn't know what they were up against, but after being stuck in a battle without any magic against the trolls, she wanted to do everything she could to be prepared.

A soft chatter sounded behind her, followed by twigs and dried leaves snapping as Peadar clumsily made his way through the forest toward them. Even after bonding with his raccoon, he still hadn't grown any nimbler. The toe of his boot caught on a branch, and he stumbled after Ziggy into the small clearing where everyone waited.

Bemused, Zofia sucked in a short breath. "Nice of you to join us, Peadar."

His face turned red, and he scratched behind his semipointed ear. "Sorry. I didn't know I was late."

"You're not. Although it was a spectacular entrance." Zofia grasped the handle of her axe as it hung from her hip.

"Since he's finally here, can we start now?" Mist swung her sword, making it cut through the air in large X's like she was itching for a fight.

Zofia shook her head. "We are waiting for two other apprentices."

"Who?" Paxton asked. "Did some others bond with their familiars?"

The weapons master grinned slyly. "No. I've decided a couple of the older ones without familiars should join us to mix things up a little."

Samara's stomach sank. They were supposed to have the hardest lesson yet, and she'd added younger, weaker apprentices to the mix. The look on Zofia's face made her wonder if the weapons master was slightly sadistic.

"Ha. Look at your faces." The instructor pulled out her axe and swung it in a twisting motion then stopped after a few swings. "You won't have the luxury of being fainthearted when you end up in a real battle. If you don't toughen up, you'll die.

Besides, where you're going today, you'll need the extra help."

The silence surrounding the apprentices grew, except for Mist, who continued to swing her sword and only stopped when the sound of footsteps approached through the forest.

Blade's brilliant red hair and its unattractive cut was the first thing Samara saw. Next came Henriette's ashen skin and long turquoise hair. Her normally mischievous expression was absent as she tied her hair back into a ponytail. As far as Samara knew, they hadn't selected a weapon of choice yet. Henriette grasped the hilt of a hand scythe hanging from her waist, and Blade clutched a double-sided axe. Although Blade and Henriette were only two summers younger than Samara, they were only kids in the majority of the apprentices' eyes.

"Good. You're here," Zofia said. "It's time to go."

"Where are we going?" Henriette asked, her cheeks somehow looking paler than normal.

The weapons master returned her axe to its holder. "You're going to be in a real fight."

"What?" Her face turned a ghostly white.

Frowning, Paxton protested, "But they haven't had much practice, and they don't have familiars, so their magic isn't powerful."

Zofia's face remained stern. "We have been too

soft on you, apprentices. This will happen no more." She turned and called over her shoulder, "Now, follow me."

She led them through the forest. Usually, they practiced against one another, but something felt off. Zofia was taking them farther away from the coterie building than normal, and she was making it sound like they were going against other beings.

Samara thought of the time she and Kaine had fought for their lives against the trolls, and shivers ran down her spine. Walking beside her, Kaine glanced her way, concern in his eyes, as though he was reliving the same thing. Samara hooked her arm through his and hugged him close. They had nearly died that day, and Kaine had suffered more. It didn't help that they had been stripped of all magic before they started. She hoped there wouldn't be a repeat of that, as she still had nightmares.

"Are we going to be able to use our magic?" Kaine asked, his voice breaking.

Samara's grip tightened on his arm as they waited for Zofia's response.

A glint flashed through the instructor's eyes as she turned back to address them. "You will have to wait and see."

The tension in the air thickened, and Henriette let out a small sob. Samara reached for her, and she hooked her arm through Samara's spare one. It felt like they were being led away to be slaughtered, especially Henriette and Blade.

"Stick with me," Samara whispered, trying to calm her fears. She would be no good to anyone otherwise.

Zofia led them farther into the forest. None of the apprentices had traveled so far from the building for class. They walked until the sun was high in the sky, the heat burning their skin when they passed through an opening in the trees.

Samara paused and took a long drink from a canteen that hung from the side of her quiver,. Her stomach growled, as it had been hours since they had eaten, but she hadn't brought any food. She hadn't known she would need it. But even if she ate, she didn't think she would be able to keep it down. She hooked the canteen back on her quiver and hurried to catch up with Kaine and Henriette, spooking Gray from her shoulder. He flew ahead, and Samara wondered if he knew where Ulrieg was.

When she caught up with the others, Ulrieg's voice cut through her thoughts. *Dragon moon! I hope she's not leading you there.*

Samara frowned when he didn't continue, and she let her irritation leak through. *Lead us where?*

If she is, she is one deranged instructor.

Panicked, she scowled. *Ulrieg, tell me what you're on about.*

Dragon forbid! It's the only thing around that I can see.

Wingless flight, Ulrieg! Get to the point! You're killing me.

He let out a sigh. *I didn't want to tell you when I saw it much earlier, but I haven't found any other reason for her taking you this far. She is one sick instructor. Is this her idea or Callista's?*

I don't know! Get to the point!

She's leading you directly to a camp of ten ogres.

Samara's feet stopped working, and all feeling left her limbs.

Kaine stopped and turned back to her. "Are you all right?"

Samara slowly shook her head. Then she caught sight of Henriette's terrified face and pulled it together for her sake. She didn't know what to tell them. She didn't want to terrify them more than they already were, but they would find out soon. *How far, Ulrieg?*

About two hundred wing beats.

CHAPTER TWENTY-THREE

Noticing the commotion, Paxton dropped back to join Samara, Kaine, and Henriette. "Is everything all right?"

Kaine stood between him and Samara. "Everything's fine. I have this sorted."

Samara grabbed Kaine's arm and pulled him back. "No. You don't have this sorted, Kaine. None of us do."

Paxton moved closer, lowering his voice. "Do you know something we don't?"

She nodded, concern filling her as she glanced at Henriette. "You stick by me or one of these two. Fight if you can, but let the more experienced apprentices do most of the fighting."

Henriette nodded, her eyes wide and face ghostly white.

"Gray flew ahead, and if he's right, we're heading toward an encampment of ten ogres." Paxton caught her gaze and nodded his understanding of her lie over her familiar. "I didn't think our lessons would become this dangerous. I hope he's wrong, but if he's not, we're in for a tough battle. I can only hope they let us keep our magic."

Kaine's face went pale. He was most likely remembering their battle against the trolls, and it took him a moment to recoup his usual confidence. "Surely, between all these fighters, we can defeat them. We've got this."

Samara gave him an incredulous look until she remembered the last time he acted charming and confident before it became serious.

Paxton shook his head in disbelief before asking Samara, "Should we warn the others?"

She glanced at Zofia's back. The teacher's long cloak billowed around her as she led them toward the threat.

Samara shook her head. "I don't think so. We don't know for sure that's where we're going, and I'd like to give our instructor the benefit of the doubt and hope she's not leading us there. Maybe there's something Ul—my owl hasn't seen up ahead. Or maybe we're bypassing the group. I don't want everyone to panic if there's no reason to." She glanced around the small group to see if anyone had noticed her mistake, but only Paxton acknowledged it with an eyebrow raise.

Zofia turned around. "What are you lot doing?" She planted her fists on her hips. "You can't stop. Come on. You're falling behind." She swept her hand. "You need to keep up."

Hurrying, they caught up quickly and fell into an awkward silence. Ginger trailed behind them.

Ulrieg, let me know if we change direction away from the ogres' camp.

Of course.

They walked in silence except for the crunch of dried leaves and the rustling of the foliage as a breeze forced its way through the trees. The farther they traveled, the quieter and rarer the birds became. Only Okak and Gray traveled with them. That in itself was not a good sign. Loud grunts and the sounds of creatures moving came through the trees, earning expressions of curiosity from the group.

With Henriette's arm still looped through hers, Samara felt her body stiffen. She didn't blame her. Henriette didn't have a familiar, nor had she experienced the level of fighting that would be required.

Zofia stopped and raised a hand for them to halt.

I can't believe she's doing it. Wait. I can. It only

confirms what I think of the coterie. Is there any way you can get out of this? Ulrieg's voice was almost pleading.

Unfortunately, no. I must partake in their "training," or they won't look after my family. We all have to.

We seriously have to find another way to look after your family. This isn't a healthy lifestyle.

It was until I had to fight the trolls without magic. But now, they seem to be upping the training to a dangerous level. I thought when we bonded with a familiar, they were supposed to ease off on us a bit.

Clearly not.

Zofia shifted, circling behind them, with Jet close to her side. Magic pulsed around them, reminding Samara of when they had to fight the trolls.

Wingless flight! That hurt!

Filled with dread, Samara asked, *What is it?*

I just flew into something solid, but there was nothing there. I was trying to get higher, away from the ogres. It's like an invisible barrier has been placed above them.

Probably around them, too, trapping us in with them. It's what Callista did when Kaine and I had to fight the trolls. I don't like the sound of this.

Confused, the apprentices faced Zofia.

"Are we going back?" Peadar asked, seemingly oblivious to the strange sounds of the ogres only moments before. Ziggy chattered at his feet, and his face turned wan as he glanced over his shoulder toward the noises they'd heard. "Ziggy tells me there are ogres not far away from us. Shouldn't we be leaving? Is that why you've turned around?"

Amusement in her eyes, Zofia replied, "No. You aren't turning around. Ziggy is correct. There are ogres behind you. I've found you a small camp. Between the eight of you, you should be able to defeat them."

"But they're ogres, and two of us don't have familiars and haven't been trained," Henriette protested.

The weapons master smirked. "Then there is no better time to learn than now."

Even Blade went pale. "This is ridiculous. We should have more training before being thrown into this." He pulled the double-sided axe from its holder on his back.

Lifting her chin, the weapons master replied, "I'm sure you know how to swing an axe. It even has two blades, giving you an extra advantage. There's no turning back now. You're all here to fight."

"Are there any rules?" Luna braced herself against her bo staff. Her rabbit, Coco, sat by her feet. Her soft, velvety voice quavered. "Do they know we're coming and that this is only practice?"

Zofia planted her hands on her hips. "When did I give you the impression that these were friendlies?

These are no acquaintances of ours. This is a real fight."

"But that's not fair on the ogres either. They're only minding their own business, and we're about to attack them for it." Paxton leaned on one leg.

Unmoved, Zofia fixed her gaze on him "Ogres aren't a friendly race. They must be ruled, or they'll cause devastating destruction to the villages. As young witches and wizards of the coven, you must prove that you are above them by defeating their leaders and showing them who is stronger. You will never be an esteemed sorcerer in our coterie if you don't. Today, because you are a team, you have the advantage. As you get stronger, you must prove you can handle things yourself."

That confirms it. This coterie is sick. What chance do the few dragons have if this is how they treat their own? Ulrieg said.

"Does Callista know about this?" Paxton asked.

"Of course she does. All your teachers had to go through this to become part of the coterie," she replied with pride in her voice.

"Even Eliphas?" Paxton asked in disbelief.

Zofia smirked. "Yes, I know these days it's surprising, but even the old herbology specialist had to fight ogres."

"So when will we stop talking and start fighting?"

Mist had pulled out her sword, causing Blade and Luna to shift away to avoid being hit by the swinging weapon.

"I've already secured you all in with a magical boundary. You can start whenever you want to." Zofia slowly backed away.

"With the ogres as well?" Henriette's body shook.

Zofia scowled. "Of course. Otherwise, what's the point?"

"Are you coming with us?" With a shaky hand, Henriette reached for her scythe.

"No. It's your test, not mine. I'm here to observe and give pointers for next time." Zofia glared down her nose at Henriette. "You need to toughen up if you want to remain in this coterie."

"But I've had hardly any training, and I don't have a familiar," Henriette protested.

"Then think of it as good practice if you don't find a familiar soon. This test resembles what Samara and Kaine faced when they didn't bond with their familiars in time." She waved a hand. "Now, off you go. I'm not waiting all day. We have a long walk back. If you don't start soon, I'll bring the ogres to you."

CHAPTER TWENTY-FOUR

Wrapping her arm around Henriette's shoulders, Samara walked beside her as Mist led them toward the ogres. *Ulrieg, can you please watch over Henriette as much as you can? I know she's not your bonded, but she's so young.*

You're asking me to protect members of the coterie. Are you kidding me?

I know you hate the coterie, but she's young, and I'm sure she has no idea what they're like. Samara's eyes landed on Blade. His strange hairstyle made his red hair stand out more. *And Blade too? Please.*

Ulrieg grumbled, *Wingless flight! I can't believe you're asking me to do this. Actually, what I can't believe is that you're going along with this. Why aren't you all rebelling and refusing to do it?*

Samara sighed. *Because we know if we don't, our families will suffer. All the apprentices are here because it helps their families. Remember? It doesn't make them instantly bad or tainted by the rotten coterie members.*

Then you lot need to put your heads together and work out a better way to look after your families without the help of the coterie. The way they're treating you is ridiculous.

I know, Samara replied. *Now that I've seen what either the coterie or senior coterie members do to dragons and dragon elves, I'm horrified. Trust me—if I knew how to provide for my family in another way, I would. It wouldn't surprise me if some of the other apprentices would do the same. But it's not as though we get paid. All our reward goes to our families.*

A loud sigh passed through their bond. *I guess I could look out for the two newbies without familiars. At least I have the advantage of turning invisible. But you are always going to come first. So it depends on how much trouble you get into.*

I hope not too much. That's why I've stuck to the bow and arrow as my weapon of choice. I don't want to get up close and personal with an enemy.

Then let's hope it stays that way. I'll keep as close to you as I can.

The branches above Samara rustled as she

walked under the tree, and she glanced up. *Have you seen Gray lately?*

Yeah, he's fine. He's perched on a branch at the top of a tall tree, taking a nap.

At least someone can rest. I don't know how I'll explain his absence, though.

Just say he's been locked out of the barrier. He very well could be. He's perched higher than when I was flying and ran into the barrier's ceiling.

That knowledge made Samara happy. The owl had been roped into many things that had nothing to do with him, so it was nice to know he could sit out one fight.

The senior apprentices looked to be gathering their courage and setting their focus. All seemed to have a slight look of fear except Mist, whose face and posture were determined and eager, and Kaine, who had put on his charming, carefree facade. He caught Samara looking at him and winked.

She shook her head in disbelief. He must be terrified inside, especially after how the last battle with the trolls ended for him.

Blade walked in silence, his knuckles white as he clutched the handle of the double-sided axe. Samara didn't need to look at Henriette to know she was scared. She was shaking, the feeling vibrating up

Samara's arm. Samara squeezed her shoulders, trying to reassure her.

Henriette's hood fell off her head, exposing her long turquoise hair, and Samara pulled it back up. She didn't want any attention drawn toward her.

A strange noise greeted them, and Mist stopped, the rest of the apprentices falling in behind her.

On a small plain through the foliage, several creatures that appeared like larger, extremely ugly humans or elves were going about their business. A couple of makeshift shelters had been constructed out of small tree trunks leaning up against larger trees and covered with long branches. Other ogres were camped under large boulders, exactly like where Samara had left Daena and Byzarid. It appeared as though the ogres didn't know that the apprentices were there. It felt wrong to attack creatures that weren't threatening them or others. A dirty loincloth covering both sides slightly concealed their muscly green-grey bodies. Their faces were hideously ugly and malformed. Ogres had a reputation for being fierce and aggressive, but they weren't doing any of that at the moment.

Unease filled the air around the apprentices as they removed their cloaks and placed them inside the tree line. Of all of them, only Kaine and Samara had fought someone who wasn't another apprentice or an instructor. Samara hoped Zofia hadn't stripped them of their magic.

Before Samara could pull out an arrow and try to enchant it, Mist charged into the small clearing with her sword held high, expelling a war cry.

It would have been wiser to sneak up on the larger creatures. All the ogres turned to face the screaming apprentice, their strange faces filled with bafflement.

When they didn't attack her, Mist stopped several feet away and cried, "Bow to me, and I will spare you!"

After a moment of silence, the ogres burst into laughter. The guttural sounds were disturbing, and some of them sounded like snorts.

Mist shifted into a ready stance. Though Samara couldn't see her face, her posture screamed determination. She thrust a hand forward, expelling a burst of lightning at the closest ogre. His body convulsed, and he dropped to his knees before Mist released him from her electricity. "That's better."

Samara expelled a breath. Their magic still worked. At least they had that.

The ogre roared and climbed to his feet. "I wasn't bowing to yo—"

Mist hit him with another shock.

The other ogres sprang into action, grabbing

their weapons and charging at Mist. She swung her sword, nicking some of them on their stomachs, legs, and arms. Although she was causing them pain, the ogres were surprisingly fast for large creatures. Only moments passed before they had her surrounded, leaving the rest of the apprentices no choice. They had to run into the fight to help her.

Samara stood at the edge of the clearing and nocked an enchanted arrow as Henriette cowered behind some shrubs.

Blade spotted her and knelt beside her. "I know you're scared. I am too. We're not ready. But if we stay here and don't step onto that field to have a go, we won't be welcome in the coterie, and our families will suffer."

With tears streaming down her face, Henriette asked, "But what if we die? Our families won't be protected then either."

He paused and looked to be thinking. "That's true. But at least we would know that we tried to keep them safe."

The amount of courage it took for the apprentices, only sixteen summers old, was admirable.

Henriette wiped her eyes, used Blade's body to pull herself up, and grabbed the hilt of her scythe from under her cloak. After straightening her shoulders, she marched after the older apprentices. Blade followed her. She moved behind Kaine and Paxton, just like Samara had told her to, with Blade sticking by her side.

Ulrieg, please keep an eye on them.

Yes, yes. I'm already on it.

Happy with his answer despite his attitude, Samara nocked her arrow again and hit the ogre closest to Kaine in the leg. The ogre halted midstep before crumpling to the ground, asleep. The guttural snore was louder than the noise of the initiating battle.

Another ogre weaved past the sleeping ogre and headed for Kaine. With a knife in each hand, Kaine braced, bending his knees, ready to spring into action. Henriette and Blade stood a few feet behind him, holding their weapons ready.

Samara nocked another enchanted arrow and shot it at the ogre. He shifted, and it skimmed past his arm. She groaned and fired another arrow before calling the missed arrow back to her. When she looked back to check whether the last arrow had hit, the ogre was heading toward her instead. It must have missed.

Kaine sliced at the ogre's ankles, cutting the tendons at the back. The ogre roared and swiped at him but knocked Henriette instead. She flew backward for a few feet and landed on her backside.

Blade shifted to stand in front of Henriette, his double-sided axe ready, but the ogre was only interested in Samara.

She quickly nocked the recovered arrow and found the ogre was only a few feet away.

CHAPTER TWENTY-FIVE

Samara backed up to the forest's edge, where her foot caught on a root. She righted herself and realized the ogre was getting too close for her to shoot. She fired the arrow, but the ogre managed to twist, avoiding the hit. He moved quickly, even with a limp from the cut tendons.

Suddenly, the ogre cried out and leaned back. Kaine, Henriette, and Blade looked on, confused. Ulrieg must have attacked the ogre.

The distraction gave Samara enough time to gather her focus and remember the latest spell they had learned. She thrust out her hand. *"Elevorto."*

The ogre rose into the air, kicking and roaring. Samara twisted her hand, and the ogre flipped and hung upside down. He expressed his displeasure with a roar.

Samara held him, wondering what to do next. She didn't want to drop him on his head but couldn't do anything else until she released her hold on him.

As she pondered what to do, she caught a glimpse of Paxton fighting an ogre with his flail. The spikes were embedding into the ogre's flesh, but he was taking hits as well as the ogre fought back with his sword. Another ogre had descended on Kaine, leaving Henriette and Blade on their own.

The ogre trapped in her magic wriggled, causing Samara's hold on him to waver. She focused on her magic, straightening the ogre's position. Her strength was waning. Holding the ogre in the air for an extended period was using more magic than she was used to.

Another ogre was targeting Henriette. She held her scythe high. The ogre swung his sword, and Blade darted forward, blocking the strike. Metal clanged as the sword hit the double-sided axe. Blade pushed forward, knocking the sword's edge away, spun, and swung his axe at the ogre. The ogre swerved out of the way then struck back, nicking Blade's shoulder.

Blood oozed down Blade's bare arm as he raised his axe and swung again. The ogre howled in pain as the axe sliced through the skin of his abdomen, but he didn't stop. He swung his sword at Blade, catching him off guard. Henriette jumped to her feet and stopped the sword with the back of her scythe, her whole body shaking from terror and the impact.

One of the ogres fell to the ground. Luna and Mist had taken him down, leaving him lifeless. They turned and started toward another ogre who was fighting Peadar. He was fighting well even while struggling to stay on his feet.

An ogre cry sounded from the other side of the field, and Samara turned back to see one clasping his back with one hand and thrusting his sword with the other. Scratches streaked down the ogre's bare back, but Ulrieg's distraction didn't help. Blade fell to the ground, a sword embedded in his abdomen. Henriette screamed, watching as the ogre pulled the sword out of Blade.

The ogre threw his head back again as more talon scratches marked his back, but Ulrieg's attempts still didn't stop the ogre from readying to attack Henriette. She held up her scythe, her arm shaking.

Samara pulled the last of her magic from within and threw it into the spell she was using to hold the ogre, and she threw him against a tree, knocking him out. She felt weak from the exertion. Still, she pulled her strength together and pulled a new arrow from her quiver. She couldn't remember what she had enchanted it with, but she didn't care. The string twanged as she released it, and the arrow hit the ogre towering over Henriette in the back. The ogre froze, and Henriette crumpled to her knees next to Blade.

Wingless flight! I tried. I wish I could use my fire and teeth. Ulrieg sounded devastated.

Cursing herself that she hadn't helped them sooner, Samara jogged toward Blade. Both he and Henriette were clutching the wound in his stomach, blood oozing from the deep laceration and his mouth.

"We can't leave him here. It's in the middle of the battle," Samara said. "I'll grab his shoulders. You get his feet. We'll place him inside the shelter of the forest."

Henriette nodded and shifted to her feet, as though getting a direct instruction had brought her back to her senses. As quickly as they could, they lifted Blade and placed him behind a cluster of bushes, leaving him out of sight.

"Stay with him." Samara rubbed Henriette's shoulders. "Heal him as much as you can, and we'll get him the attention he needs as soon as we're done."

Tears streaming down her face, Henriette nodded.

"I'm going back out to help."

Facing the battle from a distance gave Samara a better view of what was happening. Peadar was narrowly avoiding the strikes from an ogre. The way he moved, sometimes even before the strike, convinced Samara that Ziggy was telling him what to expect next as the raccoon clawed at the ogre's shoulders.

Luna's rabbit familiar dug madly behind the ogre they were fighting, creating deep holes to try to throw the ogre off balance.

Okak swooped from the trees, aiming his beak at the eyes of the ogre Mist was fighting. The ogre swiped at the crow before he connected. The crow swerved, still creating enough distraction for Mist to plant her sword in the ogre's chest. The ogre groaned in pain and dropped to his knees as Mist yanked out her sword, pulling him forward to flop to the ground.

Paxton crouched several feet away from an ogre as Ulrieg's claw marks trailed down the beast's back. He pulled something out of his pocket in his gloved hand that looked like part of a plant then rubbed the spikes of his morning star with the item before shoving it back into his pocket and returning to the ogre with his weapon swinging. The ogre cried out in pain again as more talon cuts appeared on his shoulder, and Paxton's morning star collided with the ogre's leg. The creature bellowed in pain but fought back with his sword as Paxton yanked his morning star out of his flesh. He only had to dodge a few more swings before the ogre stopped fighting and convulsed to the ground.

After taking a few moments to recover, Paxton rejoined the battle to help Kaine.

Samara aimed an enchanted arrow at a female ogre, joining the one battling against Kaine. The female ogre dropped to the ground. Then she nocked another arrow and hit the leg of the ogre battling Kaine. But the ogre continued to fight. Samara cursed. She must have used one of the arrows she hadn't gotten a chance to enchant.

Loading another arrow, she hoped that one was enchanted. It hit the ogre in the arm. She roared before pulling at her hair, screaming in distress. The spell must have been the one that caused the victim to see their worst fears. From what Samara had been told, the fears were distressing, but the spell would wear off eventually, even without help from magic.

A loud crack sounded as Luna hit an ogre in the head with her bo staff, and Mist sparked him with electricity. The ogre fell to the ground, and Mist finished him off with a sword to his heart.

One ogre remained, but when she saw the six senior apprentices heading her way, she ran in the opposite direction.

Samara searched the small clearing to ensure all the ogres were out of the fight. They weren't all dead, but the alive ones were either unconscious or incapacitated in some way.

A movement caught her eye, and she spotted the small form of Zofia standing in the distance between the trees, Jet shadowing her. Seeing that sent shivers down Samara's spine. It reminded her of when Mystique had watched her and Kaine being slaughtered. Not only that, but Blade needed healing from a more powerful witch, if he was still alive. Zofia would know that, but she wasn't moving.

Don't forget about the boy. The girl doesn't seem to be healing him. Distress filled Ulrieg's voice.

I haven't forgotten. Now I've confirmed everyone is safe, I'm on my way there. Samara caught Paxton's eye. He approached her quickly, apparently reading the urgency on her face.

Samara spoke softly, not wanting to reveal Paxton's gift he had kept from the rest of the coterie. "I don't know if you know, but Blade needs your help."

His face paled. "What happened?"

"He was protecting Henriette, and an ogre thrust his sword right through him. He's in a bad way, if he's still alive."

Paxton nodded. "Where is he?"

CHAPTER TWENTY-SIX

Aware that Zofia was watching every move, Samara led Paxton to where she and Henriette had carried Blade. Henriette bent over him, trying her best to heal his wounds and failing. Tears ran down her face as she muttered healing incantations.

When she heard Samara and Paxton approach, she blubbered, "It's not working. My magic's not strong enough."

Samara pulled her up and led her a few feet away, ensuring she blocked Zofia's view of Paxton's actions. "Have a break. Paxton's had his familiar for longer, making his magic stronger. Let him see if he can help him." She embraced her, letting her sob onto her chest.

Paxton checked Blade's wounds, paying particular attention to the large one through his chest. He then felt his carotid artery, and the worry on his face deepened. He poised his ear over Blade's mouth and gazed down his body, his green ponytail falling on Blade's face. With sad eyes, he gently placed a hand on Blade's chest. Moments later, he sat back on his heels and shook his head at Samara.

Wingless flight! Can't he do anything? Ulrieg sounded distressed.

Samara swallowed. *He can't raise someone from the dead.*

Henriette continued sobbing against Samara's chest, and she didn't want to cause her any more grief, but she had to tell her. Gently, she pushed her off her chest and lifted her chin to meet her eyes.

Samara took a slow, deep breath. "It wasn't your magic that wasn't good enough."

"But I couldn't heal him!" Henriette wailed. "Not one bit of his wound healed when I tried."

Samara nodded. "That's because..." She closed her eyes, trying to gather strength. "You can only heal wounds on people who are alive."

Confused, Henriette wiped away her tears with the back of her hand. "But Blade is alive, and I couldn't heal any part of him."

Samara's mouth stretched into a thin line, and

she cradled Henriette's face in her palms. "No, he's not."

"What?" Henriette pulled out of Samara's grasp and looked at Blade. "Yes, he is. He's just really still because he's badly injured."

Samara squeezed her arm. "I'm sorry. He's not with us anymore."

Disbelief plastered on her face, Henriette studied Paxton and cringed when he shook his head, his face filled with regret. "No. No, he's got to be alive. We were supposed to start training together and go into the forest to see if we could find our familiars."

"I'm really sorry," Paxton said. "I would have tried to heal him if he were still alive. But I can't do anything."

A wail left Henriette's mouth, catching the attention of all the other apprentices. "No, no, no! He has to be alive. This was just a practice to see if we would fight, not a test we would die in."

Samara glanced at Zofia, who was still watching from a distance. "Unfortunately, that's not so in this case, and it wasn't the case for Kaine and me when we had to prove our worth to the coterie. They were more than prepared to let us die under an enemy's hand." She pulled her back into her arms, cradling her head against her chest. "Once the coterie decides to throw you into the deep end, you quickly discover it's not as friendly as we thought. It's a tough life we've been given, but we do it not only for ourselves but also for our families."

Henriette pulled back to look into Samara's eyes. "But if we die, they aren't cared for either. Now Blade's family is helpless."

More tears streamed down her face, and Samara couldn't bear to look at them, so she pulled her close again. Being one of the oldest in her family, Samara had grown up quickly, unlike Henriette, who was the youngest. Still, it was heartbreaking to see the normally mischievous teen broken by the mess of reality and the unfairness of their world.

I tried, Samara. I really did, Ulrieg said.

I know, Ulrieg. I know. It was a difficult situation. It's not your fault. These two were too young and weak to be in this battle.

Footsteps from behind broke Samara's concentration. She turned to see Peadar approaching. His face was splattered with blood. He spotted Henriette pressed against Samara's chest. "Is everything all right?"

Samara shook her head then pointed. "Blade didn't make it."

Henriette bawled, tears soaking Samara's fitted leather tunic as Peadar's face paled. Ziggy chattered by his side, swiping at the tall male's pants when he didn't respond or move and pulling him out of his horrified trance.

The other senior apprentices finished inspecting the ogres and joined them at the edge of the forest.

"What's going on?" Mist asked.

Already tired of telling everyone individually, Samara nodded to Blade's still form, letting the others work it out for themselves. Most of the older apprentices hadn't had much to do with Blade, but they had the decency to look regretful.

Here she comes.

Samara didn't know who Ulrieg was talking about until branches cracked deeper in the forest. She turned to find Zofia and Jet coming their way. The instructor's face told her she knew Blade was deceased.

Henriette's eyes narrowed, and she turned on the weapons master. "Why didn't you come and help Blade?"

Good girl. Showing strength even though her heart is broken, Ulrieg complimented her.

Zofia shrugged. "I couldn't help him until all the ogres were taken care of, or I'd be seen as breaking the rules."

Ha! Now there's a lie. Why doesn't someone question this? You should say something.

I don't want to bring attention that will have her watching us. Maybe someone else will ask, Samara said.

"What rules?" Peadar sounded annoyed, a rare thing for him. "We haven't been told of any rules like this."

Wow! I never thought he had it in him. His clumsiness is deceiving.

Zofia lifted her chin. "That's because you don't need to be told everything. You simply need to follow orders. You're here to train to be powerful magic wielders and to serve under Callista to protect the kingdoms. If you don't have the sustainability to do that, you shouldn't be here. The younger you learn how to cope, the stronger you will be and the more beneficial you will be to the high sorceress."

Ha! What a load of rubbish. To make a strong team, they should nurture and guide you, not try to kill you.

Peadar crossed his arms, his face set with anger. "We weren't told our lives would be like this."

Annoyance flickered across Zofia's face. "Do you want your family to be cared for or not?"

Such a caring coterie you've got here. They clearly don't care about any of you. It was all a front. Are you still going to say Callista has the good of the realms in mind?

Ulrieg, Samara said impatiently, *until I see them committing the crime you're accusing them of, I won't write them off as being bad. Remember, Callista stood up for us against Vexx and Kellam.*

Peadar fumed but held his tongue.

"I thought so." Zofia stomped toward Blade and investigated him quickly before standing. "Let's go." She marched back the way that they'd come, with Jet following closely.

"What about Blade?" Henriette called.

Exactly!

Impatient, Zofia turned back. "We leave him here."

Dragon moon! She's heartless.

"What? We can't do that!" Henriette flung her arms out to the sides.

Zofia crossed her arms and put all her weight on one hip. "We have a long trek back. I'm not carrying him, nor do I expect the other apprentices to have enough energy to do it. In case you've forgotten, it's quite a distance."

Henriette's frown deepened. "But we can't just leave him here out in the open. Won't the ogres eat him when they wake?"

The instructor shrugged. "Possibly. Or wild animals."

"Then we at least have to bury him!" Henriette cried.

Zofia huffed. "We don't have shovels."

"No, but we have magic." The desperation was growing in Henriette's voice.

The weapons master gazed around at the students. "Do any of you know how to make a huge, deep hole in the hardened soil?"

Everyone shook their heads.

"So that leaves only me, and I won't waste my energy burying a body. Now grab your cloaks and come, or you'll be left behind to fend for yourself." She started to leave then paused, turning back to the apprentices. "Oh, and breathe a word of this lesson to any of the younger apprentices, and you will face my wrath. And trust me when I say you have seen nothing yet." Without looking back, Zofia marched forward.

Honestly, we have to get you out of this coterie somehow.

Trust me—I want to leave and probably would if I only had to think about myself and not my family, but I also don't think my job is done here yet. Who's going to save all the captured dragons if I leave?

Slowly and sadly, the apprentices gathered their cloaks and fell in behind Zofia. Samara gathered Henriette's, Blade's, and Paxton's cloaks and put her arm around Henriette's shoulders as she wailed.

Paxton had remained by Blade's body. He spoke loudly enough for only Samara and Henriette to hear. "Direct her, and follow the others. I'll stay back and see what I can do to cover him. I've never tried anything like this, but I've been studying it in the library. I'll only know if I give it a go."

Thankful, Samara nodded, handed him his cloak, and led Henriette forward.

After they'd walked several yards, Henriette asked, "What will Paxton do?"

Samara squeezed her arm, trying to comfort her. "I don't know. But he won't leave Blade out in the open if he can find a way to hide him."

Henriette let out a breath. "I hope he finds a way to look after him. It's just not right, leaving him there. It was almost me."

"I know." Samara rubbed her arm. "He was courageous, protecting you, and deserves respect for what he's done."

"I didn't think the leaders of the coterie would leave us like that if we died under their care. I thought it was a nice place to live until today." She rubbed away the wet streaks under her eyes.

Samara nodded. "I know what you mean. I'm not sure whether Callista approves of all this. She's gone away again."

"If she doesn't approve, she should get rid of Zofia." Henriette glared at the back of the weapons master's head.

"Unfortunately, I don't think it works that way. To find trained magic wielders as powerful as the instructors would be difficult." They had passed through the barrier, and Samara looked for Gray but couldn't find him. She hoped he hadn't gone too far. *Ulrieg, have you seen Gray?*

He's still at the top of the tree, taking a nap. I'll grab him.

Thanks, Ulrieg. You're the best.

And don't you forget it!

Running footsteps approached them from behind, and Samara glanced over her shoulder to find Paxton catching up to them, Jojo sitting on his shoulder.

"How did it go?" Samara asked.

"Did you cover him?" Henriette asked before he could answer.

"I managed to cover him so no ogres or wild animals would find him."

Henriette's eyes filled with admiration. "Thank you."

Paxton placed a hand on her shoulder. "I was happy to."

Samara looked at his hands. Blood and cuts marked them, but there was no sign of dirt. His face looked more drained than usual.

A fluttering sounded behind them, and Samara

turned to see Gray being dragged from branch to branch. She shook her head. The owl wasn't pleased and expressed as much, but he had mellowed since the first time Ulrieg had done that to him. Samara held out her hand, and Ulrieg shoved the owl in her direction. Gray flipped right side up and landed on Samara's gloved hand before taking his position on her shoulder.

Thanks, Ulrieg.

No problem. Besides, we still need him as a cover.

Did you see what Paxton did with Blade?

Sure did. That's what took me so long. It was very touching. He used his plant magic, had the roots grow all around him and pull him into the ground.

You sound impressed.

I was. How often do I have to tell you he's the better guy?

Samara rolled her eyes.

CHAPTER TWENTY-SEVEN

Darkness filled the sky when they reached the coterie building. The trip back had been mostly silent, the grief of what had happened weighing heavily on all the apprentices. The only ones who didn't seem affected were Zofia and Mist.

Mist exclaimed when they entered the building, "I'm famished!" She quickly veered toward the dining hall, where the clatter of the younger apprentices who had stayed behind filled the air.

Under a sconce's dull light, Paxton's face looked drawn. Black rings lined his eyes as he braced Henriette's arm gently, and Jojo stuck his head from under his cloak's sleeve. "Are you going to be all right?"

Henriette's eyes were red and puffy. "Possibly, after a good sleep. But I won't forget what he did for me. We were starting to get along quite well before today."

"I'm sorry we couldn't protect him." He was so genuine with her that it softened Samara's heart.

"Thank you for ensuring he wasn't left out in the open," she said.

Paxton smiled sadly. "Anytime. You're right. He should be treated with respect, especially after dying so honorably."

Henriette nodded before turning to Samara. "I'm going to go to bed. I've lost my appetite, and I'm tired."

Samara watched her wearily climb the stairs. When she turned back to Paxton, he looked even more drained. "You should go to bed too. You look more exhausted than anyone else."

He nodded. "I'm going to get a bit of sleep." He moved in closer and lowered his voice. "I hope to wake later and check on Byzarid. He still needs more healing."

"He does, but are you sure that's wise? You honestly don't look much more alive than Blade."

"I should be all right after a bit of rest. Are you going to the food hall?"

Samara nodded. "I'm not that hungry, but I'm going to do my best to eat and grab a few things for Daena. I'll get some food for you too."

"Thanks. I appreciate it."

"Make sure you wake me before you go."

Paxton nodded. "I will."

"Although we're going to have to go there separately."

He frowned. "Why?"

"Because someone else saw us come back together last time and got jealous." She indicated with a slight jerk of her head toward Kaine, who was chatting with Luna on his way to the dining hall.

"Yet look at him." Paxton rolled his eyes. "All right. I'll do my best to do as I said." He left to take the stairs.

I'm going hunting. Is your window open?

Samara shook her head. *I'll open it for you, and I might put Gray on his perch.*

All right. I'll catch him something to keep him satisfied until he can go out later.

Samara headed for the other set of stairs and to her room, feeling the breeze from Ulrieg's wings as he flew past her. *Thanks. I imagine he's worn out after the long day that we've had, though I suppose he did sleep.*

After she had looked after Ulrieg and Gray, Samara entered the dining hall and let Forgrac's cooking entice her to eat something. Her newly found dwarf friend made the most delicious-smelling foods. Despite her sadness, her stomach growled. She scooped stew into her bowl and grabbed a large piece of bread then got another two plates and filled them with food that wouldn't spoil before the trip to the forest or before Paxton woke.

Even though Forgrac had provided a delicious meal, he often put out extra snacks during meal-times, like dried fruits and nuts along with large helpings of bread and dried meats. Sometimes, the apprentices didn't get a chance to come back to eat and needed things to snack on until they could return for a meal.

She went to the tables and spotted Kaine sitting close to Luna, with Ginger sitting beside him and Luna's rabbit snuggled on her lap. Surprisingly, Ginger wasn't trying to eat Coco or glare at her like she often did to Gray. A pang of jealousy hit Samara as she noticed Luna leaning over Kaine's arm and seductively selecting food off Kaine's plate with a playful smile.

Instantly, she heard Ulrieg's voice in her imagi-nation, telling her what a lousy choice Kaine was for her. She shook her head. Ulrieg's insistence was starting to become implanted in her. Even if it wasn't, Samara wasn't going to watch such a specta-cle. If Kaine was truthful about how he felt about her, he would have to show it.

She headed toward an empty table some junior

apprentices had recently vacated. Nearby, Peadar ran into a table, too focused on Luna and what she was doing with Kaine. He was so clumsy that if she didn't know he was half human, Samara might have suspected he was a dragon elf. At least his magic was more focused and powerful than Daena's was without her guardian dragon, nor did his skin break out in gray scales when he was emotional.

"Peadar!" Samara called.

He pulled his attention away from Luna and looked at Samara. He'd cleaned his face since the battle.

"Come sit with me." Samara indicated with a wave of the hand.

Peadar ran a hand through his short yellow hair, and after a last look at Luna, he nodded and headed her way, toward the opposite side of the table.

"Don't sit on that side. It's too easy to see those two, and it'll put you off your meal." Samara patted the bench seat next to her.

He sat beside her, and they faced the window. The full moon was high, illuminating the trees and the flowered plain around the building.

"Thanks for the distraction." Peadar spooned stew into his mouth.

"You don't have to thank me. You can sit with me

anytime." She realized she hadn't spent much time with him before.

He didn't ask about her and Kaine's relationship, as he probably didn't know. Only Paxton knew about them.

Samara tore off a piece of bread and dunked it into her stew then blew it lightly before placing it in her mouth. The right balance of herbs, vegetables, and chicken sparked her taste buds. It tasted delicious. "Wingless flight! Forgrac can cook."

"Who's Forgrac?" His brow furrowed.

Samara looked at him in shock. "He's only the dwarf in the kitchen who cooks every meal and cleans up our messes and tends to the maintenance of the building. I can't believe how many apprentices don't notice him."

Peadar had the decency to look embarrassed. "I guess I should be more appreciative. I never thought of who makes the meals and cleans up."

"If you're nice to him and give him some attention, he's quite nice. However, he's a grump at first. I don't blame him, since he's worked endlessly for this coterie for eighteen years."

"Wow! Now I feel terrible."

"Good!" She grinned and nudged him with her elbow. "That's what I wanted."

She was bumped from behind as Kaine leaned

over her and took some dried meat from her plate for Daena. "Geez. You must be hungry. You've got three plates." He shoved the piece into his mouth and sat opposite her.

"Hey!" She frowned. "That's for Paxton and Henriette. They've both gone to bed without food." She made a mental note to take some food to Henriette later to back up her story.

"Oh, so you're thinking of Paxton, but you don't come and sit with me."

Samara stirred her stew with another piece of bread, annoyed. "You looked rather busy with Luna, so I thought I'd leave you to it."

Kaine grinned and leaned back, holding up his hands. "I wasn't doing anything. I was simply giving Luna company."

"Well, it looked rather cozy from here. Didn't it, Peadar?"

Peadar nodded. "Sure did." He spun to look behind him. "Where is Luna?"

"She's gone to get cleaned up. So I thought I'd come over and see why my girl didn't join me but decided to sit with another male and get food for another one." He reached for Samara's hand, and she reluctantly let him as he smiled charmingly at her. "Surely my lovely lady isn't getting tired of me. She can't blame Luna for wanting to be with this charming specimen of a man."

A strange peace washed over her, starting from the hand Kaine was holding, and pushed away all her annoyance, and her shoulders softened. "No. Of course not."

"Good. I would hate to think you're growing resistant to my charms."

Samara felt that something was missing, but she couldn't place it, and the more Kaine touched her and looked into her eyes, the less she cared. It was hard to pull her eyes away from his.

"Ahh. What is going on?" Peadar's voice broke through her trance. "Are you two a couple?"

Kaine shifted his gaze to look at him. "Yes. We are."

Peadar frowned. "But didn't I just see you with Luna? You looked kind of cozy."

Annoyed, Kaine replied, "I can't help that Luna can't resist my charm."

Peadar shook his head. "I don't know. I think you put it on for all the females, especially Luna. It's unfair to them and Samara."

Releasing Samara's hand, Kaine placed it on Peadar's arm, erasing his frown. Kaine held his gaze, and only moments later, Peadar's attitude changed, softening toward Kaine.

"I wouldn't do that. I can't help how the ladies feel about me."

Confused, Samara tried to piece together what was happening.

Kaine placed his other hand back on hers, dissipating her confusion, and said, "It was lovely catching up and straightening out the misunderstandings. I'm going to leave you now to enjoy your meal while I go and clean up."

Samara and Peadar nodded and watched him leave before returning to their meal.

CHAPTER TWENTY-EIGHT

After placing a small plate of food in front of Henriette's door, Samara cleaned herself up and packed a small bag with food for Daena and another for Paxton. Gray slept on his perch, and Ulrieg was still out hunting. She curled up on her bed and was asleep in just a few moments.

She woke with a start as a loud tap sounded on the door. Sitting up, she gazed out the window. It was still dark, with the moon casting shadows under the trees. The window was closed. She had left it slightly open for Ulrieg to get back inside when he was finished hunting.

Something moved near her legs. *I'm pretty sure it's only Paxton. I'd say he's here to let you know he's about to head out.* She could barely make out Ulrieg's black form curled beside her legs.

She threw back her blanket then padded to the door and opened it a crack. Paxton was fully dressed, his flail attached to his back and Jojo sitting on his shoulder. He still looked tired although better than he had earlier.

"Come in."

He stepped through, and Samara closed the door behind him. She reached for the bag she'd prepared for him. "I grabbed you some food. You'll need to eat it on the way to gather some more strength."

"Thank you." He dipped his hand inside and pulled out a piece of dried fruit.

She looked down at her plain shift that flowed to her knees. "I'll get dressed when you leave, then I'll follow you. Have you got an excuse to be out?"

He nods. "I'll tell them that Jojo was restless and wanted fresh air and a dip in the little creek I found him in."

Samara led him to the door and placed her hand on the handle. "That should work. I'll see you soon." She opened the door, and he left, trying to keep his bootsteps quiet.

As soon as she closed the door, Samara started to get ready. She had to take Gray as well for her cover, and the owl should be well rested and ready for a flight in the forest. After pulling on leather gloves and leather arm straps, she threaded her quiver onto her back and hung the bow from it.

Wandering through the corridors while heading to the front door, she kept her eyes peeled for any sight of the monkey or the yellow snake. She hadn't seen the two senior commanders for a couple of days. However, she had spent most of the day away from the building. As far as she knew, Callista wasn't around. Still, that didn't calm her nerves while looking for Mystique. The high sorceress was known to arrive at the most unusual times.

Samara made it through the common room, and her nerves had almost settled when she spotted Jet sleeping by the front door. She froze. The black bear was on duty. Last time, that hadn't bothered her much. But after what they'd just gone through, that was no longer the case. Her nerves fired in all directions, weakening her limbs. She forced herself to move on.

Even though Samara was allowed to go outside, having the sun bear guard the door after what Zofia had done, with Jet by her side, gave her the same sense of dread she'd felt after Mystique had watched her battle the trolls. It seemed like the familiars loved to see them suffer. The only difference was that Jet didn't have eerie yellow eyes that cut through the forest as he watched them being slaughtered.

He's asleep.

Are you sure? Samara asked.

His breathing is relaxed and in an easy rhythm.

Let's hope he stays that way.

She snuck around Jet and edged toward the front door then slowly turned the handle and pushed through. She stopped the door before it reached the point it usually groaned. Gray sat on her shoulder the whole time, his movements limited, as though he understood the situation.

Are you outside? Unable to see or hear Ulrieg, she had to check.

Yes. I'm on the stair railing.

Samara closed the door, careful not to let the latch click, and slowly descended the stairs, ensuring her boots didn't make noise on the way down. Even though she had Gray with her, it would still seem strange for them to sneak out late in the night or early morning.

Eerie shadows carpeted the forest as she made her way through it toward the area where Daena and Byzarid were hiding, hoping Paxton had been successful in reaching it first.

Seeing the dark shadows cast by the almost-full moon, Samara remembered Ulrieg's gift. *Can you sense anything out of the ordinary?* She paused to set Gray free to hunt. He took flight without looking back.

No. Everything seems as normal as it could be. I can't sense anything out here other than us.

I hope your senses are correct. What about under the building? We haven't checked under there for a few nights.

I can't sense anything. However, I haven't been close enough. We've been busy trying to look after Byzarid and Daena along with fighting off death.

True. There may not be any more captives. I don't think the two senior commanders are here at the moment.

Along with Callista. Ulrieg reinforced.

Yes, yes. But we have to catch Callista in the act to prove her guilty. She has protected us against her commanders, so I'm not sure she's involved with the torture.

I still wouldn't write her off as innocent.

She could honestly be trying to run the kingdoms for the good of the people.

Uh-huh! We'll see.

When they had traveled far away from the building, Ulrieg turned visible. Even then, his black form was hard to spot against the night sky. He almost looked like an oversized bat from underneath until his red eyes cut through the darkness.

They had traveled for quite some time when a soft hum of voices reached Samara's ears. She slowed, making sure all was in order before joining the group. She peered around the corner of the boulder.

Paxton still looked drained against the orange glow of the fire, yet he continued to work on Byzarid. He had already been through so much today. It would have taken a lot of effort to bury Blade. His thoughtfulness and caring were both touching and surprising for someone who preferred the company of books, plants, or animals. His true character shone through, putting many of the other coterie members to shame.

Byzarid stirred, and Paxton ran a hand gently over his forehead and down his back, avoiding his horns. The injured dragon wasn't as spikey as Ulrieg, but his horns still looked menacing.

Daena looked healthy and cleaner, wearing the clothes Samara had brought her. Samara wished she could bring them more than the few meager supplies she could sneak out of the coterie grounds.

She approached the group noisily to avoid scaring them. "It's just me."

Paxton smiled as he continued to work on Byzarid's wounds, and Samara held out her bag to Daena.

The dragon elf's face lit up in anticipation. "Is that more food?"

Samara nodded, and Daena rose to her feet and grabbed the bag to pull out the different foods, groaning as she put a couple in her mouth. "This is the best food I've tasted since I was home."

Samara sat down next to Paxton and observed Byzarid's still form. "How is he doing?"

Jojo creeped out of Paxton's tunic and stood on the dragon's nose.

Paxton's plain face lit up with compassion. He placed a hand on the side of Byzarid's nose, stroking it gently. "Believe it or not, he's looking better. He seems to be breathing easier, and the infection is starting to subside."

"That's great news! How about you? How are you coping after the day we've had?"

After a moment's silence, he frowned. "I'm pretty weak. I won't be able to finish healing him tonight. I'm too exhausted after burying Blade. That took a lot of energy."

Samara nodded.

"He may be able to heal on his own after some time." He gently stroked the scales on Byzarid's nose. "But I'll return as soon as possible to heal him more. That way, these two can leave and find a safer spot."

A twig snapped, and everyone's eyes shot up.

Samara thought she saw a shadow move around the forest, but try as she might, she couldn't see it again.

I'm on it. Ulrieg had turned invisible, and the leaves on the ground around the campfire suddenly fluttered as Ulrieg pumped his wings.

The silence ate at Samara as she waited for him to report back.

Paxton gazed at Samara as though looking for answers. He had put together how the dragon would act in such a situation.

Samara shrugged in response.

A moment later, Ulrieg's voice cut through her panic. *I can't see anything. There doesn't seem to be anyone or thing out here.*

Are you sure?

I can't see through shrubs, but I can't find any other movement. And I was quick to come and investigate, so I doubt anyone couldn't have gotten far. I can't see any animals or humans. The sound may have been a branch falling from the treetops, making it seem louder than usual.

All right. That makes sense. I guess we're all on edge.

Samara turned to Paxton and Daena and shook her head. "Ulrieg can't find anything."

Color washed away the gray scales that had suddenly risen to the surface of Daena's face. She nodded. "That's good. I must admit every sudden noise out here has me on edge. I'll be glad when I can leave and find a safer location."

Samara placed a hand on her knee. "We appreciate your staying to watch over Byzarid."

Daena huffed. "It's the least I can do after you rescued me." Her eyes turned dark, and splotches of gray grew on her skin. Samara guessed she was thinking about Kaida.

Paxton looked to be in deep concentration. "I read that the dragon elves' magic runs through their blood."

Daena frowned. "I don't know. I've never met anyone else like me. I haven't seen anyone's skin change like mine. My mother is an ordinary elf. Although my father died when I was young."

"Oh, I'm sorry to hear that. What happened?" Samara asked.

"I believe it was a magic accident." Daena rubbed her arm. "My mother was never open about it. I think it embarrassed her somehow."

"Did you have any siblings?" Paxton asked.

She shook her head.

"What about cousins? Did your father have any siblings?" Paxton lowered Byzarid's head gently to the ground and pulled his knees up to his chest, wrapping his arms around them.

"I believe he had a brother, but I never met him.

From what my mother told me, he also died quite young."

"What? Was it the same kind of death?" Paxton offered Jojo his palm, and the frog climbed on.

Daena chewed her bottom lip. "No. I believe ogres killed him in one of the village raids."

A shocked silence filled the air, broken only by the crackling of the fire.

She gave a wry smile. "I know. It doesn't give me hope that I'll live a long life. But I believe he had a daughter before he was killed. I think she's younger than me."

Samara and Paxton exchanged looks.

"Do you know where she lives?" Samara asked.

"Apparently, in a small village in Clialarion called Felfalune. It's more than a day's travel from my village, so we never visited. I guess also because my mother is embarrassed to be associated with my father's family." She shrugged. "I think she should get over it. But then again, without Kaida, my magic seems to be as uncoordinated and dangerous as I'm told my father's was."

Samara didn't know where the village was, but surely, it couldn't be too hard to find if she could get into Clialarion and past Vexx's border control. That would be more of a problem. "Do you know what her name is?"

Daena frowned and chewed her bottom lip again. "If I remember correctly, it's Tanila Darora. She kept her father's last name because he didn't die in shame. My mother made me change my family name to Wynstone after her family."

Paxton tilted his head to one side in contemplation. "It would be interesting to find out if she has the same skin condition as you."

Daena shrugged. "I have no idea. I guess I should have called in and introduced myself when I was on the merchant trail. I didn't think it was that important at the time."

CHAPTER TWENTY-NINE

Paxton and Samara traveled together for most of the journey back to the building. Occasionally, Samara thought she saw the shadows moving. However, her nerves were probably on edge because they were doing something that might get them in trouble with some of the teachers. It brought her comfort to know Ulrieg was invisible, flying close by, and he would alert her immediately if he spotted anyone.

The air had taken on a light, fresh smell, signaling the early-morning hours. There was no sign of light in the sky, and Samara hoped they would have time to get some sleep before they were required to go to their first lesson.

Once they reached the edge of the pine forest, Samara paused. "You go ahead. I'll stay back and call

Gray. That way, we won't go in together and raise suspicion if anyone sees us."

Paxton nodded as Jojo flicked his tongue at a spider's web near his shoulder. "That's probably the best idea." He turned to leave.

"Paxton."

He turned back, and the moonlight cast his eyes into darkness, making his sockets look hollow.

"Thank you for helping us, especially Byzarid. You've won Ulrieg's approval even more, and he's grateful for your help."

He smiled. "Of course. It's my pleasure. It's been very educational and eye-opening. I'm glad to be involved."

Samara rubbed her arm, which was cold in the morning air. "I'm worried we might have placed you in danger, though."

Paxton clasped his elbows. "I think I already did that when I started digging around the library and found the book about the coterie."

Samara tilted her head to one side. "Maybe. But I'm pretty sure sneaking out with us in the middle of the night to visit the captives Ulrieg and I rescued from Vexx and Kellam's torture would put you in more danger. Be careful."

Paxton nodded. "If I'd found them under the building, I would probably have done the same as you. It's nice that someone else in the coterie genuinely cares for others. I'm honestly not sure about the other apprentices." He turned to leave and called over his shoulder, "I'll see you in the morning."

Samara watched him for a few moments before searching the top of the trees. *Have you seen Gray, Ulrieg?*

A grunt sounded through their bond. *Yes. He's playing hard to get. I think he's enjoying the fresh air too much.*

Panic surged through Samara. They needed to get the owl back if they were going to continue their act. She had tried to respect him as much as possible, but sometimes, she had to contain him against his will. *That's worrying. Can you catch him?*

Yes. I'll get him eventually, without hurting him. It could be the full moon that's making him act differently. I've seen other animals do weird things when the full moon is near. It's like it affects many creatures in strange ways.

Do their emotions become extra sensitive like yours?

No. I don't think so. What I mean is it seems to affect their personality and can make particular creatures hyperactive.

Oh.

A rustle of leaves sounded in a tree several yards

away. Her eyes wide, Samara spun to see if anyone was coming her way. Instead, she spotted a pale-gray creature in the treetops, urgently flapping and twisting. Ulrieg must have caught the owl. Samara felt sorry for the owl and wished they didn't need him.

Gray fought his invisible captor the whole way down.

Brace yourself. I'm coming in.

Samara pulled strength from her core just in time to support Ulrieg's weight as he landed on her back, his talons digging into her quiver and leather shoulder protector. Still protesting, Gray landed forcefully on Samara's shoulder. She ducked before the owl's wings hit her in the head for the fourth time. She dug into a small bag hanging from her hip and pulled out a tiny piece of meat then offered it to the bird. Gray paused his protests, considering the bribe. He didn't act hungry, but he rarely turned down a treat. After careful consideration, the owl took the meat and settled down.

She whispered to him, trying to calm him. "I'm sorry. I know you don't want to come inside tonight. If things change, and we don't need you as a cover, I will gladly set you free." She softly stroked his pale-gray chest feathers with the back of her finger, earning herself a nip. It was enough to cause slight pain but not enough to cut her skin. "All right. I accept that. You're expressing your frustration with the situation. I completely agree. We're frustrated too."

Ulrieg remained on her back, securing Gray with a hold on one of his legs, allowing the other freedom to hold his treat.

On their trip back to the building, there was no sign of Paxton. She hoped that meant that he'd managed to get to the building undetected.

When she reached the stairs, a shadow emerged from under them. Samara jumped back, calling on her magic, ready to defend herself.

Ginger emerged from the shadows.

"It's only us." Kaine's voice seemed slightly edgier than normal, but when he stepped out into the moonlight, he flashed her his usual overconfident grin. His eyes were shadowed, making it impossible to see if the smile was genuine.

Gray grew unsettled the closer Ginger moved to them. Samara attempted to settle the owl with a soft stroke to the wings while cooing.

"What are you doing out here so late?" It took all of her efforts to sound relaxed as she wondered whether he'd followed them out to where Daena and Byzarid were hidden. She remembered the strange sound they'd heard in the forest. Ulrieg had investigated and found nothing, but foxes were fantastic hiders.

He moved closer, his movements confident. "I could ask you the same thing."

Ulrieg suddenly pushed off her back, and she struggled to keep steady from the sudden weight shift. Since Gray's restraint was gone, he quickly followed.

"I see your familiar is still skittish." Kaine watched the owl as he headed for the trees.

"I was just letting Gray hunt. After what we did today, I'm having trouble sleeping."

Kaine wrapped his arms around her. "Why don't you talk to me about it? Remember, I was there, too, and with you when we fought the trolls."

Samara nodded, her cheek rubbing against his firm chest under his tunic. "I know." She wanted to melt into the comforting embrace, but she couldn't shake the thought that he might have been following them. Suddenly, a strange peace flooded her, pushing away the niggling worries. He stroked her hair, the gesture strangely comforting and softening her resolve.

"You know you can take me with you on these trips. I want to be with you and help you through any worries you may have." His voice was warm, and she wanted to tell him her secrets and worries about the coterie.

She managed to pull slightly away from him and looked into his eyes. Although it was still hard to see them through the shadows, she was still mesmerized. She opened her mouth to say something.

Don't you dare. Ulrieg's voice cut through the trance she seemed to be in. *Even if you think he may have followed us, don't. Just don't. I don't trust him.*

She closed her mouth and blinked, still looking deep into the shadows where his eyes should be.

Kaine stroked the strands of hair resting over her ear. "You were going to say something."

Again, her defense softened.

Samara! I'm warning you! Ulrieg's voice poked at her again as though he were wielding a sharp stick.

Gently, Samara pulled out of Kaine's embrace. "I'm so sorry. It's been a hectic day and night. Now that Gray is fed, I should be able to get some sleep before our lessons." She squeezed his arm. "It was a nice surprise to see you out here." The trance lessened when she stopped touching him and looking into his eyes. "Maybe you should get some sleep also." She turned to leave, calling to Gray on her way up the stairs. Ulrieg captured the owl and brought him down as inconspicuously as possible.

You and I need to talk. Ulrieg placed Gray on her shoulder and walked up the steps beside her.

About what?

About Kaine and how he constantly uses a charming spell over you when he touches you.

Samara frowned. *What do you mean?*

Ever since Kaine bonded with the fox, his charming skills have been accentuated, and judging by his actions, I can tell he knows it. He's been using it against you and other females he comes near. He also tries it against the instructors from time to time. It's dangerous when we have so many secrets we don't want to share with him.

Oh. I had no idea. Samara opened the front door to find Jet still resting by it. The bear didn't even open an eye. *Some kind of guard bear he is. How do you know this?*

It's obvious when you're the one watching. Judging by your reactions, it's not apparent to the person he's using it on.

Samara frowned, feeling a deep anger rising. Even though she hadn't involved Kaine in the coterie's secrets or her own, she had trusted Kaine with almost everything else. The thought of him abusing that or using magical power against her to draw out information she didn't want to share irked her. It wasn't right.

CHAPTER THIRTY

When Samara woke, her thoughts were filled with how the apprentices with familiars often had a more substantial magical power. Her brow pinched with a frown. As far as she knew, she didn't have a power that had exceeded the others after she bonded with Ulrieg, and it bothered her. Perhaps it was because he was a dragon, and she pretended an ordinary animal was her familiar, or she was simply lacking in that department. The way things were going, she would need every magical advantage to survive and help others. She didn't stand a chance if she tried to do all of that without enhanced magic.

She looked out the window, and the position of the sun told her she had missed breakfast. Her stomach rumbled. She would have to visit the kitchen and see if Forgrac had something she could eat before class.

Samara dressed quickly and headed for the kitchen, leaving Gray to sleep on his perch. In his invisible form, Ulrieg came with her, clinging to her shoulders to avoid having his talons clack on the stone floor or a sudden breeze from his wings brush someone as he flew over.

She passed through the apprentices as they chatted in the common room then entered the kitchen, finding Forgrac washing the dishes after the rush of breakfast.

"Still working, I see."

"The work for the day 'as only jus' started," he grumbled. The dwarf turned, smiling instantly when he spotted Samara. "An' there's my favorite apprentice." He glanced at her shoulder. "Where's your familiar?"

Samara was too aware of Ulrieg's weight on her back. "Gray is resting in our room."

"I 'ave some food for 'im." The dwarf wiped his wet hands down his pants.

"That's nice of you. We were actually out hunting last night. That's why I'm late for breakfast. Would you happen to have some food for me?" She tried to look endearing.

"Of course I'll find some food for ya. Anytime."

He stepped down from the stool. "Come on. Let's 'ave a look."

Samara followed him through the double doors into the food preparation area. Fresh bread, bacon, and eggs lay in trays on the bench.

"I was jus' about to put these into cooling. 'Elp y'self." He handed her a clean plate.

"Thank you." Her stomach growled as she dished some food onto her plate. Ulrieg climbed off her back as Forgrac disappeared then returned with some cutlery for her to use. He then pulled a stool over for her to sit on while he packed the remaining food away. She rested her head on her hand as she forked food into her mouth, not even tasting the delicious cooking, even though Forgrac was a fantastic cook.

The dwarf studied her from the corner of his eye. "Is everything all right?"

"Hmm?" She frowned as though remembering what he'd asked. "Oh. Yes. Right. No, everything is as normal as it can be in this coterie."

Forgrac chuckled. "There wasn't much sarcasm in 'at." He stacked the bowls of food on top of one another. "Why don't ya try to tell me the truth? You know that I'm not the biggest fan of their teaching methods 'ere."

Samara poked at a bit of egg with her finger. "Yes,

I know. I just automatically go on the defensive when someone asks me what I've been doing."

"Understandable, from what I've seen over my eighteen summers here. But this is me you're talkin' to. I've told ya things 'bout this place that could get me into trouble, so I'm not 'bout to give away all ya secrets."

Samara stopped eating and watched Forgrac as he continued working. "True." She chewed a piece of bacon while contemplating what to share.

Just tell him the truth.

Which part?

Start with your lesson yesterday.

Samara swallowed. "We lost an apprentice yesterday."

Forgrac stopped what he was doing. "Wha' do ya mean exactly?"

Samara jabbed at her eggs. "Zofia, our weapons master, took the apprentices with familiars and two of the apprentices who should connect with theirs soon to fight ogres. We lost one of the apprentices without a familiar. They shouldn't have been with us. It was a horrifying battle, and they weren't strong enough or trained enough to fight them."

The dwarf placed a hand on her back. "I'm so sorry. Were you close to them?"

"No. But that doesn't make it any less distressing.

We're all here to help our families, and at first, it was a nice sacrifice to make, for it was an honor to be trained to protect the kingdoms. But now I don't know what to believe." She pushed the eggs around her plate. "Callista isn't here, so I'm unsure whether she approved this harsh training. I know she likes to train us hard for life outside the building, but they were so young, and we had no warning about these terrifying battles. They could have left the younger ones out of it until they had more training and stronger magic from bonding with a familiar."

"I didn't know they went to 'at extreme. I 'aven't talked to any other apprentices 'ere. Many acted too superior to talk to the likes of a dwarf. But I did notice the numbers dropping off at some stage. I thought they might 'ave been taken away to serve. But now I think 'bout it, they could've died. Often, there was an eerie silence among the apprentices after their disappearance. The food hall used to get spookily quiet."

Samara stared at him. "That's terrible! Do you know if any apprentices left of their own accord?"

"It would be impossible for me to tell. As I said, no one talked to me. Why? Are you thinking of leaving?"

Samara's shoulders sagged. "To be honest, I can't. I like learning the magic and training, but since I bonded with my familiar, things haven't been the same here."

"What? When you bonded with ya owl?"

Samara's mouth spread into a thin line. She didn't want to lie. "It's like my eyes have been opened. It was worse when the two senior sorcerers arrived and treated us so poorly, then yesterday's lesson with Zofia happened. But if I leave, my family will be put back into poverty and most likely slavery, and it will all be my fault."

The dwarf asked again, "So all this 'as come to light after ya bonded with ya owl?"

Samara's lips thinned again.

"Either the owl 'as some powerful magic, or he's an extremely wise familiar."

"I guess you could say my familiar is very wise."

Forgrac frowned, as though he knew she was sidestepping his question.

A loud clang sounded in the far corner of the kitchen, and Forgrac spun, his eyes wide. "Who's there?"

Realizing Ulrieg had knocked some pots off their stand, Samara said, "The pots must have been unbalanced."

"Nope. That, they weren't. I'm cautious with stacking me pots." His eyes narrowed with suspicion as he surveyed the area. Another pot rocked on its own. "Where are ya? I know someone's there." He shifted to the wall and pulled the broom off its hook then held it ready to strike.

A loud sigh sounded from the corner. *All right. I'll come out. I mostly trust you because of what you've told Samara anyway.*

Forgrac froze, his eyes flicking around the room, searching for the owner of the voice.

Ulrieg turned visible. He was standing in the middle of the collapsed pots. *It was me. I'm Ulrieg. I've been watching you with Samara for a while now.*

The dwarf blinked, surprise and disbelief all over his face. He lowered the broom handle. "Why, ya a dragon. An' ya can turn invisible?"

Ulrieg's red eyes narrowed, and Samara knew he was ready to spurt out insults and sarcasm. Instead, he eyed Samara then swallowed. *Yes. That's right.*

Samara took the broom from the dwarf and returned it to the wall. "Forgrac, this is my true familiar, Ulrieg. The owl is just a cover."

Surprise and excitement lit the dwarf's face as he slapped his thigh. "Ha-ha! 'At's jus' gold! No wonder you've become suspicious 'bout the coterie since ya bonded with ya familiar." He went over to Ulrieg and bent slightly to look at him closer. "Wow! Look at ya. I 'aven't seen one of ya since I ran into that family on me acting trail. You look just like 'em."

They were probably my cousins.

The dwarf placed a hand on his forehead. "And ya can talk to more than ya witch. How fantastic!"

Ulrieg raised an eyebrow and looked at Samara. *Oh, it is so difficult not to make snarky comments.*

Forgrac gazed at Samara. "Did I do somethin'?"

Samara shook her head. "No. He's just very sarcastic and grumpy with most people. I'm slowly training him to be nice when he meets people. Even then, he only tries when he likes the person."

A look of pride crossed the dwarf's face. "Well, I like 'im too." He paused. "Has he met others in the coterie?"

"Only one. I leave it up to him who he trusts enough to expose himself to."

"So you've been actin' with everyone this whole time."

Samara frowned. "I guess that's one way to put it. I'd call it lying or keeping a secret."

"Well, I call it actin' to protect somethin' worth protectin'. Every day you're here, ya act to all the teachers and students as though everythin' is normal. Maybe when I earn me way out of here, I can take you with me, and you can act in our group of traveling performers and earn enough to pay for ya family to survive, if they 'aven't found a way by then."

"That's lovely for you to think of my family and me. I don't know what will have changed by the end of two more summers. A lot has happened in the last one and a half moon cycles. I've also found a creature who needs protecting, and if I leave here, I won't be able to protect them anymore. On the other hand, with all this power I'm growing and nurturing, I want to help protect the kingdoms. Even then, I'm not sure if staying here with Callista is the right thing to do. So far, Callista is keeping her hands clean of harsh treatment, except when I had to prove my worth and fight the trolls."

"That's quite a lot to have on your shoulders. Let me know if there's any way I can help." Forgrac had hardly removed his gaze from Ulrieg while Samara was talking. He walked over to a nearby bench, grabbed a large cut of raw rabbit, and took it to Ulrieg. "I'm guessin' ya like some raw meat."

Ulrieg sniffed. *It's fresh.*

"That, it is. I caught it this mornin'." He smiled proudly then cut a few small chunks off another rabbit on the bench and handed them to Samara. "Here's a few bites for your pet owl." His grin was childish, like he was happy to know a dark secret. "I thought your owl was a perfect familiar. You've blown me away even more with the dragon. I knew there was somethin' extra special about ya, besides ya being the only one to pay attention to me. I never knew a witch could bond with a dragon."

Neither did I. Trust me—it was a great surprise to both of us. Ulrieg tore his rabbit to shreds, making a mess on Forgrac's floor. The dwarf was too ecstatic to care.

CHAPTER THIRTY-ONE

Having someone else know about Ulrieg was both a relief and a worry. Although she trusted Paxton and Forgrac, it was still risky. If something happened with their friendship, they could tell others about Ulrieg, but also, it was putting them in more danger.

You're worrying about Forgrac knowing about me, aren't you?

Samara blinked and glanced over her shoulder at the invisible Ulrieg clinging to her back. *How did you know?*

I can feel the tension in your shoulders and over our bond, and you've been walking as though you're not seeing things.

Oh. Samara focused on the path before her. *Of course.*

Forgrac is already in danger with them, and he's on our side.

And what about Paxton?

He's already digging his own hole by researching and questioning what he's reading or can't read. That's the danger of being intelligent.

Samara nodded. *That's true. I just don't like thinking that we could be putting them both in a lot of danger—more than what they're already causing for themselves.* She weaved down another stone-walled corridor as she headed to the potions room.

"There she is. My favorite girl."

Samara's shoulders tightened. Since she'd found out that Kaine had been using his charming magic to try to coerce her to tell him more than she wanted to, he was the last person she wanted to see.

Relax. I'm here to jolt you out of it, and you know it'll be my pleasure doing it.

Samara barely resisted rolling her eyes, remembering how Ulrieg had despised Kaine from the start.

Remember not to look too long into his eyes, and don't let him touch you. Then you won't need my help. Ulrieg's weight suddenly lifted as he pushed off her back so that Kaine wouldn't accidentally touch him.

When the blue-haired apprentice reached her side, a whiff of something inviting tickled her nose.

"What's that smell?" she inhaled, savoring the smell.

Kaine moved closer. "Do you like it?"

Samara nodded, her eyes already locked with his as she breathed deeply.

"It's lavender oil. I've started dabbing it on my skin. Maybe it'll get the lovely ladies like you to relax around me."

Samara giggled and pretended to slap him on his arm. "Oh, stop it. Like the females aren't relaxed around you."

Wow! That was quick. I'm impressed, Ulrieg said sarcastically. *That wasn't even one of his forceful attempts. That guy has a strong charming spell. All right, Samara. You can back off now.*

It took all Samara's effort to pull her eyes off Kaine. She blinked then shook her head, trying to clear it. Ulrieg's voice had helped, but her thoughts were still fogged. *How did that happen so quickly? I was trying not to look.*

You failed spectacularly.

"Are you all right?" Kaine placed a hand on Samara's shoulder.

Ginger sauntered behind him, sniffing and scanning the area as if looking for something.

Samara jumped away, ignoring Kaine's disappointment. "Yes. I'm fine. Just lacking sleep. I don't know how you're thinking so clearly. My brain is wrecked." She rubbed the spot he'd touched as though it could wipe away the magic he was undoubtedly using on her. She smiled at him without looking into his eyes.

That wasn't very subtle. You'll have to do better at moving away from his contact without being so obvious.

I know. I guess I'm jumpy because I didn't think his magic would work so fast.

Someone moved next to Samara, separating her from Kaine. Paxton gave her a friendly smile, but it also seemed like he knew he was protecting her from Kaine, who gave him an annoyed look.

Samara smiled back at the welcome intruder. *Did you put Paxton up to this?*

I didn't have to. I suspect he can see through people's nonsense and cut to the truth. He probably also spotted your jerking away from Kaine's touch. I'm guessing he also knew something was off with Gray being your familiar, but he couldn't see me, making him question his ability.

I'll have to remember that if I ever try to tell him a lie.

I'm sure he already knows your biggest secrets, so I don't think you need to lie to him.

Kaine dropped back and shifted to Samara's other side. Jojo croaked, and at the same time,

Paxton slowly maneuvered behind Samara, blocking Kaine's access to her.

Samara struggled to hold back a grin. Paxton was becoming a good friend. It was what Ulrieg wanted. Knowing this made her wonder if Ulrieg was telling her the truth that Paxton was doing this on his own without the dragon's prompts.

Not being able to get access to Samara, Kaine shifted and moved toward Luna. Samara frowned.

His voice low, Paxton said, "Sorry. I didn't mean for him to do that. I was trying to stop him from using his charming magic on you to get information out of you."

Samara shook her head at how Kaine was inching closer to the tall, beautiful elf. "If he cared for me, he wouldn't do that."

"Unless he's acting out of jealousy." Paxton pushed his long green ponytail over his shoulder.

"True. He's been showing some of that since he spotted us returning from the forest together. I appreciate your help. Ulrieg was pulling me out of the magic's spell, but completely blocking him off was more effective. I didn't know what he was doing until last night when he approached me on my way back into the building. Ulrieg told me."

Paxton's brown eyes filled with concern. "Did he spot us again?"

"I don't know about us in particular. But he definitely spotted me."

"Have you told him anything?"

Samara shook her head. "Ulrieg was there to pull me out of his charms."

"Good." He smiled. "You have an intelligent familiar."

"Don't tell him that. It'll only make his head grow." Samara chuckled, only to be cut off by Ulrieg.

He doesn't need to. I can hear what he's saying.

Connecting their gazes, Samara and Paxton laughed, receiving a disapproving look from Kaine. Samara shrugged. She was only being friendly with Paxton, and they were keeping a secret together.

Kaine snuggled closer to Luna, wrapping his arm around her shoulders, instantly setting her swooning. Samara had never seen Kaine do anything other than flirt with other females, but she still hated that he did it when he claimed he was only interested in her.

Someone nudged her, and she glanced over to meet Paxton's caring brown eyes. At that moment, his plain face turned into the most enticing one she had ever seen.

He brought his mouth closer to her ear. "It's up to you what you do, but if he's not committed to you, he's not worth having, no matter how handsome and charming he is. You should be with someone who cares only for you. You deserve that much if not more."

She looped her arm through his, his long-sleeved tunic rubbing gently against her skin, and leaned her head on his shoulder briefly. "Thanks." Warmth rushed through her. It was nice to know that someone genuinely cared.

You should kiss him. That's a relationship I'd approve of.

I'm not going to kiss him. I'm with Kaine. I'm not a cheater.

You can't say for sure Kaine isn't.

The words hurt, and she wanted to snap at Ulrieg. But she knew they were true. She wasn't confident that Kaine was loyal. *I'm still not going to cheat. Besides, Paxton deserves better than that, and I don't want to wreck our friendship.*

CHAPTER THIRTY-TWO

They reached the dingy room where their potions lessons were held. The scent of combined ingredients siding on acidic wafted to them as they entered the room, which was decorated with spices, drying herbs, and creature parts, either dried or stored in jars with clear preserving solutions.

The enormous cauldron at the front of the room bubbled over a fire, and the small, elderly potions master slaved over it, stirring the liquid with a large wooden stick. Tabatha lay on a corner of the bench, her tail flicking with annoyance.

Hearing their footsteps, Artemise looked up and grinned, showing off her brown teeth. "About time you lot arrived. I've almost finished my potion, and I'm looking for some guinea pigs."

Peadar shifted to the back of the room, trying not to make eye contact with the instructor.

"You. Young mischievous one. Don't you want to try this first?" Artemise pointed at Henriette as she tried to hide at the back of the room with Peadar.

Her pale face blanched some more, darkening her freckles. She looked like she was still processing Blade's death and not wanting to participate in something else that could harm her. In the past, she had often thought it hilarious to try different potions that would temporarily cause her to do strange things. After the battle with the ogres, she must have realized that some things the coterie expected them to take part in could kill her. Samara didn't blame her.

Artemise looked around at the other apprentices arriving, searching for her next victim with a gleam in her eyes.

Paxton breathed in deeply. "What potion is it?"

Artemise flashed her brown teeth. "If you don't know, then I won't tell."

He frowned and took another long, deep breath. "It doesn't smell complete."

Artemise clapped and rubbed her hands together, her wrinkled face filling with mischief. "I was waiting for the final ingredient." She searched him from head to toe. "Where's that frog of yours?" She cackled.

Paxton froze then moved away from the instructor.

The instructor's playful smile dropped over ten summers off her face. She waved a hand dismissively at Paxton. "Relax. I'm just joking with you. But it *is* missing an ingredient, although this time, it's not someone's familiar." She cackled, though the apprentices weren't amused. "Cauldron's failure! You lot need to lighten up. Life's too short to be this grim."

"I can't do this. I'm going back to my room." Henriette stormed toward the door, only to be stopped when Artemise threw a small pouch at her. It exploded when it hit the ground in front of her. Henriette stood motionless, her hands pinned to her sides.

Artemise narrowed her eyes at the exiting apprentice. "No one leaves this room unless I permit them. Because you were so keen to leave early, you will be my test subject."

Henriette's stationary body shook as fear radiated out of her. The younger apprentices were also frozen with uncertainty. The safe, secure place where they had come to learn and help their families had suddenly turned unpredictable.

Paxton sniffed again, his brow furrowing. "Potions Master, are you simply missing lavender?"

Artemise pulled her attention away from Henriette to narrow her eyes at Paxton. "How did you know?"

He shrugged. "The smell. I recognized most of the ingredients but noticed it was on the pungent side and smelled slightly sour. After careful consideration, I narrowed down the type of potions I know and decided it was one that would be finished nicely with a few sprigs of dried lavender." He pointed above the instructor's head. "Plus, you have lavender hanging close to the cauldron, making it seem like the obvious choice."

Artemise screwed up her nose. "Very clever." She rubbed her pointy chin between her thumb and forefinger. "Since you're boasting about how smart you are, tell me what potion I'm making."

Paxton pulled his shoulders back. "You're making the *Maginot* potion."

Artemise pursed her lips, and her eyes narrowed. "That's correct. Do you know what it does?"

"It makes people imagine things and act crazy. It's one of the nicer potions that can potentially stop someone from doing something you don't like."

The potions instructor nodded then eyed the room. "So, who's going to be the test subject?"

Though Henriette had shied away, Artemise raised an eyebrow and beckoned her forward after releasing her from her spell.

Before Henriette moved, Rehan raised his hand. "I'll do it."

He seemed unafraid, and Samara thought it must be because he hadn't had to face the harsh realities of the coterie's testing. Strangely, none of the younger apprentices had asked about Blade when he didn't show up for lessons. It was almost as though he'd never been in the coterie. That thought made Samara's heart ache. Many hadn't known him well, but his death had clearly rocked Henriette.

Artemise nodded. "And who else? I'd like more than one volunteer, or it'll still be the little miss I froze at the back." She indicated the large cauldron. "As you can see, I've made more than enough. I'd like to see how two different people act." She took the lavender from above her, broke off the dried leaves, scrunched them in her hand, then dropped them into the cauldron. After stirring the ingredients, she got another handful and did the same. When she was finished, the brew's smell was sweeter.

Paxton raised his hand. "I'll be the test subject instead of Henriette."

Samara yanked his arm back down. "What are you doing?" she hissed.

Gently, Paxton removed her hand and raised it again, whispering over his shoulder, "At least if they catch me doing anything they disapprove of later, I can blame it on this potion." He lowered his voice further. "I have an antidote in my room. I'll take it after class if you remind me."

"Absolutely, I will." She cast him a side glance. It was weird for him to have an antidote for the potion, and it caused her to wonder what other potions he had in his room.

"Very good, Frog Boy." Artemise pointed at Paxton with a gnarled finger. "You will make an excellent guinea pig. Well, come on! Don't just stand there. You need to come up to the front to get the potion. I'm not carrying it to you. How much pressure do you think these old legs can take?"

The rest of the apprentices parted, leaving a younger female apprentice with long pink hair in Paxton's way. The young elf stood fixated, staring up at him as though infatuated. It was a strange sight to see, and with the way Paxton reacted, it must have been a new experience for him also.

Although Samara was confident that if they saw a glimpse into Paxton's heart, they would automatically swoon if they valued loyalty and respect.

She shook her head, trying to clear her thoughts. *I'm starting to sound like Ulrieg.*

She focused on the young apprentice as Paxton smiled , grabbed her upper arms, and gently shifted her aside. Her pale, pointy face turned red with embarrassment.

Samara had thought Rehan was the youngest in the coterie, but recently, she had discovered some of the quieter apprentices were younger than he was. Before, she had only thought they were shorter.

The elf's thin body remained rigid, as though she were worried for Paxton as he partook of the potion.

I'd watch out if I were you. That young female really likes Paxton.

Samara frowned at Ulrieg's interruption, although she felt a strange pang of jealousy.

You forget that I'm with Kaine, not Paxton, Samara retorted.

Oh. But are you? I'm not an expert at relationships, but I'm pretty sure that if someone is using their powers against you or manipulating you to tell them things you're not ready to disclose, that's a warning sign that they aren't the right person for you and don't care for you properly.

Knowing he was right, Samara didn't respond. She had never seen her father or mother be as deceptive as Kaine had been to her, nor how she had been to Kaine. As far as she knew, her parents were always open with each other. She shook her head, trying to get rid of the thought.

It's not like I plan to marry Kaine. He's only a love interest.

And probably the same for nearly every other female in the coterie, Ulrieg grumbled.

Samara ignored him and concentrated on Paxton and Rehan as they stood before Artemise. After scooping the potion's contents into clay cups, the instructor handed one to each of the males. Rehan took it with untainted enthusiasm, unaware of the devastation the older apprentices had faced the previous day. Judging by the stiffness of Paxton's shoulders, he hoped his educated guess had been correct. If not, they could be killed within moments.

CHAPTER THIRTY-THREE

Samara held her breath as Rehan and Paxton lifted the cups to their lips. Tension radiated off the older apprentices.

After neither Paxton nor Rehan started to show any signs of poisoning, the older apprentices' shoulders relaxed.

Suddenly, Rehan yanked hard at the front of Paxton's tunic and peered inside the crack. "Where's that turtle?"

Paxton flicked him on the forehead. "What turtle, you turkey head? I have a butterfly. See? it's sitting on my nose." He touched the tip of his nose with his forefinger, his eyes crossed.

A rumble of laughter echoed through the room.

"That's your chin, you dingbat," Rehan retorted, giving Paxton a weird look.

Paxton knocked him on the head with his palm, the slap radiating throughout the room. Rehan hit his fingers on the underside of Paxton's chin.

"All right, you two. You can move back to your places now." Artemise looked pleased with herself although keen to eliminate the distraction.

Playfully slapping each other, Rehan and Paxton made their way toward Samara, leaving her unsure of what to do. It was clear that they would need the potion in Paxton's room.

The potions instructor turned back to the room. "As you can see, this potion works. I won't give it to any more of you because I think it'll make teaching you too chaotic." She indicated several benches with ten small cauldrons on the room's far side. "As you can see, I've set up for the next part of the class. But first, I want you to nominate potions you wish to create. Do you have any ideas?" She stood on a small stool that raised her slightly higher than Peadar and Luna.

Henriette grinned, apparently appeased by the boys' antics. "How about one that makes facial hair grow?"

At first, Artemise looked bored, then she raised one eyebrow, and her faded eyes twinkled. "That sounds interesting. I would have preferred to make something more sinister, but I like a bit of mischief."

Henriette clapped and jumped on the spot. She was smiling for the first time since Blade had died to save her. She looked around the room, and her eagerness faded. Blade was usually her potions partner, and she'd momentarily forgotten.

Samara's heart sank. Usually, she tried to pair up with Paxton or Kaine, but Kaine seemed to have settled in with Luna, much to Peadar's disappointment. And Paxton was acting strange with Rehan. Unless he could mix potions even when in some weird state of mind, their potion would be interesting.

Samara squeezed Henriette's shoulders. "Do you want to be my potions partner today?"

Sadly, Henriette nodded. "That would be nice."

Even though none of Samara's sisters had Henriette's mischievousness, she was starting to feel like a little sister.

Thinking of her family made her heart pang. There was no way she could let them starve. She would do whatever it took to keep them well looked after.

Samara led Henriette over to the bench where the cauldrons sat half filled with water. She was taking in the ingredients lying on the bench when someone a couple of tables over fell to the ground.

She looked around to see Peadar lying on the floor, unconscious.

Raucous laughter filled the room, and all eyes turned to Artemise.

The instructor shrugged. "He fell for the oldest trick in the book—assuming that the ingredient in front of you is the right one."

The young human apprentice with large ears and short aqua hair stood beside Peadar, looking forlorn. His feet were pigeon-toed, and his knees shook slightly. "He only licked the water off his finger." The boy kneeled to observe Peadar as Ziggy climbed on Peadar's chest and slapped him in the face before pinching his nose and roughly dragging it from side to side.

It took a few moments before Peadar opened his eyes slightly. "What happened?" he croaked. "Why am I on the ground?"

"You tasted a potent sleeping potion." Artemise struggled to overcome her laughter. "You're lucky you only licked your finger and didn't take a sip, or you would have been out for a lot longer."

Peadar shook his head and rose to his feet with the help of his partner. "Why am I not surprised?"

Artemise shrugged. "That'll teach you not to taste solutions you didn't oversee." The potions instructor turned to the other students. "All of you have a sleeping potion in your cauldrons. In small doses, it's not harmful, although I don't recommend sampling it, even a small dose. If you take too much, you won't wake up without some powerful magic."

The younger apprentices giggled, though the older students fell into silence.

"All right." Artemise clapped her hands. "We don't need a sleeping potion to make the potion young Henriette suggested. So I'll get you all to pour your caldrons' contents into the empty jars on the floor against the wall." She pointed to the left side of the room, where ten large jars sat empty. "Then I want you to gather these ingredients." She called out the ingredients as she scribbled them on the stone wall in chalk—goat's beard, pig's hoof, comfrey stems, raspberries, pinecone seeds, and spit. Then she wrote the method under the ingredients.

Samara scrunched her nose. "It sounds disgusting."

Henriette smiled. "That's why I wanted to make it. Also, it will brighten my day if it has the desired effect. I think all the senior students could use some brightening. Even Mist, who loves to fight."

As Henriette had said, Mist also looked apprehensive and a little down.

Henriette gathered the ingredients while Samara began grinding the pig's hoof with the goat's beard then crushing the comfrey stem with the raspberries to add some flavor and juices before adding the ground pinecone seeds. When Henriette returned with the last ingredients, she spat into the bowl.

Samara wrinkled her nose as her taste buds turned sour. The potion wasn't one she wanted to consume. It looked and sounded disgusting. The only normal ingredient was the raspberries.

When she was sure it was mixed properly, they heated it over a small burner, churning the ingredients until they boiled, then placed it aside to cool.

"Cauldron knows! What have you two done?" Artemise sounded more amused than upset as she went over to Paxton and Rehan's table.

Rehan squatted to half his normal size, appearing stuck, and Paxton was lying on his back, his legs up in the air, kicking as though stuck.

"My shell is weighing me down!" Paxton yelled before laughing at Rehan. "Look at shorty."

Meanwhile, Rehan was laughing at Paxton, thinking he was a turtle. "You've turned into a turtle. I guess you do take on your familiar's personality." He held his stomach as he laughed.

Although amused, Samara shook her head over how much the potion had affected them. She spotted Jojo sitting on the edge of their bench and offered the frog her hand to move him to safety within a small pocket of her tunic. "Don't worry. I'll give him the antidote after class," she whispered to the frog, unsure if he could understand her.

The apprentices around her laughed, and the noise grew louder, drawing her attention away from Paxton and Rehan. Half the apprentices had grown bushy beards, including Henriette.

Samara's jaw dropped. "What happened? I only looked away for a moment."

Henriette was holding her stomach, bending over as she laughed, feeling her beard. "Half of us drank the potion."

Samara did see the humor, especially when she spotted Luna with a black beard so long that it covered her normally exposed cleavage. "How long does it last?"

When Henriette shrugged, Samara turned to Artemise, who was catching her breath after pulling Paxton off the ground. "Is there a potion that will take away the beard?"

Artemise's eyes glinted, and she shook her head. "No. It usually wears off in about an hour, depending on how much they drank." She looked around at the chaos and cackled. "This is one of my favorite teaching methods, second to the ones when I make the apprentices sick."

CHAPTER THIRTY-FOUR

Samara helped Paxton back to his room, accompanied by Kaine. She couldn't help wondering if Luna with a beard was a little too much for him.

Each holding one of Paxton's arms, they staggered up the stairs. Suddenly, Paxton stopped and yanked his arm free from Kaine and pointed at a dark corner. "Hey! That looks like a dragon."

Samara's heart skipped a beat, and she kicked Paxton's calf.

"Ow!" Paxton yelled then laughed. "Did you just kick me?"

"I'm sorry. I stumbled up the step." She gave Kaine a look that said Paxton had lost his mind, and he nodded. She hoped that meant that Kaine didn't believe that he saw a dragon.

"Come on. Let's keep you moving," Samara said when Paxton opened his mouth to speak. She didn't want him to yell any more secrets that couldn't be explained. She looked at Kaine past Paxton's back. "He said he has an antidote for the potion in his room."

Kaine frowned. "That's a strange thing to keep in your room."

Samara shrugged. "It's Paxton. He does a lot of things the average apprentices don't do."

Paxton puffed out his chest. "You bet I do."

Still trying to keep him quiet, Samara prodded him along. "Come on. Let's keep moving. We need to find your antidote."

Paxton swerved and slurred, "I don't need an antidote. There's nothing wrong with me."

Bewildered, Samara said to Kaine, "I wonder how Henriette is doing with Rehan. I believe the potion wears off eventually, but it will probably be at least tomorrow or later before that happens."

Kaine's hand gently caressed Samara's. "Maybe we can leave him like this and let it wear off naturally."

Trying not to be too obvious, Samara pulled her hand away from Kaine's and shook her head. "I think he has something he wants to take care of today, and poor Jojo is stressing over Paxton's behavior. It would be disturbing when you're used to someone being intelligent."

Ginger snorted, and Samara heard talons clacking in the spot where Paxton had pointed earlier. She wondered if Paxton had seen Ulrieg or was imagining him from the shape of the dark shadow. Or maybe Paxton's brain and sight were scrambled from the potion.

When they reached the door to Paxton's room, he wobbled forward and turned the handle, pushing the door open.

Samara turned to Kaine. "Thanks for helping me take him upstairs. How's Luna? Does she need your help to get rid of her beard?" She knew the beard potion would leave her body soon, but she wanted to get Kaine to go in case Paxton had things lying around that Kaine shouldn't see or in case Paxton blurted something that others shouldn't know.

"Maybe Paxton has an antidote for the beard potion too." Kaine rubbed his chin.

Paxton cackled and poked Kaine's nose. "Nope. I don't have anything for that one." He almost sounded intoxicated. "It's not like I'm worried about having a beard."

"Luna might need a little of your uplifting charm."

Kaine sighed. "All right. I should see how she is.

Her pride is probably suffering. Although I thought my tending to her might make you jealous."

Samara scoffed, "You think I'm going to get jealous over a bearded woman? I've seen you flirt with females much prettier."

Kaine pouted. "Are you keen to get rid of me so you can spend more time alone with Paxton?"

"Look who's the one getting jealous." Samara quirked an eyebrow. "Trust me. Paxton is only a friend in need. I hope he'll direct me to the right antidote for this particular potion and not something that'll make him worse. I don't know that I could handle worse."

After Kaine turned and walked down the stairs, Samara helped Paxton open his door and directed him inside. His room was small, like hers, except the walls were lined with bookshelves loaded with books that spilled onto the floor. It seemed overcrowded, and as she coaxed Jojo out of her pocket, careful not to touch his skin and burn it, and put him in a tiny green enclosure Paxton had made him, she realized a frog familiar was one of the few that would be happy living in such a crowded place. The frog dived into the small pond in the middle of the enclosure, which was surrounded by natural rock, green furs, mosses, and shrubs. Paxton had gone to a lot of effort to make sure Jojo had a nice home.

On another bench beside the enclosure were all kinds of tools for making potions, and finished potions covered the workbench and sat in boxes on the floor. If someone looked at his room, not understanding the importance of the items within it, they would think Paxton was a hoarder. Except all the items were part of the additional studies Paxton did on his own time and the reason he excelled in potions. Samara could tell that he worked on keeping things orderly. The clutter of the potions was much neater than Artemise's classroom.

"All right. Where do I start looking for the antidote for this potion?" She bent over one section of bottled potions and read the labels, but none made sense.

"It's the purple bottle," he slurred.

Samara dug through the bottles and found a purple one. The label read Swollen Lips. "Ah, I don't think this is it. Are you sure it's a purple bottle?"

Paxton nodded.

"Is there more than one?"

"Yes, of course. You've also got to read the label."

Samara pursed her lips. "I figured that, or you would have swollen lips right now."

Paxton laughed. "That would be hilarious."

Samara frowned. He was definitely not himself.

She kept sorting through the bottles and finally

came across another purple one. She lifted it and read the label. "Pink hands. How does having pink hands help anyone?"

Paxton plunked down on his bed, studying his fingernails as though they were the most impressive things he had ever seen. "They can always be picked out of a crowd if you didn't get to take in their face properly."

Samara nodded. "I guess that makes sense. But it's not going to help us here."

She kept digging. Every purple bottle held a potion that changed the body weirdly but had nothing to do with the problem of the mind Paxton was dealing with. She began looking at other colors and reading all the labels, hoping he had named them all in the same easy fashion as the purple ones. After much sorting, she eventually found a pink bottle that read Mind Restorer. She held it up to him. "Is this the one?"

Paxton nodded. "That's it. The one in the purple bottle."

Samara stared at the bottle and held it under the window's light. "I'm pretty sure it's pink."

"Same thing." Paxton chuckled.

Though she was unsure it was the right one from his strange reaction, at least the label sounded better for his problem than the ones on the purple bottles.

She uncorked the bottle and gave it to Paxton then watched as he downed the contents.

Ulrieg took that moment to turn visible.

"Oh, good. You're here." Samara let out a breath.

Of course I'm here. Where else did you think I would be?

"I didn't know. You've been rather quiet, and I know this is hard for you to believe, but I can't see you when you're invisible."

Ulrieg exposed his teeth in what looked like a nasty grin. *Funny, that. I thought you could see me when I'm invisible.*

Paxton frowned and flopped back onto his back, resting on his thick blanket. His eyes stilled on the ceiling.

Is he all right? Ulrieg swapped his sarcasm for concern.

"I'm honestly not sure. I hope it's the right potion. He was so far gone that he couldn't give me a proper answer. I hope the label was correct."

Ulrieg scoffed. *When is he slack with his work?*

Samara frowned. "Never. He's always been on top of everything, except when he works with his flail."

Exactly! That should mean his label was correct.

"If he was the only one who touched his potions."

Ulrieg recoiled with his red eyes wide. *You're honestly starting to sound like me when it comes to the occupants of this coterie.*

"I've learned a lot about them since I came back after we bonded. But I hope it's only a couple of bad eggs, and they're not all like that. I'd hate to think that Devi is evil, and I hope that Callista is good. If that's the case, we have much more on our side to see if we can find and release Dragoria from its binding spell."

No one wants that more than me, but don't let your guard down.

Ulrieg climbed onto Paxton's bed and stared at his face, watching every unusual twist of the muscles until they eventually stopped, and Paxton seemed to fall into a deep sleep. Ulrieg curled his tail around himself.

It's times like this that I wish I could read minds. That's the only way to know if the potion is working.

"If he doesn't snap out of it soon, I'm going to have to get some lunch for the both of us and bring it back here." Samara felt his arms under the long sleeves of his jerkin. They seemed to be the correct temperature. "I wish I had a talent like Paxton's and could heal him."

From what I understand, he doesn't need healing, as it's only temporary. And it looks like what you gave him is the only thing that will clear out the potion before it has run its course.

Samara studied Paxton's face as its color changed repeatedly until his normal color finally won the battle.

Not long after, Paxton's eyes slitted open. "Is it safe to come out yet?" His voice was croaky.

Samara chuckled. "I don't know about safe, but it's only me, Ulrieg, and Jojo. How are you feeling?"

"Kind of strange." Slowly, he rose to a sitting position, and Samara helped him.

She smiled, earning herself a strange look from Paxton.

"What?"

She shook her head. "Nothing. It's just good to see you acting normal again."

"Was I that bad?"

"Yes. It was hilarious."

His cheeks reddened.

Samara touched his arm. "In a good way. Embarrassing for an introvert, but you only did things an extrovert would be proud of."

"So in other words, I'd be embarrassed."

Samara shrugged. "Probably. I'd be embarrassed, too, but you didn't do anything that bad. Except I did have to look after Jojo. He looked lost and a little scared."

Paxton went to the enclosure and lowered his hand. Jojo climbed onto it, and Paxton raised him to his eye level. "I'm sorry. I didn't know I'd make you uncomfortable."

Silently, they eyed each other, the frog's throat moving monotonously.

After a while, Paxton lifted Jojo to his shoulder, and the frog climbed on. "He's all right about it. He said it was a bit daunting, but you took good care of him, and he knows it was the potion, not me."

That's what I thought he would say. Ulrieg uncoiled his tail, his red eyes trained on Paxton and Jojo. *I didn't think he'd be upset. Every day in this coterie is a fight for our lives, even for frogs.*

Paxton studied Ulrieg. It seemed the novelty of seeing a dragon up close still hadn't worn off. "It would be much more dangerous for you if what I'm reading is true." He turned to Samara. "I noticed something around Artimese's neck before I took the potion. It looked like the emblem you asked me about, but it was on the end of some trinket and hung from her neck like a necklace."

Samara looked at the ground.

"You know about it?"

She nodded. "Yes. That's the key we borrowed for a couple of nights without her knowing. Ulrieg took it, and it allowed us to get into the area under the school where we found Daena and Byzarid."

We'll have to borrow one again and check to see if there are any more captives under the building.

Samara nodded. "Yes. Just in case it isn't only Vexx and Kellam taking captives down there."

"Who has these keys?" Paxton asked.

"We believe it's all the senior members of the coterie, so I'd imagine all the instructors would have one. As to how many use it regularly, that would be different."

"So you don't know exactly?"

Samara shook her head. "No. We haven't spotted one on every teacher, but some may not keep it on them as much as others."

"At least I can help you look for them. But if I find the next one first, you have to take me to the underground level."

Samara frowned. She didn't want to get Paxton into more trouble, although she had a lot of faith that Ulrieg could get the next one when he was invisible. "I guess we can do that."

CHAPTER THIRTY-FIVE

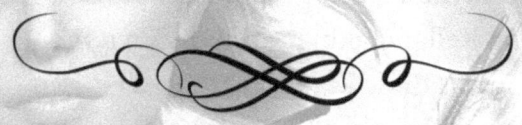

They entered Eliphas's greenhouse, watching and waiting for the herbology specialist to instruct them for their afternoon lesson. With Phobae, his extra-long stick insect familiar, on his green ponytail, the instructor's eyes narrowed, deepening the wrinkles framing them. He was acting weirder than usual, silently pulling potted plants out of the grouped plant area and slowly placing them on the barren bench.

Paxton leaned closer to Samara and whispered, "Notice they're all the same types of plants?"

Samara watched as the instructor pulled over a few more potted plants and placed them on the additional bench. She nodded. "What do you think he's doing?"

It looked like how other instructors prepared for

their lessons, except he was doing it while the apprentices were there and waiting, wasting their lesson time.

Paxton shrugged. "I guess we'll find out eventually."

Eliphas turned to Paxton and rubbed his sizeable hooked nose with a dirt-covered finger, leaving a trail along the bridge. Phobae had perched her long front legs on the top of his rounded ear, and it looked like she was talking to the absent-minded instructor. Eliphas nodded. "Phobae says I should get you to help me."

Paxton clasped his hands at the front, looking unsure. "All right. As a warning, though, Artemise had me drinking the *Maginot* potion last lesson, and I don't think my senses are completely back to normal yet."

Eliphas rolled his eyes. "That woman is always up to some kind of trouble." He shrugged. "This task shouldn't be hard for you, as plants are one of your passions."

Paxton unclasped his hands. "What do you want me to do?"

The herbology instructor pointed at the mixed plants then at the small amount he had selected and placed on the side. "I need you to help find the monstera deliciosa plants. I know I've got twenty in here somewhere. That's enough for one each."

Everyone stopped talking as they realized he was including Blade in that number. Eliphas must not talk with the other instructors often.

Paxton set to work finding the plants.

With tear-filled eyes, Henriette called in a rough voice, "We only need nineteen plants, unless you use one as an example."

The herbology instructor stopped digging through the potted plants to look her in the eye. "No, young lady. We have twenty apprentices, so we need twenty plants."

Henriette wiped the tears from one side of her face. "We lost Blade yesterday."

The herbology instructor looked taken aback. "No one told me that."

Samara tensed. She hoped Henriette remembered the threat Zofia had made at the end of the battle about not telling any of the younger apprentices about their brutal lesson.

Peadar placed a hand on Henriette's back. "I'm sorry the other instructors didn't tell you. Perhaps they were waiting for Callista to return." It seemed like he was taking over the conversation before Henriette said too much.

Eliphas looked around at the older apprentices'

sad faces before understanding dawned on him. "That's too bad. He will be missed."

The apprentices fell silent. It was hard to imagine the extremely introverted herbology instructor caring, except for Phobae and his plants.

He turned and continued setting up for the lesson, leaning over the plants he and Paxton had gathered to ensure they were all the same type. All the plants lacked a central stem and grew more like vines with large holes in the leaves, making them look similar to palms.

Samara noticed Paxton inching his way behind Eliphas to another bench in the far corner. Scattered over the top were all kinds of plants and empty pots. After Paxton reached the bench, he did a quick survey of the room, then his hand darted out and grabbed something. He spotted Samara watching him, and he opened his palm, exposing an inner circle key for the Sacred Flame coterie looped on a long leather cord. Grinning, he slipped it into a pocket in his tunic, only to have Jojo climb out of it, looking annoyed that his hidey hole had been infiltrated.

Samara gritted her teeth. *Paxton has found Eliphas's inner circle key. Now we're going to have to take him to the underground cave.*

Isn't that a good thing? Ulrieg sounded undeterred. *You'll have someone else to lean on for helping the dragons escape. Who else is better than Paxton?*

No one. But the point is that it'll be putting him in more danger. I appreciate his friendship and don't want to do that.

He could be more than a friend.

Ulrieg! Will you concentrate on what I'm saying?

All right, all right. I can only hope. If Paxton is willing to face the danger to help you, then so be it. You put your life in danger helping my kind, and I worry about you. Now it's your turn to worry about someone.

But I already worry about you.

Ulrieg fell silent.

You know that, don't you?

Of course I do. It just sounds so soppy when you say it out loud. I mean, geesh!

There's my nasty dragon who can't stand too much kindness. Samara frowned at Paxton as she watched him return to the group.

Since he's already put himself in danger by stealing the key, we should go down to the underground level tonight.

But we still need to check on Byzarid.

We can check on him after. I think it's a good idea if someone like Paxton knows about the cave in case we get caught.

Samara's heart leaped with panic. Ulrieg was

right. If they were caught, they could end up down there as well, and she doubted her family would be provided for if she was held prisoner, and they would never know what had happened to her. She shook her head. Callista hadn't been proven guilty. A lot of things had happened while Callista was away. She had to stand by her belief that people were innocent until proven guilty.

Eliphas clasped his hands behind his back, and Phobae climbed onto one of the plants. "Now, who can tell me about these plants?"

Paxton started to speak, only to be cut off by the instructor.

"Anyone who isn't Mr. Vigil." Eliphas smirked at him. "It would be nice to have one of you other apprentices know a little about plants." He rocked onto his toes as he scanned the room. When no one volunteered, he let out a loud sigh. "All right, Mr. Vigil. I guess you get to answer this one too."

Paxton puffed out his chest. "These are monstera deliciosa plants. They grow a delicious fruit that tastes like none other. Although if eaten while unripe, they can cause bad irritations of the throat and intestinal tract, copious salivation, and difficulty breathing, swallowing, or speaking."

The apprentices gathered closer to the table holding the monstera deliciosa, each one pulling a potted plant toward them and turning them slowly, looking for evidence of fruit.

Eliphas nodded. "As per usual, very good. You know your plants. But there is one thing you missed that not many people know about."

Paxton scratched behind his ear, deep in concentration, before his eyes lit up. "Oh. I know. There is a magical eye at the base, near the roots, that can cause more destruction than its unripe fruit."

Eliphas shook a finger at Paxton. "Very good. And what exactly does that eye do?"

Excitedly, Paxton explained, "If triggered, it will send out a new root as fast as a—"

A sudden strangled noise came from the table's far end, and all apprentices turned to find Peadar wrestling with a fresh green root wrapped around his neck.

Sakaala, the thin young elf with long pink hair, grabbed the root, whipped a small knife from the back of her pants, and cut it. The plant crashed to the ground, the pot shattered, and the dirt scattered, leaving the roots bare.

Sakaala set to work unwrapping the wayward root from around Peadar's neck, having the coils undone before Eliphas made it to Peadar's side to help.

Peadar gasped, his hand at his throat and the color returning to his face.

Sakaala held the root out for Eliphas. "Here. I don't want it."

Cautiously, the herbology teacher took it from her then dropped it to the ground in the far corner of the greenhouse. "Well done, Sakaala." He turned to Peadar. "And of course, it had to be you, Mr. Mongan. It always seems to be you who experiences the worst kind of luck."

Peadar stared at him in disbelief. "How was I supposed to know it would do that?"

Eliphas leveled his gaze. "If you had stopped touching and spinning the plants and listened first, you could have been saved from an extremely sore neck."

Still holding his throat with one hand, Peadar pointed at the rest of the apprentices with the other. "I was only doing what the rest of the class was doing."

"Yet none of them were strangled by their plants." The instructor squatted to pick up the pottery pieces and threw them into a box near the door before picking up the plant, careful not to damage it further. "Once the monstera deliciosa has sent out one of these strangling roots, it has to rest for a while, or else it will die. If the plant is in a pot like this, it must be treated with care. If growing in the wild, then it simply needs to be left alone."

Eliphas walked over to the bench, carefully placed the plant on the top, dug through the empty pots, then pulled out one that was the correct size. He paused, frowning at the bench top, and muttered something.

"Is everything all right?" Paxton asked casually.

"Hmm?" Eliphas looked up. "Oh, yes. I just thought I left something here I'm not supposed to let out of my sight."

"Did you need us to look for it for you?" Samara asked, casting Paxton a side glance. If she took it back from Paxton, he wouldn't be able to get himself into more danger.

Eliphas waved a hand dismissively. "Oh, no. It's only a stupid key anyway. It's no good to anyone. I'll find it later."

Paxton gave her a grin, and Samara responded with a scowl.

The herbology instructor gathered some nutrient-rich soil and packed it gently around the root of the monstera deliciosa, watered it with a watering can, then placed it in front of Peadar. "Now, be very careful with the plant."

Peadar nodded.

Eliphas turned the plant to one side and pointed

at a small circle at the base near the root. "This is the spot you must watch out for in the future. The rest of you, make sure you don't face a small circle with a dot in the center toward you. If it catches you, it will shoot out the root exactly like what happened to Mr. Mongan."

As the class went on, a couple more roots shot out. One of them came from Mist's plant because she wanted to test the reaction time. She barely missed being strangled. The other plant was Henriette's. Her mischievous streak seemed to be slowly returning. She turned the circle toward her then immediately spun the plant, and the root took hold of Kaleb's wrist. He pulled back, trying to free himself. Henriette tickled his large, rounded ears with the plant leaves, giggling with glee. It felt nice to hear her laugh again, even if it was at the expense of a younger apprentice. Although Kaleb was restrained, he didn't seem too concerned.

After a while, Eliphas intervened. Samara wondered whether he'd taken so long to allow Henriette time to enjoy the lighthearted moment.

CHAPTER THIRTY-SIX

Later that night, Samara met Paxton under the stairs at the front of the building. She hoped they could escape without Kaine knowing, and to ensure that no one would see them leaving together, she waited inside until no one was around before she followed Paxton. Kaine had already been acting weirdly since Samara had started pulling away from his touch. He was probably finding it hard to deal with someone being able to evade his charms. She felt grateful that Ulrieg could see what was going on. Otherwise, it could have been dangerous. As much as she liked Kaine, it seemed Ulrieg had been correct when he said the familiar was like their bonded. A fox was known to be a sly creature. That didn't mean that Kaine would necessarily be against them, but it was best to be safe until she worked out his intentions.

Samara released Gray into the night sky to hunt and have some free time before heading to the meeting spot under the stairs. Paxton stood in the shadows cast by the full moon with Jojo sitting on his shoulder.

He jumped when Ulrieg turned visible right next to him. Jojo snuck closer to his bonded's neck.

Ulrieg chuckled, a weird sound squeezing out of his throat as he tried to remain quiet.

Paxton put a hand over his heart and hissed, "You scared me half to death."

It wouldn't be because you're doing something you shouldn't, would it? Ulrieg arched a hairless eyebrow.

"Yes, that too." Paxton waved a hand before pulling at the leather cord around his neck, which was tucked under his tunic. "I have the key. Can we get this over with before we're discovered?"

"Follow me. Stay low and out of sight of the windows."

As Samara led Paxton toward the hole, ensuring he followed her every move, Ulrieg turned invisible again. It was still early, and they had to spend most of the way crawling so that no one would see them from the windows.

When they entered the hole behind the bush, Paxton's eyes were wide in the light of the sconce on the wall. They looked hollow and full of fear, and Samara wondered if hers had been the same on her first time entering the chamber.

"Where are we?" Paxton studied the corridor lined with doors and very little light.

"We're entering the back way to the underground level where Callista goes to consult with the higher magical power." Samara pulled the torch from the wall and led him down the corridor. "Keep your ears peeled for unusual sounds." She turned to the visible Ulrieg. "What are your senses telling you about the caves now?"

Ulrieg moved next to her. *I don't feel anything. Maybe that means there aren't any captives trapped in there this time.*

"Let's hope not." Paxton walked close behind him. "But I still want to see where it is."

They arrived at the door shortly afterward, and Samara held out her hand. "We need the key." She pointed at the emblem. "It has to be inserted here, or the door won't open by any other magic or tools. Believe me—I've tried."

Paxton looped the cord over his head and placed the key against the emblem as Samara opened the lock. It clicked, and she pushed the door open, the corridor flooding with the bright light of the orb.

Paxton's jaw dropped. "I had no idea it was that big."

Samara nodded. "Me either, but that's not what we're here for." With Ulrieg by her side, she led Paxton to one of the small caves around the larger one. "This is where we found Byzarid."

The table he was lying on had been cleaned, and the utensils lay polished on the side tables.

Paxton whispered, "It looks like a room where they treat sick people."

Ulrieg's face clouded.

Samara nodded to a large case on the utensil bench. "Go and open that and see what's inside."

He moved slowly, his steps hesitant as he approached the case. A sharp click sounded as he undid the clasps, followed by the creak of a hinge as he tilted the top open.

His face paled. Clearly displayed on the top level of the box were instruments that weren't used for medical purposes. They were strange and looked nasty, ready to inflict pain. Paxton dropped the lid, which gave a loud clank.

Her eyes wide, Samara scanned the large cave around the orb. When nothing moved after a few moments, she relaxed and turned back to the room to find Paxton standing not far from her, looking horrified as he surveyed all the smaller rooms.

"Are those all torture rooms?"

"I believe so."

"And there are twenty of them. One for each apprentice before Blade was killed." His mouth hardly moved to form the words, which came out muffled.

"Unfortunately, yes. At first, I thought they were for sick people who needed special care. Maybe the orb had powers to heal us when the instructors couldn't, but then we found Byzarid, Daena, and her deceased guardian dragon. Our hopes died quickly."

Paxton pulled at the end of his sleeve. "Wouldn't you think Callista knows about this if she comes down here to consult with the orb regularly?"

Thank you. My words exactly. Ulrieg looked at him proudly before turning to glare at Samara.

Samara's spine tingled. "There doesn't seem to be anyone down here at the moment, and if Callista comes down here at times like this, then she wouldn't know about the dragon torture. That's why we have to remain open-minded and only say someone is guilty after finding evidence against them."

Pfft! You're too *open-minded.* Ulrieg grumbled as he sauntered to the next room.

Paxton hurried after him. "She's right, though. You can't just write everyone here off. I'd find it hard to believe that all the instructors support the torture of creatures, especially dragons. I'd like to think that some of them have good hearts and believe they're serving a better purpose."

Ulrieg jerked his head around. *Dragon moon! Two optimistic idiots accompany me. You've seen what happened to my cousin and Daena and heard what happened to her bonded dragon, yet you still want to believe that there are good people in the coterie. Please!*

Paxton followed him into the next room. "Jojo says he would also like to see evidence of a guilty person before accusing them."

Wingless flight! And I thought Jojo would have more sense than that, since he's a familiar.

Samara peered into the next room to find it also empty. She moved to the next then the next. All were empty. Each one she found eased her mind some more. Maybe there wasn't anyone down there. "It's looking clear at this stage. Vexx and Kellam aren't here. Maybe they're the only ones responsible for the torture and death of Daena's dragon."

Ulrieg passed her to look into the next room and

expelled a sigh. *Whatever! One can only hope for your sake. I guess.*

"Your optimism and understanding are astounding." Samara nudged him.

Ha-ha. I've seen too many dragons hunted down and killed. And I've heard of many more from the few dragons I've encountered. It's not something I'm going to be optimistic over. Someone is responsible, and I've heard it's this coterie and its leaders.

Paxton nodded. "There's truth to what you've heard and seen. You've proven that by finding your cousin and the guardian dragon. And you also know it was Vexx and Kellam, so two of the senior coterie members are guilty. Perhaps that's it."

Ulrieg growled. *We'll have to see.* He finished searching the last of the smaller caves. *At least there isn't anyone captured in here this time.*

"That's good news." Paxton went over to the orb and stood just outside of its barrier. He looked mesmerized. "Feel that magic. It's so powerful."

Samara grabbed his hand, pulling him away. "And dangerous if misused. We're not sure whether it knows we're here. If it does, it may report us to Callista. We should go."

Reluctantly Paxton followed her then stopped and pointed. "Did you see that?"

Samara followed his finger to the door where

they'd entered. It remained open a few inches so they could make a quick exit, but she couldn't see anything out of the ordinary. "See what?"

Paxton squinted. "I thought I saw something orange peering through the blackness." He shook his head. "Maybe I was imagining it."

Dread filled the pit of Samara's stomach. Something orange could be the face of a fox or Kellam's monkey familiar if they had returned. She crossed her fingers and hoped Paxton's eyes were playing up after he'd stared too hard into the orb. That thought didn't comfort her, though.

Ulrieg, keep your eyes open. If Paxton saw something orange, Kaine or Kellam may be in the corridor or above.

Let's hope he's wrong.

Following Ulrieg's lead, they hurried to the exit. Samara closed the door gently and locked it before taking the torch off the sconce and holding it high so the light would bathe the area.

Ulrieg, remember to keep your eyes peeled for the shiny eyes of a fox or monkey.

Already on it. I'll scout up ahead in my invisible form.

Great! But she thought of another worry. If Ginger or the monkey were spying on them, they would have seen Ulrieg. She closed her eyes for a moment and breathed deeply. There was nothing they could do about it. They would have to tackle the problem if it arose. For the moment, the best they could do was prevent anyone or thing from seeing them.

Slowly, she led the way up the stairs toward the exit.

CHAPTER THIRTY-SEVEN

I've been out here for a while now, and I haven't seen anyone or their familiar. Perhaps Paxton's eyes went funny after staring into the orb.

The fresh air on Samara's face revitalized her spirit, especially after hearing Ulrieg's report. *That's great news. Maybe you should remain invisible and keep watch, just in case.*

Sounds like a good plan.

Feeling slightly safer with Ulrieg on watch, Samara gave Paxton a head start then followed him into the forest. She hoped it was the last time Paxton needed to go out to heal Ulrieg's cousin. Then he wouldn't be in as much danger, and they wouldn't catch Kaine's attention so easily.

They met up several yards away from the edge of the pine forest and finished the trek together.

Samara felt surprised at how easy it was to talk to him. Once they shared a secret, everything else fell into place, and it was easy to find common ground. She'd never really had that with Kaine. Even though she was attracted to him, so was every other female, and their conversations didn't flow easily. She wondered if she would ever have a good relationship with Kaine, even after applying effort. Their best bonding time had been when she rescued him from the trolls' dungeons. Not long after they returned, things had mostly gone back to normal but with more tension, since Kaine had made a move on her directly.

She looked at Paxton out of the corner of her eye. He seemed distracted, though it was hard to tell in the moonlight. "So, how do you feel after seeing the cave with all the rooms?"

A frown creased his forehead. "To be honest, I feel confused but also justified." He chuckled. "If that makes sense."

Samara shook her head. "Not really."

"I mean that after I found the book on the coterie's history with so much blacked out, it doesn't seem as surprising that there are secret caves under the building and that you've found creatures being tortured. But at the same time, this used to be our haven, and we thought the coterie had our interests in mind when they looked after our families. If Zofia hadn't taken us to fight the ogres and Vexx and Kellam hadn't mistreated us, it would be easier to believe that the members of the coterie were on our sides."

"Exactly. That's how I felt after being sent to fight the trolls and stripped of my magic."

I don't know. You were still very pro coterie until we bonded. I guess I'm rubbing off on you. Ulrieg's wing pushed breeze down onto Samara and Paxton.

Paxton looked up, but Ulrieg was still invisible. "Is that so?"

"Unfortunately, yes. Ulrieg implanted my doubts, but I still had to see for myself before I believed him."

She only really believed me once we found Byzarid and when Vexx and Kellam basically owned up to it not long after. It was obvious when they got upset about our helping their prisoners escape.

Paxton studied Samara under the moonlight shining through a break in the trees, making her squirm. It felt like he was looking at her for the first time, which was ridiculous. Maybe he thought she lacked a few brain cells after what Ulrieg had said.

Eventually, she looked straight at him. "What?"

"It's nice to know that others believe people are good until proven otherwise."

"Oh." Her cheeks heated, and she was glad her face was in shadow. "So you're not looking at me as though I'm an idiot?"

Paxton chuckled, something he didn't do often. It was rich, sincere, and deep, making her want more. "No, of course not. I think you're quite intelligent."

She curtsied. "Why, thank you. I think you're intelligent—actually, I know you're intelligent, and I'm flattered that you think the same of me."

Paxton nodded. "Absolutely. But it's your heart that impresses me more."

Samara didn't know how to react, and it was a not-so-welcome yet welcome sound when Ulrieg interrupted her thoughts.

See? I told you he'd be better for you. Listen to how genuine he is. Your conversations are interesting and not about how he's always looking at or flirting with other girls. If you want loyalty and friendship, you have it right here.

Samara glared above her, hoping it was aimed directly at Ulrieg. *Yes, yes. I heard you the first time. You adore Paxton and hate Kaine. It's not that simple for me.*

And why not? It should be.

Just leave it, all right?

"You look upset. Did I say something wrong?" He

gently took hold of her elbow and turned her to face him.

She shook her head and met his gaze. "No. I was arguing with Ulrieg. He just won't let something go."

Paxton's mouth twitched. "Sounds like an interesting relationship you have with your familiar. I guess that's what you get for bonding with one so unique. Jojo rarely argues with me."

Or maybe you never argue with Jojo, and you actually listen to his advice.

Paxton thought for a moment. "You know, you may be on to something there."

Trust me—I know I am. Somehow, I was lumped together with an argumentative young witch who won't listen to my never-ending wisdom.

Samara's jaw dropped. "Let me ask you something, Paxton. Does Jojo constantly go against everything you believe?"

Paxton looked at Jojo on his shoulder. "No. He rarely tells me to do something I think is wrong."

Samara slapped her thigh. "Exactly! And that is why you don't need to argue with him all the time."

Or maybe it's because Paxton is intelligent enough to listen to the wisdom that Jojo is guiding him with.

Samara groaned. "Whatever, Ulrieg. You win. I can't be bothered arguing anymore."

Yes! About time. See, Paxton? That didn't take very long.

Paxton chuckled but stopped suddenly when he caught Samara's glare. He held up his hands in surrender.

They reached the boulders where they had left Byzarid and Daena and spotted the small fire still burning. Daena sat by it with the dragon's head resting in her lap. She stroked his head gently, seeming lost in thought and sadness. Samara could only imagine that she missed her dragon, Kaida, and being so close to another dragon would only fuel that grief.

When they moved closer, dried leaves crackled under their feet, and Daena spun to look in their direction, gray scales flaring across her face. To Samara's surprise, Byzarid's eyes opened, although his head remained in Daena's lap.

Ulrieg turned visible and dropped to the ground. *Byzarid, you're awake!* He was so excited that he nearly ran through the fire.

Byzarid lifted his head slightly, obviously still lethargic, although his eyes lit up with excitement. *Ulrieg! I thought I'd never see you again. We didn't know where you went, so I looked for you.*

You did what? That was careless of you. Is that how

you ended up as a captive? Although he chastised his cousin, his red eyes burned with affection.

Byzarid nodded. *That's very likely, but it's not your fault I was captured. It was only a matter of time.*

Ulrieg nudged him with his nose. *You fool!*

Byzarid frowned. *But where did you go? And how are you here now?*

You wouldn't believe me if I told you.

Try me. Byzarid's eyes narrowed at Paxton as he moved closer to him.

"Do you mind if I sit by you while you talk to your cousin? It's great to see you conscious, but you still look as though you could do with some more healing." Paxton squatted a few feet away from the dragons.

Uncertain, Byzarid looked at Ulrieg, who nodded.

He's been healing you.

What? Byzarid lifted his head as far as he could.

Ulrieg shrugged, spreading his wings wide. *As I said, you wouldn't believe me about where I've been if I told you.*

Go on. Byzarid spoke to Ulrieg but nodded to Paxton, who moved closer.

Ulrieg looked at the ground. *I've bonded with a young witch from the Sacred Flame coterie.*

You've done what? Byzarid's voice rose an octave.

I know. I'm as shocked as you are. I hate the coterie for what they've done to our kind, and I didn't realize bonding was a thing, but I was drawn to this half-elf and half-human young woman trapped in the trolls' dungeons. It was the full moon. Ulrieg looked at the sky. *And you know what I'm like when its shining in all its glory. We touched by accident and bonded in a second. She took me back to the coterie because she couldn't leave, or her family would suffer, then we found you not long afterward.*

Deep creases formed on Byzarid's forehead, and he nodded at Paxton, who placed his palm on the dragon's side. *And who is this?*

Paxton is an apprentice wizard at the coterie, and he's the only one at the coterie who knows about me, except for Samara. And before you judge me, they're both on our side.

Samara sat next to Ulrieg. "I hope we'll be able to help find Dragoria one day or at least stop the mistreatment of the dragons in our realms."

Byzarid seemed to be weighing up Samara and Paxton. *I guess we don't have a choice on whether to trust you.*

"I helped you escape with Daena and Ulrieg, and I only told Paxton about you and Ulrieg because he was starting to do his own homework and question things about the coterie. Plus, he's an excellent healer. We needed his help to heal you."

Byzarid faced Paxton as he placed his hand on different places on his body and injected him with healing magic. *I can feel your magic enter me.*

Paxton gave him a small smile. "I hope it feels nice as it weaves through your body."

It does feel strangely nice. If it weren't for Ulrieg, I'd be attacking you for simply looking at me.

"I'm sorry your kind is getting mistreated. I hope we'll have you out of here soon so you can return to your family and let them know you and Ulrieg are all right."

Byzarid turned to Ulrieg. *Are you ever going to leave here?*

Ulrieg nodded. *As soon as I can. Just because I'm here doesn't mean I like it. I'm only here for Samara and now Paxton.*

Byzarid sniffed Paxton's hand. *You do seem rather trustworthy. Forgive me for my disbelief.*

Paxton looked deep into the dragon's eyes. "There's nothing to forgive. You and your kind have been mistreated. I don't blame you for acting the way you did. I would, too, if I were in your shoes."

Daena sat quietly by the fire as the exchange took place.

"I've brought you some more food." Samara dug into her quiver and fished out a small bag.

Daena nodded appreciatively, holding out her hand. "Thank you."

Samara passed the bag to the dragon elf. "How long has Byzarid been awake?"

"Since early this morning. It seems like the last lot of healing helped more than the first, or his body was already starting to heal itself."

"That's great! Then you can both head for safety. Will you be going back to your village?"

Daena kept staring at the brown dragon, a strange longing in her eyes. "I don't know if I'll even be able to pass through the border to get to my village. I was given permission to travel and sell our blankets, but now, if I have to pass Vexx, I might not get through." She poked at the fire with a stick. "It would be nice to bond with another dragon, but I don't think it's possible with any ordinary dragon. Perhaps I'm doomed to mourn my Kaida for the rest of my life."

Saddened, Samara replied, "I hope that's not true." She nudged the ground with the tip of her boot. "Once Byzarid is healed enough, I want you two to leave. I don't know how long you'll remain undiscovered here. Don't wait for us so you can say goodbye. I'm sure Ulrieg would be happier knowing his cousin had left to find a safer place. Isn't that right, Ulrieg?"

Ulrieg nodded and nudged Byzarid. *Absolutely. The second you think you're strong enough, I want you to leave for somewhere safe. Tell the others I'm all right. Even though I'm bonded to a witch in the Sacred Flame coterie. Tell them I'm being cautious, and I don't want any of them to come and look for me. Understand?*

With a sad expression, Byzarid nodded. *We'll leave a message of some sort if we leave, though. So that you won't worry.*

Daena nodded.

CHAPTER THIRTY-EIGHT

As they left the camp that night, it felt like they'd seen Byzarid and Daena for the last time. At least, Samara hoped it would be. Paxton had spent the whole time healing Byzarid, and the brown dragon had become more robust by the time they left.

With Jojo on Paxton's shoulder, he, Ulrieg, and Samara walked together in the darkness. According to the moon's position, it was late, maybe even the early-morning hours. Ulrieg had spent a long time catching up with his cousin.

They had walked for a while and were almost back at the pine forest's edge when a twig snapped off to the left, deep in the woods. Ulrieg turned invisible, and the leaves scattered where he once stood as he took flight.

Jojo croaked, and Paxton spun. He tugged at Samara's arm, and she turned to find Kaine.

He stood alone with his eyebrows raised and his arms crossed. "What are you two doing out here in the middle of the night?"

Guilt wracked Samara, but she tried to force it away. They hadn't done anything wrong to Kaine. "We're out hunting. Gray's in the forest somewhere, catching his meal, and Jojo wanted fresh air. Paxton and I ran into each other and did a little weapons practice."

Looking annoyed, Kaine scratched the back of his head. "That doesn't sound that convincing. Are you sure you weren't cheating on me?"

Paxton let out a long groan. "Honestly, that's your question? I mean, seriously, that coming from you, of all people."

Kaine looked taken aback. "What are you saying?"

Paxton stood taller, though he was still half a head shorter than Kaine. "I'm saying you are the biggest flirt in the coterie, and you know it. Besides, Samara and I are friends. Maybe you should try it sometime. It's quite rewarding."

Kaine's brow furrowed, and it looked like he would lose it. Then he took a deep breath and laughed. With the moonlight casting shadows over his eyes, it was hard to see his expression to tell if he was being sincere. He placed an arm around Samara's shoulders. The gesture set her nerves on fire in the wrong way. She tried to relax, hoping it would soothe Kaine's envy so he would stop questioning them. She hoped Ulrieg would keep an eye on her and pull her out of any charming trance he might place her in.

Paxton shifted away slightly, and Kaine trailed his fingers down Samara's bare skin.

She needed to be sure before she played along and got caught up in Kaine's charms. *Ulrieg, are you close? I think I'm going to need your help with Kaine soon.*

I'm not too far away. The noise back there was Ginger. I think she's been spying on us.

Wingless flight! Maybe Paxton did see her in the cave. Samara gazed at Paxton, who had suddenly gone quiet as though deep in thought.

Kaine squeezed her shoulders.

Kaine's all over me. If I pull away, he'll get upset.

Paxton looked Samara in the eyes then looked quickly at Kaine then back at her as though he was trying to tell her something.

Ulrieg broke through her confusion again. *I will watch over Ginger to try to work out whether she knows about me. I've told Paxton about what Kaine is capable of*

and asked if he can keep an eye on you to ensure you
don't do anything unusual while Kaine's touching you.

Samara couldn't read Paxton's expression. *Did*
Paxton say he was going to do it?

Oh, Samara. Sometimes I wonder about you.

What do you mean?

Paxton isn't bonded to me, so he can't respond without
Kaine hearing him. But I get the feeling that he already
knows what Kaine can do.

Oh. Samara smiled shyly at Paxton and
mouthed, "Thank you."

He smiled back at her.

Kaine ran the back of his hand down her arm
again, instantly making her relax. "Don't you want to
share with me what you've been doing tonight?"

Samara smiled sweetly at Kaine. "Of course I do."

He squeezed her shoulders. "I'm all ears."

Meeting his gaze, she leaned in, pressing against
his chest. "Paxton and I weren't doing anything to
give you a reason to be upset. Were we, Paxton?"

Paxton shook his head, looking grumpier than
usual.

Kaine glanced at Paxton sideways. "You seem
quite convincing."

He made a wry face. "Of course we do. We
weren't doing anything that would make you
jealous."

Stroking Samara's cheek, Kaine asked, "Then why all the secrecy?"

She opened her mouth to speak, but Paxton answered for her. "There is no secrecy. Samara told you what we were up to. We've just adapted to be good practice partners for our weapons, and when we run into each other by chance, we don't think to call you. That's all."

Kaine set his palm on Samara's upper arm, and she had a sudden urge to tell him everything.

"Are you sure that's all? You seem to be keeping something from me." Kaine traced his thumb over a small mole on her arm.

Samara opened her mouth to answer.

Samara! Ulrieg yelled.

She giggled and playfully pushed Kaine's nose with her finger to hide her almost saying something. "What are you talking about? And how do you keep running into me while I'm out late at night, anyway? Have you been spying on me or something?" She giggled again, making her miss Kaine's response, but she caught Paxton's frown.

She looked up at him with adoring eyes. "What did you say?"

Kaine's face had suddenly turned serious. "I said I haven't been following you. Ginger has, and she's been reporting back to me."

Samara suddenly sobered and pulled out of Kaine's embrace. "You've sent Ginger out to spy on me?"

Kaine nodded, looking quite pleased with himself. "Yes. I had Ginger follow you when I sensed you weren't telling me the truth, even when I used my charm on you. How you could resist my charms puzzled me."

She dug her fingernails into her palms. "And what did she report back to you? And how do you know she's not telling you lies to split us up because she's jealous?"

Kaine shook his head and reached out to push some strands of Samara's hair behind her ear. When Samara recoiled, his face hardened. "She's my familiar. She has no reason to lie to me."

"How do you know?" Samara crossed her arms across her chest.

"Because she confirmed that you and Paxton weren't doing anything to make me jealous, but you were up to things you were hiding from everyone in the coterie. Like how your owl isn't your real familiar, and you've been sneaking out to a fire in the forest to meet with another elf with strange skin and two weird creatures, one of which is your true familiar." His eyebrow rose as he studied her reaction. "What is this unusual creature you're bonded with, and why aren't you telling the rest of the coterie?"

Samara spluttered, "S-She's... making things up. I could sense she never liked me."

Kaine cocked his head. "I don't think so. Your reactions confirm it. I can understand you keeping a secret from me, but I can't understand why you told Paxton. I'm the one you should be telling, not him. And the audacity of you sneaking out with him and not me. Not inviting or including me in what you are doing."

Samara rubbed her arm. "There were things that Paxton did that encouraged me to tell him before anyone else. As for not telling you, I had to try to work out how you would react if I told you. I needed to work out if I could trust you or not."

Kaine huffed. "So you can't even trust me with anything?"

Samara flailed her arms. "You're always using your charms to influence me to tell you things without giving me space and time to make up my mind. That's why I decided I couldn't trust you."

Kaine raised his voice and flailed his arms. "I used my charming magic against you because I could sense you weren't telling me things!" He ran a hand through his hair. "Knowing that you were keeping things from me made me use my biggest gift."

Samara shook her head. "You should have just given me time, and I would have been able to work out for myself whether you're trustworthy. I don't respond well to being tricked."

Kaine backed against a tree and rested his weight against it. "So I guess that means you're not going to tell me why the two of you were sneaking around in the sacred room under the building, then?"

Samara was lost for words.

Paxton squinted. "I knew I wasn't seeing things down there. It was Ginger's face peeking through the crack in the door."

Not knowing what else to do, Samara grabbed Kaine's hand. "Look. I'm sorry I didn't tell you what I was doing. It's been tough for me to trust anyone."

Kaine pulled away. "Yet you still won't tell me what kind of animal your familiar is or what you two were doing way out in the forest, associating with that creature and the elf with the weird skin."

Samara put as much sincerity into her words that she could manage. "I'll tell you more if you can prove you can keep what you know so far a secret. Don't tell anyone, including the instructors. If you do that, you will earn my trust, and I will tell you more."

Kaine crossed his arms. "That sounds like a lot to ask after what you've already done."

She rubbed the back of her neck. "That's how hard it is to trust people. Do we have a deal?"

"I'll think about it."

Kaine headed toward the coterie building, and Samara and Paxton followed.

CHAPTER THIRTY-NINE

After a bad night's sleep, Samara tried to pull herself together. She rolled to a sitting position and rubbed her eyes while accidentally touching one of Ulrieg's horns. "Ow!"

Are you all right? Ulrieg raised his head, blinking slowly.

Blood oozed from Samara's finger. She sucked on it and nodded. "I should have been more careful. It's not like you haven't slept there every night since we bonded. My brain just hasn't woken up yet." She frowned as everything that had happened the previous night flooded back into her memory. It hadn't been a bad dream. It was real. "What are we going to do about Kaine?"

Ulrieg stretched his front legs out in front of him. *I honestly don't know. I haven't kept my mistrust of* him a secret, and my point of view hasn't changed. But I hope I'm wrong for all our sakes.

"Me too. Although I don't remember a time you've been wrong so far." She nudged him with her fist. "It's kind of annoying."

Ulrieg grinned, although it looked more vicious than friendly. *It's probably my fault you didn't tell him anything. Still, I don't know if it would have made a difference. If he's decent and honestly cares about you, he'll come around.*

"What are we going to do if he tells them everything? If the coterie is a true enemy, then we'll have to leave for our safety, and if Paxton and I leave, then our families will suffer again."

Ulrieg nudged her leg with his nose. *We'll worry about that if it comes to it. One thing at a time, or you won't be able to function because of worry.*

Samara nodded. "Of course, you're right again."

She threw back her blanket and stood then walked over to feed Gray some meat scraps out of a bowl. The owl was content to rest again after having a chance to stretch his wings the night before.

Ulrieg climbed out from the blanket, which Samara had accidentally thrown over him. *We should check on Byzarid and Daena tonight and make sure they're safe. I know we weren't going to revisit them so soon, but after discovering that Kaine had Ginger follow us, we will need to give them some extra protection and tell them to move on as soon as possible. They're in more danger if Kaine tells any of the instructors where they are.*

Samara rubbed the back of her neck. "You're right. Just in case Kaine goes against us before he confirms which side he's on."

She slid on her pants and laced up her tunic. "Maybe I should pack a flight bag in case we're in danger."

Um. You don't fly. Ulrieg gave her a look like he thought she'd lost her mind.

Samara chuckled. "I didn't mean that kind of flying. A flight bag is a bag of essentials you pack in case you have to run away in a hurry."

Oh. Then yes. I think that would be a good idea. Ulrieg climbed off the bed.

"I'll get some food from breakfast to add to it." She screwed up her nose. "Although I may need to change the food almost daily." She packed a few pieces of clothing and a blanket then added a few pieces of food she had sitting on her table, ready to take to Daena.

Then she left her room, with Ulrieg following her in his invisible form. When she reached the stairs, Kaine was descending them from a higher level with Ginger at his side.

The blood drained from her face. Trying to sound lighthearted, she asked, "Is Callista back?"

The broad smile Kaine gave her chilled her to the bone. "She certainly is. Isn't that fantastic?"

Ginger sniffed the air, not even trying to make it inconspicuous, as Kaine strolled past and down the stairs before Samara could answer.

Something poked her leg. *You need to keep moving, or else you'll look extra guilty. I'm worried that if Kaine thinks he has something over you, it'll entice him more to expose our secret. Maybe it's a good thing he hasn't asked to meet me yet.*

Let's hope so. Maybe he'll protect me, since I saved him from the trolls. Actually, we rescued him from the trolls. Maybe I should remind him of that. She started to increase her pace to catch up to Kaine.

Just leave it. I don't think he needs reminding. It may even do the opposite and encourage him to tell them everything because he wants to redeem himself for not being the successful one in your battle.

But I haven't told anyone that, so he shouldn't need to feel like he has to compensate.

That one is full of pride. If he knows he's failed, then he may think he still has to redeem himself in his own eyes by making himself more important.

Wingless flight! This is getting difficult. So many secrets to sort out and keep, and so many lives are in danger. Samara tugged at her hair and plodded down the stairs. *I wish I had someone who wasn't directly involved to talk to.*

There is one person who might have some grown-up input.

Who? Samara nearly stopped on the steps, only to be nudged by Ulrieg again.

Forgrac.

Samara's heart lightened, and her footsteps quickened as she headed for the kitchen.

Forgrac was stirring something in a large pot, the fire burning heartily underneath. When he heard footsteps, he turned with a deep scowl. "Who dares enter the kitchen without me permission?"

"It's only me, Forgrac. May I come in? I'd love to speak with you."

The dwarf's square beard spread wider as he grinned. "Oh. Samara, love. Ya don't need permission. Excuse me temper. Someone broke into the kitchen last night an' left the place a mess. They had meat scraps lying 'round everywhere an' breadcrumbs left all over the benches. It took me a while to clean up."

"That wasn't me." She raised her hands. "I admit I've taken food from the kitchen in the middle of the night before, but I cleaned up after myself. I figured you wouldn't mind."

Forgrac nodded and stirred the contents of the pot some more. "'At's true. I'd let ya raid me kitchen, especially if ya left it neat." He dipped a spoon into the pot and tasted the food before taking a few herbs from the bench and sprinkling them into the pot. "What'd ya want to speak to me 'bout?"

"I have a problem and wanted to pick your brains." Samara peered over the edge of the pot he was stirring, and her mouth watered when she smelled the stew.

"What's the problem?" He picked up another spoon and filled it with the stew before handing it to Samara.

She blew on it before placing it in her mouth and moaning. It tasted so good. "Do you remember Kaine?"

Forgrac picked up a bowl and spooned some of the stew into it then handed it to Samara. "This is actually for lunch, but you look like you could use some comfort food right now."

Samara took it gratefully. "Thank you."

"And to answer ya question, yes. He's the one hangin' 'round ya an' likes to lean all over the girls."

Surprised, she paused her spoon in midair. "Yes. That's the one. Clearly, everyone sees what he does."

The dwarf shrugged. "He doesn't hide it. Why do ya ask?"

"He and I are partners."

Forgrac whistled and shook his head.

That's exactly my reaction. Ulrieg turned visible.

Forgrac picked up a piece of rabbit he had cut on the bench and gave it to him. "He's bad news, 'at one. I would be most upset if I had a daughter pairin' with him."

Samara frowned, not happy that her dwarf friend was siding with Ulrieg. "Anyway, I hadn't told him about Ulrieg and another huge secret about dragons, but I told Paxton."

"The quiet one with the long green ponytail?" Forgrac asked.

"Yes."

"Good choice. I woulda trusted 'at one more too."

Ha. I told you, Ulrieg said while ripping off a bit of rabbit.

After grinning at Ulrieg, Forgrac stirred the stew some more before catching Samara's frown. "Let me guess—Kaine discovered ya had told Paxton, but ya 'adn't told 'im."

Samara nodded. "But now I'm worried he'll tell others about my secrets, including Ulrieg, to get back at me."

The dwarf rubbed his beard. "A valid concern."

"What should I do? If Ulrieg is an enemy of the

coterie, like we're worried about, aren't we in deep trouble?"

"I'm afraid so." The dwarf clanked the spoon on top of the pot before resting it on the edge. His brow creased in thought. "Then again, Callista is still a wild card in all this, as are most of the instructors. She, or they, may be on the dragons' side, and it may be jus' her senior commanders who are the enemies."

"I get all that. So what do I do?"

"Whichever way ya turn, it's going to be risky. If ya leave, you'd 'ave to take Paxton with ya because he could still be in trouble if this is enemy territory an' Kaine tells the wrong people. Then both ya families will be cut off."

"Exactly!" Samara pushed her stew around with the spoon.

"On the other hand, if you stay, you might have more control over what happens with ya families. Maybe. Then again, if ya both end up in trouble with the coterie, then ya families will be cut off anyway."

"And if I stay, and Kaine doesn't inform the wrong people about what we're doing, then I may be able to help more dragons that get captured, and I may find out more and rise within the coterie's ranks to help Dragoria."

Forgrac wiped his brow with the back of his sleeve. "It sounds like you've made up ya mind.

Although ya will have to be very careful in how ya go about things, and you and Paxton will have to watch for anythin' that may put you in danger. That way, ya can react accordingly."

"That doesn't sound very comforting." Samara's stomach growled, and she spooned some of the stew into her mouth.

"I'm sorry I ain't got anythin' that can help ya further. You've dug yourself a big, nasty hole, love. Although if Callista ain't like the senior commanders, then ya got nothin' to worry 'bout." He shuffled over to her and pinched her cheek affectionately. "I 'ope ya can stay 'round and leave with me. Ya may find this ain't the place for ya. But 'at's up to ya."

CHAPTER FORTY

With her stomach full, Samara worked her way to defense class. She was lost in thought as she turned the corner to enter the room, and something jolted out and hit her. She fell to the floor, writhing. Her body stung everywhere, and her blood felt like it was sizzling.

Paxton raced to her side and placed a hand on her, and his calming, healing power washed through her. She caught a glimpse of Mist's satisfied face as she realized that Mist must have hit her with her lightning. Okak cawed from a stand in the corner of the room as though he was cheering his bonded on.

Suddenly, she and Paxton rose and hung upside down, held in place by an *Elevorto* spell. Jojo fell from Paxton's tunic pocket, his eyes wide, and Luna's face filled with pride as Coco hopped toward the frog, making him run.

Paxton whispered, *"Liborte,"* and fell to the ground. He tucked his chin to his chest and rolled out of the fall then held out his hand for Jojo.

Before Samara could pull her thoughts together, Kaine had placed a hand on her, making her calm, and she suddenly wanted to yell every secret she held.

Snap out of it, Samara. Ulrieg's grumpy voice cut through the charming spell once again.

She shook her head, clearing away the strange fog, and said, *"Liborte."* She forgot to tuck her chin, but the fall wasn't far. She rolled to the side, trying to focus on the ones attacking her before they struck again. She chastised herself. She didn't execute the one thing they were always taught upon arriving at this class. She should have been alert and protected herself. Although when she looked at Kaine, his face was filled with glee, and she wondered if he was getting rid of some of his frustration with her, and perhaps he would keep their secret and wait to decide on giving them away. Even though she would happily take a bit of his aggression if he kept his mouth closed, she still prepared herself for more onslaughts. She didn't think her head could take on much more that day. Slowly, she rolled to all fours before climbing to her feet.

"Samara, you should know better when coming into this lesson." Devi stood at the back with Zion, her copper wolf familiar, sitting by her side. Shock filled the instructor's face over what she had witnessed.

Samara gave her a small smile. "I know. It's completely my fault. I should have been more prepared." She held up a hand. "And I know a bad night's sleep is no excuse." She rubbed her head where it had hit when she landed on the floor. She had been the last one to arrive, so everyone had witnessed her failure. She scolded herself again. She was already in danger. She didn't need to add more unwanted attention to her list. Her eyes traveled from Ginger up to Kaine. "I deserved that." Samara let her eyes travel to Mist and Luna to try and not make it as obvious that she was only talking to Kaine, still trying to persuade him from exposing her and Paxton's secret.

Kaine's easy, charming smile didn't come, and her blood ran cold.

She moved into the circle, closing the gap, and prepared for a rough lesson of being attacked by Kaine, Mist, and Luna. With the way Mist and Luna were looking at her, she wondered if Kaine had already told them.

As though reading her thoughts, Paxton shifted to stand by her, his knees bent, ready for the onslaught.

Devi had moved closer to the circle to watch the apprentices attack one another. Her eyes were sharp, as though she sensed an overly aggressive undercurrent, yet at the same time, confusion seemed to muddy her assertiveness. Her hands twitched by her sides, as though she was preparing to stop any unfair treatment.

Movement behind Kaine caught Samara's eye. Ginger had raised her nose, sniffing toward the back corner of the room.

Is that you she's sniffing, Ulrieg?

I'm afraid so. I'm sure she knows about me, and it looks like she doesn't want to be subtle about it.

You should leave the room. It might be safer for you outside. It would look strange if Ginger followed you.

What? And leave you here on your own?

If you hang around in the corridor, I'll still have access to your power for more potent magic. Go! I'll be fine.

Ginger continued to sniff, and Samara worried Ulrieg was having trouble leaving.

I've made it. I made sure I released some extra-strong odor for the fox to be overwhelmed by.

The fox was wiping her nose as though she had something horrid stuck up her nostrils. *What did you do, Ulrieg?*

Chuckling, he replied, *If I have to explain it to you, you'll be disgusted, and it may take away your fighting edge.*

Ginger snorted, as did Kaine. Mist and Luna's faces were contorted with disgust.

All right. I think I've worked it out. And if I'm right, I want you to refrain from explaining it to me.

Disgusting yet highly effective. Ulrieg's chuckle loudened.

"Now, remember. You're all friends and fellow apprentices in this class. This is practice, not an excuse to hurt one another severely. I know some other classes at this coterie have taught you otherwise." Devi took in the expressions on Kaine, Luna, and Mist's faces and seemed to realize the friendly battle would not be that friendly. She clapped, drawing everyone's attention. "All right. Let me be clear. If you get too rough in this class and I deem you an aggressor, not a learner or practitioner, you will face punishment and feel my wrath. So far, I haven't had to punish, but mark my words, I will if you don't practice nicely. I won't stand for it in my class." Although she sounded confident, when she finished the little speech, her gaze landed on Samara, and she looked almost apologetic.

Samara nodded, trying to tell her it would be all right. Even though she didn't know how it would go, if it turned nasty, it was mostly her fault, and Kaine was only treating her poorly because he felt betrayed. As for the other two, she didn't know whether he'd told them, or they were siding with Kaine because they liked him or he'd charmed them into doing it.

They stood ready, waiting for Devi's command for practice to begin. The older apprentices' muscles twitched, their familiars restless in the background. Jojo climbed into Paxton's tunic, making Samara feel far away from Ulrieg, even though she knew he wouldn't be far.

Paxton and Kaine eyed each other, shifting their weight on their feet rapidly, their fingers twitching. The tension was growing unbearable.

Samara.

She barely refrained from jumping when Ulrieg's voice entered her head.

What is it?

We have unwanted company coming.

I'm busy, Ulrieg. Get to the point.

A yellow snake and an orange monkey are waltzing

down the corridor. Oh, and Vexx and Kellam are following them.

The tension in her shoulders intensified, and her stomach roiled, making her want to retch. Before she could react, the senior commanders and their familiars entered the room.

The men stood on either side of the door, their feet shoulder-width apart and their arms crossed over their chests. Their familiars stopped beside them. Their gazes traveled over the apprentices and Devi before stopping on Samara.

"Respected senior commanders, what can we do for you?" Devi moved between the apprentices and the men.

"We are here for one person." Vexx straightened his tall frame.

"Oh. Who may that be?" Devi's voice was mostly calm, but it wavered slightly at the end.

Kellam's mouth twitched into a sadistic smile, and he pointed at Samara. "That one. Callista requested that we escort her to her office, and she didn't say in good condition." His grin widened.

Samara's knees shook. It seemed like overkill to send two senior sorcerers to escort her, a measly apprentice, up to see Callista.

Devi lifted her chin and shifted to stand in front of Samara. "Very well. Although I need to finish this lesson, which I require Samara to take part in, then I'll personally escort the apprentice up to the high sorceress myself."

Vexx shook his head. "No. We were told to bring her up."

"Respected sorcerers, I'm sure a few minutes won't make any difference to Callista. Now, you two look exhausted, and I'm sure you could use some rest after your long journey here. Why don't you catch up on some sleep? I promise to deliver her to Callista as soon as the lesson ends." She inclined her head.

Vexx pursed his lips. "I'm not keen on letting someone else take her, but I *am* tired." He looked at Kellam. "We can always have our fun later."

It took Kellam a while, but he eventually nodded. "All right. I guess we could let you do that."

Devi smiled widely. "Great! It's settled, then." She waved a hand. "Now, run along and get some much-needed rest, and you can check with Callista later to see if she has seen Samara."

Reluctantly, the two men left the room and disappeared down the corridor.

Samara breathed a sigh of relief only to be lifted into the air and smashed against the back wall, hitting her head. The room went black.

CHAPTER FORTY-ONE

A strange noise woke Samara, and she cracked open an eye. What she saw wasn't what she'd expected. Callista stood in the center of the room with her back arched, her arms spread wide above her head, and her long lilac hair cascading down her back. Samara had a clear side view of the head sorceress. She had her eyes closed and seemed to be soaking up unseen power.

Samara surveyed the room to see the four large pillars in the corners, three with large crystals sitting on top, the fourth still bare. She turned slightly to find a three-seater couch underneath her. Devi must have brought her to Callista's office, even though she had been knocked out.

Earlier in the year, that wouldn't have worried her, but lately, she didn't know whom to trust, and

she wasn't sure she liked the idea of being unconscious in a room with someone. She shook her head.
You're being paranoid, she told herself. After all, she
had just been unconscious, and nothing untoward
had happened to her, and despite the pain at the
back of her head, her brain function seemed
normal.

Ulrieg, are you around? Her head hurt when she
pushed the words out, but she had to know.

*Of course I am. Wingless flight! What kind of animal
companion would I be if I left you whenever you were
knocked unconscious?*

*I know you wouldn't leave me on purpose, grumpy. I
was only checking that you hadn't been knocked out and
taken somewhere else.*

*Nope. Kaine didn't know where I was. He sent some
spell at the wall that Ginger had been sniffing, but I was
already long gone before then. He was definitely trying to
hit me with something because he seemed disappointed
when he didn't hear a thud afterward.*

I'm so sorry.

It's not your fault.

Do you know what Callista wants? The head
sorceress hadn't moved.

Not a clue.

*Do you know whether I'm a prisoner here, or this is
where Devi left me because it was requested?*

I'm not entirely sure. But you're not tied up, so I guess you've just been left under Callista's care until you regain consciousness. Maybe she hopes her weird crystal ritual will heal you faster.

Good thought. Where are you, by the way?

I'm on the back of the couch. I can't move much because my talons might rip the leather cover.

Samara moved slowly and reached up, her hand brushing his rough scales. The feeling settled her heart. *Where's Mystique?*

She's outside, at her usual spot when Callista meets with the students.

And the evil sorcerers?

I haven't seen them since they were in the defense classroom.

Samara breathed a sigh of relief, moving slowly to avoid disturbing Callista but also because she wanted to watch her while she performed her strange worship of the crystals. The head sorceress's eyes remained closed. Her diadem circled her forehead. It felt weird to see the head sorceress looking almost relaxed. Her face was always unreadable, and this was the closest Samara had gotten to seeing her show emotion. Her leaf-patterned dress flowed to the ground, occasionally swaying when the sorceress moved. She was wearing her green dress, and it seemed to make her lilac hair glow, or maybe that was the energy of the crystals.

Samara looked closer, taking in the points of the golden diadem. She couldn't remember when Callista had appeared in public without it. From the side, she could see that the jewelry was raised slightly off her forehead. It looked like there were tiny crystals under specific points, and when she looked harder, they seemed to be different colors. Samara almost gasped at how genius it was.

What is it?

Callista has crystals under her diadem, basically pressing against her mind.

What's so great about that?

I imagine that because she's a crystal witch, that would give her even greater energy, and the power is almost connected directly to her mind. So not only does she soak up all the energy from these three crystals practically every day, but she also visits the powerful magic orb under the building as well as having crystals pressed directly onto her head. If she finds the other crystal and any other sacred trinket she's been hunting, she will become too powerful to overcome.

What about that bracelet that's on her wrist? That's new, isn't it?

Samara gaped at it. A purple stone was set in the middle of the gold. *Yes. It is. I wonder where she's been and if it's one of the sacred trinkets she's been searching for.*

Callista opened her eyes to see Samara gaping at the bracelet. She clasped her hand around the hard gold shape. "Do you like it?"

Samara looked from the bracelet into Callista's piercing blue eyes, unable to read the emotion in them. "Yes. It's beautiful. I haven't seen it before."

Her sharp blue eyes softened. "It's new. I picked it up on my last trip."

"Lovely." Samara did like the bracelet, but her mind was racing with all kinds of scenarios in which she could have acquired it, making it hard to sound genuine. "Did you buy it from a trader?"

Callista laughed, the sound surprising Samara. "No. I don't have to buy things like this. It was given to me as an offering by one of the humans at the village we visited. They knew it was one of the pieces I was looking for."

"Lovely!" Samara's voice fell flat.

Suddenly, she remembered what had happened with Kaine, making her stomach flip. For a moment, she had forgotten she had been summoned. She only hoped it wasn't because of him. She stood, her nervous energy taking over.

If Callista sensed her shift in emotions, she didn't say. "Why don't you sit down? I hear you received a nasty bump on the head. You must still be dizzy." She indicated the chair in front of her desk.

Samara sat, squeezing the leather padding on the arms as she worried.

The head sorceress sat on the opposite side and steepled her hands, resting her chin on the fingertips. "I called you here today because I wanted to see how you're coping with everything. There have been reports that you've been acting weird since you bonded with your familiar." She searched the room. "Where *is* your familiar? It's strange of Devi to bring you here without him."

Samara pressed her back against the chair. "Oh, I often leave Gray in my room to rest during the day. After all, he's a nocturnal animal and would rather be out at night to search for food."

Callista's eyes glinted before her gaze flicked around the room as though she was searching for something.

Samara stirred, uneasy, as she wondered if Callista was looking for Ulrieg. "As for acting strangely, I don't think I am. The coterie curriculum has become much more intense since I bonded with my familiar."

"What do you mean?" Callista touched her fingertips together in a wave motion.

"There have been harsher battles we've had to

participate in. The coterie seemed like a kinder place before the push to get familiars."

She tapped her index fingers against her mouth. "We did have to push you to get familiars. As you know, this isn't a charity. You have to earn your place and the provisions for your family. What do you mean by harsher battles? You had that one battle with the trolls to prove your worth before you bonded with your familiar."

Samara nodded. "Then we had that impromptu battle with one another that ended when Vexx and Kellam entered and defeated us harshly."

"Yes, that was rather unhelpful of them. Please forgive their methods. They lose themselves, forgetting where they are at times."

"All right. Then there is also the lesson with Zofia." Samara made sure her eyes stayed on the high sorceress's face.

"What do you mean?"

"When you were away this last time, Zofia led the apprentices with familiars and two of the older ones out of the group who don't have familiars yet to an ogre camp. She had us fight to the death. It was a hard enough battle for the older and stronger apprentices, but Henriette and Blade were far too inexperienced."

Callista pulled back, her hands gripping the

edges of her seat. "I didn't know about this challenge."

"Blade lost his life." Samara thumped the wooden desk with her fist. "We have only nineteen apprentices left." Samara thought the head sorceress's face had turned somber, although it was still hard for her to be sure.

Callista looked to the side. "I'll have to speak to Zofia to see what she was thinking."

"Shouldn't she be removed if she acted without your consent?" Samara's voice rose.

"I completely understand why you're upset, and I'm sure other students are as well."

"They certainly are."

"I will look into this and take disciplinary action if I find it's required." She looked Samara in the eye. "But you must also be aware of how difficult it is to find instructors with Zofia's expertise willing to teach young magic wielders."

"Can't you teach us instead?"

Something that almost looked like amusement flashed across her face. "Zofia is extremely experienced with weapons and is the best instructor I can find to teach you." She hooked a strand of hair behind her pointed ear. "But I'm disappointed that we lost an apprentice while I was away, and I will look into this."

It looks like that's the best you'll get at this stage.

Samara let out a sigh, knowing Ulrieg was right.

Callista narrowed her eyes on Samara. "I hear you've been sneaking out of the building every night and in the early-morning hours."

Samara gulped. "I thought we were allowed to leave the building at night, especially if we have nocturnal familiars."

"Yes, that's true. Although I hear you've been out most nights with a certain male apprentice. And there is concern that your relationship is disturbing your ability to learn and concentrate on becoming a stronger member of the coterie."

Samara's palms turned sweaty. "Oh, no. That's not why I'm going out at night. I promise you." The words came out in a rush. "Our relationship isn't like that."

"So you're saying you only go out so your familiar can hunt and spread his wings?" As Callista spoke, her gaze traveled throughout the room again as though she was looking for something.

She tried her hardest to sound sincere. "Yes. That's the only reason I go out."

"And you're not going out to have secret rendezvous?"

Samara scoffed. "I go out alone, and sometimes I

find others out there. But my main purpose is what I've already told you."

Callista's eyes were unnervingly set on Samara. "And does your familiar always want to hunt only at night?" The sorceress fiddled with her bracelet, fingering the stone and twirling the metal around her wrist.

The way she said *familiar* worried Samara, but she wouldn't give anything away freely.

"I guess that's the main time he likes to hunt. He hasn't told me any differently."

The head sorceress sat back, still fiddling with the bracelet. "All right. As long as that's all you're doing out there and not having unsavory relationships."

Samara shook her head, not knowing what to say.

The sorceress nodded. "Try not to make it a habit. You may go."

Samara stood to leave.

Her hand was on the doorknob when Callista called, "I'd like to meet your familiar one day and get to know him."

Samara frowned. Callista had already met Gray. "Sure."

CHAPTER FORTY-TWO

When Samara exited Callista's office, she headed straight to her room to check on Gray. Her room was dark and stuffy because the windows and curtains had been closed. She thought it must be about to rain. Ulrieg turned visible and ignited the sconce on the wall, which brightened the room. She rubbed Gray on his head and fed him a small treat before opening the curtains.

The darkness surprised her when she looked out the window. "How long was I unconscious, Ulrieg?"

Quite a while. You missed lunch, and it looks like you've also missed dinner.

Samara sighed. "I don't know about you, but Callista's conversation confused me. I wanted to check on Byzarid and Daena tonight to make sure they leave, but now if I go out, I'll probably lead more people to them. I can only hope Kaine won't go out to have a look and will keep it to himself and not tell people like Vexx and Kellam."

Ulrieg gasped.

"What is it?"

That's the last thing we all need. I should go out by myself to tell them to leave.

"I don't need you being in danger as well."

He shook his head and gave her a dubious look. *If I didn't know your head was spinning with worry, I'd think you were lacking a few brain cells. I can turn invisible, remember?*

Samara pushed his shoulder with her fist. "Aw, Ulrieg. You're so nice to me. Of course I remember. But my brain *is* still spinning, and I'm finding it hard to keep up."

Will you be all right if I leave you for a little while?

Samara lay back on her bed and let her boots hang off the side. "I don't think I should go anywhere at the moment. I don't trust my brain to get me out of tricky situations."

Good thinking. If you can open the window, I'll—

A knock at the door startled them both.

Ulrieg sniffed under the door before frowning at Samara. *I think it's all clear. I can't smell a fox.* He turned invisible to remain cautious.

Samara groaned as she sat up, then she plodded

over to the door and opened it a crack before swinging it wide. "Come in."

After a quick look over his shoulder, Paxton entered, and Samara closed the door behind him as Ulrieg turned visible.

"I know it's late. I'm sorry." Paxton peered around the room, finding Gray on his perch. "Did I wake you?" He frowned when he saw that Samara was still dressed in the clothes she had worn earlier.

Samara huffed. "To be honest, I have no idea what time it is. I've been unconscious all day and woke up in Callista's office."

Paxton grimaced. "Kaine was rather nasty with his attack. You hit the wall quite hard. Are you all right now?"

She nodded, and her head spun. "I think so, just a little dizzy. I think my brain worked well enough to sidestep Callista's questioning."

She did wonderfully. Ulrieg sounded proud.

"Thanks, Ulrieg." Samara wanted to hug him.

You dodged her questioning quite well. However, the conversation was interesting. He gave a smug side glance at Paxton.

"What does he mean?"

Samara sat and fiddled with her hands. "I don't know whether this is what Kaine told her, or she was trying to find out in a weird way what I was doing outside every night. She tried to say you and I were sneaking out to have an inappropriate relationship."

"Well, that's not bad." When he caught the strange look on Samara's face, he added, "I mean, that's what males and females our age are known to do when alone. So it's not an unrealistic line of thought."

Her embarrassment fading, Samara nodded. "True. But her questioning had me suspecting she was being cryptic." She sat on her bed and held up a finger. "Or I could be reading too much into it because of my guilt." She kicked off her boots. "Either way, I don't think it's a good idea for me to go out tonight to tell Byzarid and Daena to leave before Kaine gives away their location. Ulrieg was just about to leave on his own."

Paxton smiled at him. "You don't have to go."

What do you mean? I can't risk having my cousin and his helper be captured again, especially with Vexx and Kellam back.

"No, of course not. What I meant is that I've already gone out to tell them to leave. It's the middle of the night already."

Samara looked out the window as if that would help confirm the time.

Are they leaving? Ulrieg was almost climbing Paxton's leg in his eagerness.

Paxton's smile grew wider. "They had already left."

Are you sure they left, or were they taken?

Paxton sat on the chair, bringing his head closer to Ulrieg's level. "There was an image of a house made with sticks and leaves left under their boulder. To me, that means they're heading home."

Ulrieg jumped onto Paxton's lap then back down to the ground. *Yes!*

"Ow!"

Ulrieg's talons had dug through Paxton's pants.

Ulrieg grimaced. *Sorry.*

"That's all right, I guess." Paxton shook his head with disbelief before asking Samara, "How do you cope with his talons?"

Samara tugged at the gloves and extra leather straps tied to her arms and shoulders. "That's why I always have these on me. Between Ulrieg and Gray, my skin has no chance otherwise."

Paxton studied her gloves and arms.

Samara squirmed with self-consciousness under his gaze. When she turned to face away, she caught sight of Ulrieg's self-satisfied grin. She frowned at him. When her stomach growled, she was thankful for the distraction. "You didn't happen to bring any food with you, did you?"

"No, sorry. I was too focused on making sure Daena and Byzarid got away."

Samara shook her head. "Don't be sorry. It was the right thing to do. I can sneak down later and grab some food from the kitchen. Forgrac doesn't mind if I do it. But he hates it when people steal food, makes a mess of his kitchen, and don't clean it up. And I tell you he can get very grumpy."

CHAPTER FORTY-THREE

The bright sun shone through Samara's window, reflecting off the opposite wall. It hurt to open her eyes, and she squinted and struggled to get out of bed and close the curtains. Both Ulrieg and Gray preferred to be outside at night, and she didn't blame them. They were once wild animals, and she imagined she would want the same if she were one.

With the brightness gone, she wiped the sleep from her eyes, and the previous day's events came crashing back to the front of her mind. She grimaced. Her life had become extremely complicated.

She pulled on her clothes and prepared herself for another challenging day. She had snuck into the kitchen the previous night, somehow avoiding the snake and the monkey, and had also taken enough food to eat in the morning. Though Byzarid and Daena had gotten away before Kaine could give their location to someone wishing them harm, the morning had added a different concern to her list.

The first lesson for the day was weapons training. Samara couldn't remember a lesson with the weapons master that hadn't been gruesome in some way, and they seemed to be getting worse. Usually, Kaine sided with her. After what had happened, that partnership could become her worst nightmare.

Ulrieg watched her in silence, peering at her in a way that made her think he could read her thoughts.

She paused. "You're staring."

Some would call it observing. But call it what you wish. The dragon sat on the edge of her desk.

"It feels like staring to me."

He tilted his head to one side. *Does that bother you?*

Pursing her lips, she said, "It doesn't help me relax."

The dragon dropped to his stomach and rested his chin on his front talons. *Call it concerned observation. I'm merely reading your mood by watching your actions. We will work out how to deal with this.*

"One can only hope. There's a lot at stake no matter what direction I choose."

His red eyes filled with sadness. *I know. And I'm sorry. It's because of me that you're in this situation.*

Samara shook her head. "Don't apologize. If you hadn't come into my life, I might never have known what was happening throughout the kingdoms. I was so naive."

Yes, you were. He grinned.

"Will you have my back today?"

What sort of question is that? Of course I will. I'm sure Paxton will too. His grin broadened.

She shook her head in disbelief. "You'd like that, wouldn't you? I hate to disappoint, but I have too much going on to be interested in another confusing relationship."

I think you'll find it wouldn't be confusing with Paxton.

Rolling her eyes, Samara shrugged on her quiver, looped her bow over her shoulder, and took Gray off his perch. She scratched the owl on the back of his neck before heading out the door. Ulrieg's talons scraped the floor behind her.

When she reached the steps, Kellam's monkey was sitting on the railing overlooking the common room. When he turned to Samara, he hissed, showing off his large fangs. Samara recoiled.

I'd love to take a bite out of that monkey. He would never see it coming.

Ulrieg's voice helped her relax.

I wish you could. And the snake too. Keeping her eyes on the monkey, Samara slowly descended the stairs.

Something in the way he followed her with his eyes gave her the feeling that he was boasting. He appeared more confident than she remembered, and it made her uneasy.

In the corridors, the older apprentices headed for the front door, while the younger ones went in a different direction. Samara spotted Henriette following the younger apprentices and hoped Callista had spoken to Zofia, ensuring the younger ones had more training before being thrown into dangerous battles. If that was the case, then they'd been given a small win.

Her step lightened. At least that was one fewer person she had to worry about that day. A breeze ruffled her hair as Ulrieg flew over her down the stairs. He waited for her to catch up.

Long golden hair caught Samara's attention when Luna threw her head back in laughter. Kaine leaned in close, his arm wrapped over her delicate bare shoulders. The only thing breaking the connection was her bo staff, which was tucked into the back of her low-cut, figure-hugging fighting leathers.

Peadar followed close behind, his face downcast,

and Samara felt for him. Her own emotions were also wreaking havoc on her, but hers involved more than simple jealousy.

Straightening her back, she marched down the steps.

Paxton was already there when she reached the meeting area in the forest. Okak swooped low over his shoulder, and Paxton cradled Jojo in his palm then slid him into a pocket in his tunic when he spotted Gray.

Samara smiled apologetically, happy to see a friendly face among the senior apprentices.

Zofia weaved her way through the trees from the opposite side of the forest, Jet shadowing her. Her posture seemed hostile under her large cape. "Today, it's just the older students with familiars. It appears there have been complaints lodged over our last lesson." She spotted Samara, and her face darkened. "Because of this, we're having a typical lesson in this forest."

Mist groaned. "Does that mean that we're not allowed to cause injury?"

An evil grin passed over the weapons master's face. "Oh, no. Injury still applies. It's one of the mottos of this coterie that you don't learn if you don't experience pain. Although you can't use magic, as this is your weapons training." Her gaze landed on

Samara again. "That also means you can't charm any of your arrows while participating in this lesson."

"What about if they're already charmed?" After the harsh experience with the trolls, Samara had learned that she must always precharm several, if not all, of her weapons.

The weapons master's eyes narrowed. "If they are already charmed with magic, you may use them. But if I catch you using your magic on them while you are in my lesson from this day on, I will severely punish you." Her voice was low and menacing. "I have the ability to sense magic. And trust me—it won't be a pleasant experience for you."

Samara's stomach roiled. The way Zofia was singling out Samara, she guessed that Callista had told the weapons master that she had complained. Although she found it hard to believe she was the only one. Surely, one of the others must have said something. Maybe she was simply singling out Samara because she knew she'd spent time in Callista's office the previous day.

Mist's eyes lit up with excitement. As usual, she was keen to inflict pain on the others. Samara turned and caught Kaine looking at her with an evil glint in his eye. She hated weapons lessons at the best times, but now, she had an ally determined to be her enemy. Fighting him would make the experience worse. She encouraged Gray to move onto her hand then propelled him into the air. He shouldn't be anywhere near the fight.

Zofia continued. "All right. I'll give you a few minutes to prepare for the battle. The last one standing wins."

All the apprentices slid on their hoods to cover their brightly colored hair before they spread out. Some climbed trees, some hid in the bushes, and others dug holes and covered themselves with leaves.

Samara moved as far into the area's outskirts as possible, hoping she had passed all the others. After only a few moments, she'd lost track of where they had gone. She wished she could stay hidden until it was all over, but if she did that, she would have to face Zofia's wrath and battle the master. Besides, the familiars would probably find her and give away her location.

Jet roared, indicating the start of the battle. Samara hid in some brush, trying to blend in with the dried leaves. Preparing for an attack, she pulled an arrow from her quiver and held her bow, her eyes peeled for any sign of movement. Her hands shook. She hated hurting people as much as being hurt by them. Weapons training was a nasty lesson. They used to practice against logs and trees to enhance their weapons skills, but once they became older, the training had turned sadistic.

The leaves above her rustled. Gray was at the top of the tallest tree, but she was sure the rustling had come from somewhere closer. *Ulrieg, is that you?*

Yes. I've been watching Gray, and surprisingly, he wants to stick near you. That works out for me too. Then I can keep an eye on you.

A twig snapped several yards away, and Samara squatted lower.

Dragon moon! How did he get here so quickly?

Kaine crept through the trees, his handsome face twisted in a wicked grin as he gazed at the treetops. Ginger led the way, her nose working overtime as she tracked down the scent. Besides his familiar, he seemed to be alone.

I have a pretty good idea of how he tracked us this way.

Suddenly, Kaine grabbed a knife from the holster on his back and threw it at Gray.

CHAPTER FORTY-FOUR

Samara barely stifled a cry as the knife hit Gray, sending him careening off his branch. His motionless body fell to the ground. Samara could do nothing, and she slammed her hand over her mouth, realizing she hadn't actually held in her cry. She searched for Kaine but was unable to find him where he'd been only moments before. She stayed low, checking all around her to try to pinpoint where he'd gone.

Her heart cried for Gray. She hoped it looked worse than it was. *Where did he go? Can you see him, Ulrieg?*

The dragon grunted. *Wait a moment, and I'll have a look.* He groaned. *You'll be happy to know that Gray is alive but injured. I hope it's something he can recover from. I caught him before he hit the ground. The knife handle hit him, not the blade.*

Thank you, Ulrieg. That's good news.

Something hard pressed against Samara's throat through her cloak. "There you are. I've already taken out your fake familiar. Now, where's your real one?" He pulled her up.

Samara couldn't see past her hood, although she would know that voice anywhere. "Kaine, we need to talk." With his knife pressed against her throat, she wasn't sure how far he would go. She'd never seen him angry.

"I think it's a little late for that. I gave you ample opportunity to open up and explain things to me and invite me along to your secret getaways, but you only wanted to involve Paxton—the quiet know-it-all. Ginger has been telling me for weeks that you were hiding something big, and for some reason, I didn't believe her. It's a huge shock to discover that my female fox was correct." He began dragging her backward.

"It wasn't anything against you, Kaine. I told you I didn't tell anyone. Paxton finding out was mainly because he did his own research."

"And what about me? I conducted my own research as well. I sent Ginger along, and she found out the truth for me. Yet you still didn't want to include me." The blade pressed harder against her neck. "It's a shame we're not supposed to kill in these lessons. Sometimes, I think it would make me feel better. Maybe I could slip and apologize later instead of seeking approval."

Ginger sniffed and moved off to the left as though following a scent.

"Wonderful. Ginger says she can smell that strange creature you have as your familiar. Let's go follow her." He pushed her forward with the knife still pressed against her neck. "I'd like to see this strange creature for myself."

Samara tripped on a root, and the blade cut through her cloak and grazed her skin. Her neck stung, and warmth trickled over her shoulder.

"Oops. You'll have to be more careful. I'd hate to explain how I accidentally killed you."

Something thudded softly behind them, and Kaine faltered before the knife pulled away. Then another thump sounded.

Samara turned around to find Kaine lying face-first on the ground, a small stick protruding from his calf through his cloak.

Grinning, Paxton held a small hollow tube. "I thought they might come in handy one day, especially since no one knew I was training with them."

"What is it?"

He held up the tube. "They're small darts you fire by blowing with your mouth. I've dipped the tip of the dart in sleeping potion."

"So you're saying he's still alive?"

"Unfortunately, yes. But he should be unconscious long enough to miss the rest of this lesson. Oh." He jumped into action, quickly loading the tube with a dart and firing it. The tiny dart landed in Ginger's rear end, and the fox yowled before dropping to the ground.

Wingless flight! That was close. I hadn't finished looking after Gray yet. Ulrieg turned visible several yards away. He was holding the unconscious Gray in his talons.

Paxton raced over and gently took the owl before setting to work healing him.

"Thanks, Paxton." Samara placed a hand on his shoulder. "Kaine didn't kill him, which would have been a deliberate. He's very skilled with his knives. He probably felt sorry for my fake familiar, but I don't know his intention for me."

A noise that sounded out of place in a forest came from several yards away, and their heads shot up.

I'll take a look.

Ulrieg turned invisible again, and the wind from his wings brushed the top of Samara's hood and over her face. She pulled out a new arrow and nocked it, waiting for Ulrieg's report.

It's Peadar. He's relieving himself.

Samara frowned. *What do you mean?*

Seriously? You're going to make me describe it?

Why are you making this a big deal? Just tell me what you mean by relieving him—oh. Never mind. I understand.

She crept forward, startling when Ziggy jumped from behind a tree and started chattering frantically.

A tall figure shifted behind him, the hood slipping to expose bright-yellow hair. Peadar's face paled when he spotted Samara's arrow pointing at him.

"Sorry, Peadar." She released the arrow, which hit him in the thigh, making him freeze.

Ziggy's eyes turned wild, and his chatter intensified before a slight whistle passed through the air, and the raccoon fell to the ground.

Paxton moved next to Samara. "I'm glad I made this. It's making fighting a lot easier." He smiled at her. "I learned a couple of tricks from a friend and improvised to make my own version, but mine are laced with potions, not magic."

Samara smiled back. Paxton was quickly growing

to be a loyal friend. The thought of having to go against each other in this challenge was going to be difficult. Even harder than going against Kaine in the past. She looked back over her shoulder. "How's Gray?"

"He's resting. I've healed his bones and any internal bruising. Ulrieg is putting him in a safe place until the challenge is over."

"Thanks again." She watched him for a moment. "I don't know how I'm going to go against you when it comes to it."

He held up his dart shooter. "We have ways that won't hurt each other as much. Another reason I'm glad I created this."

A noise sounded some distance behind them, and Samara spun to investigate while Paxton remained facing the inner section of the challenge. Her gaze traveled rapidly from tree trunk to tree trunk, stopping at the bushes between. *Ulrieg, can you see anyone?*

I'll take flight now and have a look.

Keeping her eyes peeled for movement, Samara waited for Ulrieg to report back, keeping her arrow nocked.

Don't shoot!

Who is it? Samara pressed her back against Paxton's.

The disbelief in Ulrieg's voice was palpable. *It's Daena.*

Really? Is Byzarid with her?

No. And she looks disheveled. I thought Paxton said they'd left for their homes.

Softly, Samara asked, "You said Daena and Byzarid left a message to say they'd gone home, didn't you?"

"Yes. Why?"

"Apparently, Daena is heading in our direction, alone and looking unkempt."

Paxton turned as Daena peered around a large tree. Her face was dirty and her clothes torn, like she had been crawling through the mud.

"Daena! What's going on? I thought you left for home," Paxton said.

Looking disoriented, she nodded and stumbled toward them. "Thank the moon! I've found you."

Samara studied the bushes behind her, hoping to find a brown dragon. "Where's Byzarid?" She embraced her, helping hold her up by the arms.

Daena ran a hand through her matted hair before giving up and hooking some blond strands behind her ear. "We were leaving when we spotted our captors hauling a couple of bound dragons toward your building. Byzarid got emotional. I did, too, but I told him we should stay away from that building and get some help." Scales began flashing on her skin. "I told him we should camp for the night and come back to see if we could find you in the morning." She clawed at the changing skin on her arm. "He agreed with me, and we went to sleep, but when I woke up at first light, he was gone." She dug her fingernails into her hand before looking up and pointing behind them. "Who's that?"

Samara spun, nocking the arrow still in her hand, and fired it at the first thing that moved. The cloaked figure dropped to the ground unconscious, and she saw the face briefly. It was Luna.

Her rabbit hopped out of the shadows, and Paxton shot her with his dart, putting her to sleep.

When Samara turned to face Daena, the elf was scratching her face.

"I'm so sorry. I was supposed to look after him, and he's gone. I don't even know how to find him."

Ulrieg had turned visible and crawled on the ground behind her, his eyes filled with worry.

Daena spun and dropped to her knees before him. "I'm so sorry."

When Ulrieg looked at Samara, her heart melted over the worry whirling in them. "We'll go as soon as we can. I promise. If we go now, we'll find ourselves in more danger than if we do it discreetly after the lesson."

Ulrieg was too distraught for words, and Daena groveled by his side.

Paxton placed a hand on the dragon elf's shoulder. "Relax. Sleep. You aren't going to find him like this." Daena crumpled to the ground, her breathing steady and deep.

Together, they placed her under a thick shrub with Gray.

"We need to finish this challenge quickly and find an unguarded key," Samara said.

I'll find the key. You two finish the challenge and somehow distract the senior commanders.

As Ulrieg turned invisible, a loud thump sounded.

Samara turned just in time to see Paxton fall face-first to the ground, his legs tied together by a rope connected to two balls. His arms were also bound to his sides in the same fashion.

Samara blinked. She hadn't seen anyone in the senior apprentices use those ropes as weapons. She searched for the person responsible, pulling out an arrow and nocking it. The only apprentice left in the competition should be Mist, and ropes weren't her style. She usually preferred a more destructive method.

Paxton groaned, and blood poured from his nose.

Ulrieg, can you see anyone? Samara's eyes were wide as she trained her poised arrow toward any noise.

No. Nothing out of the ordinary. Wait. Hang on. There's a figure coming from the south, and it's not Mist.

How do you know?

Because they're a lot more petite and less muscular than her. Oh. That explains a lot.

What does? Panic rose in her. She hated being unable to see everything around her but was glad to have Ulrieg by her side, and his eyes were sharper than hers.

A petite figure cut through the trees, heading straight for them. Long locks of purple hair tumbled out of the hood.

Samara lowed her bow. "Weapons Master. What's going on?"

Zofia's face was hard and unforgiving. "This one has been using magic, even though it's forbidden in this class."

Blood drained from Samara's face. "Yes. But he was only healing my familiar. He wasn't using it to go against anyone."

Zofia's eyes narrowed. "Why would he want to heal your familiar? You're supposed to be fighting each other."

"I don't think it's something he can help. He hates seeing animals hurt."

Zofia shook her head. "Doesn't matter. He shouldn't be healing anyone or their familiars during the competition. He should have waited."

"Maybe he didn't think Gray would make it. He was in very bad shape."

Zofia grabbed the ropes tied around Paxton's back and yanked him up. Paxton groaned as he struggled to get his footing.

"You're coming with me. You're disqualified from this competition, and I'll have an extra punishment for you later."

CHAPTER FORTY-FIVE

Dumbfounded, Samara watched helplessly as Zofia dragged Paxton out of the forest. He didn't struggle, as that would only make his punishment worse. He cast a last glance over his shoulder at Samara.

Letting her arms fall by her sides, Samara wondered what Zofia had in mind for him and hoped the punishment wouldn't be too severe, although she didn't know anymore when it came to the coterie.

A noise sounded behind her. She thought it was Ulrieg, but then came the sound of metal sliding. She spun to find Mist holding her sword high, ready to swing at her. Samara dodged, feeling the sword's breeze as it glided past her. It was strange that Ulrieg hadn't warned her she was coming.

Mist spun, her sword aiming straight for Samara's abdomen. Being so close to Mist put Samara at a disadvantage. Arrows couldn't be used at close range, and she had no other weapons. She would lose the fight if she didn't think of something quickly.

Mist swung again, her muscular arms rippling with every movement. The female warrior attacked her again and again. Samara's breathing became ragged as she dodged each strike.

Wingless flight! I can't leave you for a moment before you manage to get yourself into trouble.

Some warning would have been nice. Samara grunted as she dodged another swing. *Where have you been?*

I was seeing where Zofia was taking Paxton.

Mist shrieked, straining her neck to find what had attacked her. Ulrieg must have struck her from above. Okak cried in the distance, his caws growing closer. With Mist distracted momentarily, Samara remembered the small knife she'd attached to her quiver. She used it to craft additional arrows if needed, so it wasn't a proper weapon, but any pointy object would have to do. She unhooked her quiver and grabbed the knife before returning the quiver to her back. Even if she couldn't use the arrows, the quiver would bring additional protection from the slice of the sword.

Ulrieg dug his talons into Mist's shoulders again then pulled away before she could swipe her sword at him.

"Where is that familiar of yours?" Mist shrieked.

"He's just very good at hiding."

Okak swooped toward Samara before landing on a nearby branch. Her upper arm stung, and when she looked, a long, deep scratch ran across her flesh, blood oozing from it. The crow cawed and jumped on the branch, seeming to search for Gray. With the additional pair of eyes, Ulrieg couldn't attack freely without raising suspicion. But at least with the way Mist was questioning Samara, she didn't think Kaine had told her about Ulrieg.

The crow struck again, and while she was distracted and trying to get away from the attack, Mist charged at her with her sword.

Samara sidestepped too late, earning a slice on her hip. She chanced a quick look and felt sick at the sight of the blood flowing freely down her side. Mist lunged again, and Samara dodged, plunging her small knife into Mist's ribs. Mist gritted her teeth, spun, and attacked again, hitting Samara from behind and slicing the back of her thigh.

Ulrieg dug his claws into Mist's back.

Stop, Ulrieg. I don't need you to be exposed.

I have to do something to help you. I can't just watch you be hurt.

You're going to have to. Besides, she's not supposed to hurt me so much that I'll have permanent damage.

And like I trust this coterie to look after its members.

Samara tried to sound upbeat despite the pain and fear that engulfed her. *I will be healed. Hold back. We need to keep your secret as long as possible.*

Mist attacked again, and Samara dodged, slicing her underarm with the knife, disabling the arm. When Mist switched the sword to her other hand, she wielded it with almost as much skill as she did with the right. That didn't surprise Samara.

When Mist moved forward again, Samara twirled, aiming for an unguarded spot to stab her. As she spun, Mist quickly flipped the sword and changed directions before Samara could react accordingly, and she hit her head with the sword's handle, knocking her forward several yards before she slumped to the ground. Her face smacked into the dried leaves, and her teeth cracked on a tree root before everything went black.

～

WARM HANDS CUPPED HER HEAD, filling her with comfort. When she opened her eyes, she met Paxton's, which were filled with worry. She blinked and took a better look. Deep bruises lined his eyes. She tried to retreat from his touch.

He frowned. "No, you don't. You received a nasty blow to the head. I'm making sure it's healing."

She remained but wasn't going to do it quietly. "What about you? You look like you've been punched in the eyes. You need just as much healing as I do."

Gently, he touched the skin around his eyes. "They're hurt and probably look bad, but the bruises will go away eventually."

"What happened?"

"Zofia taught me a lesson the hard way."

She gaped. "Just for healing competitors?"

He nodded.

"That's not fair. You weren't using your magic to win."

He shrugged. "She said no magic and meant that in its totality."

"Then you should be healing yourself, not me."

"I'll need to find a healer. My healing doesn't work very well on me."

Samara felt bad as he continued to work on her

wounds after he was satisfied that her head had healed. "How long was I unconscious?"

"Quite a while. You missed lunch." He nodded to a plate on a small table near her. "I managed to pick you up a few things."

Samara realized she was in the healing room. "Shouldn't Artemise be looking after both of us?"

"She was busy with some potions and didn't see our injuries as urgent." He shrugged. "That's all right. You're nearly healed, and mine look worse than they are."

Samara gave him an incredulous look and gently touched under one eye. "I don't know. It looks pretty bad. What makes you think it's not?"

He tugged at a leather strap that dangled under his tunic and leaned closer, keeping his voice low. "Because I managed to visit Eliphas's greenhouse and pinch this, and I've gone for a quick trip underground."

Are there captives under there? Ulrieg asked, giving away that he was in the room.

Sadly, Paxton replied, "I couldn't go into the cave."

What do you mean? Couldn't you open the door?

"I opened it slightly, but cloaked figures were circulating through the room. If I'd entered, I would have been in danger and no good to anyone."

Disappointment filled Ulrieg's voice. *Wingless flight! That's exceptionally unhelpful, but I understand. We'll have to go back later.*

"Yes, we will." Paxton shoved the strap back into his pocket.

"Won't Eliphas miss his key?" Samara asked, her eyes fixed on the pocket that held the leather strap.

Paxton shook his head. "To be honest, Eliphas doesn't seem to care about it, although I will return it as soon as we don't need it, just in case."

Samara nodded.

Did you hear any signs of captives?

Paxton's mouth dropped at the edges. "There were cries of pain from creatures that could have been dragons. I think there were other people in the smaller rooms with them."

Samara's jaw dropped. "Seriously?"

"I think so."

"Could you see who the cloaked figures were?"

Paxton removed his hands from Samara, apparently satisfied that she was healed enough, and handed her the plate of food. She bit into some dried meat.

"There were three. I couldn't see one, but another was Vexx, and the third was more of a surprise."

Samara swallowed her mouthful, her eyes fixed on Paxton. "Who was it?"

"It was our lovely, caring Zofia."

Samara leaned back against her pillow. "That would explain a lot."

CHAPTER FORTY-SIX

Waiting for the day to pass was painful. Paxton had healed Samara enough for her to return to her room with Ulrieg. As soon as she regained her strength, she returned to the forest to find Gray and Daena. She hoped neither would be disoriented or confused if they woke up in the strange place.

When she and Ulrieg arrived, Daena was awake, sitting crossed-legged and cradling Gray in her arms. The owl was still peacefully asleep. Hearing them approach, Daena looked up. The dragon elf's skin was filled with gray scales. She must be a wreck, worrying about Byzarid.

"Is he still asleep?" Samara gently stroked the soft gray feathers of the owl's wing.

Daena nodded, carefully handing him to her. "Have you heard anything about Byzarid?"

Samara shook her head. "I've been unconscious for most of the day. Paxton did visit the underground cave, but he couldn't go in because the captors were there. Although he said there were sounds of pain and distress that he thought might be coming from a dragon."

The gray on Daena's skin grew more prominent as she looked at the ground.

Ulrieg moped not far from her.

Samara placed a hand on her leg. "It's not your fault. There's nothing only one person could do. Even Ulrieg knows that. We'll go down to the catacombs late tonight. Maybe all the captors will be gone by then, and we can rescue the dragons."

"I'll come and help." Daena's eyes were hopeful.

"I don't know if that's a good idea. We're going to be in enough danger if we get caught. If you get caught, too, I imagine it will be worse for you."

Daena raised her chin. "I want to help. Now that Kaida is gone, I don't have anything else to live for."

Hesitating, Samara stroked Gray's feathers. "I guess you can come. I'm not happy about you being in danger, but I understand that your bond with Kaida was powerful, so much so that it affected your physical body. Wait for us at the edge of the forest near the outside entrance to the catacombs. Do you remember where that is?"

Daena nodded. "I can't see your building, but I know the plain it was in and which side of the plain the entrance was on."

"All right. We could use some help if there are dragons to carry out. Make sure you stay hidden and out of danger. We'll probably head down when the moon is high." Samara rose to her feet, carefully cradling Gray. "Take care. I don't want to find you down there as well."

CHAPTER FORTY-SEVEN

Sneaking down the stairs, Samara barely avoided the yellow snake as it lay over one of the steps. Seeing it at the last second, she skipped the step, using the support of the railing, and almost rolled her ankle on the next step. Gray flew to the balustrade, out of the way. The snake coiled, and unsure whether it would strike, Samara descended the stairs quickly. She rounded a corner into a side corridor, only to be confronted by Kellam's orange monkey. Opening its mouth wide, it hissed, and Samara backed away. She was getting bad vibes about visiting the catacombs that night, but she didn't want to wait any longer in case they did something to the dragons. She would just have to be extra cautious.

She pretended to head to the dining hall, acting

like she was out for a feed rather than going for a late-night stroll.

I'm going to check ahead to see if there are any more nasty surprises. Ulrieg's wings pushed a soft breeze over her as he flew toward the door.

Samara waited near the dining hall, straining her ears for any strange noises from wayward familiars heading her way. They didn't seem to be following her. Still, that didn't put her at ease. She needed the way out the front door cleared more than other places in the building. Even though there was a way to access the catacombs inside the building, it would be far more dangerous than the outside access. It was almost as though the senior commanders weren't aware of the exterior entry. Her mind spun. *Perhaps that's the way that the familiars are guarding, and they're not worried about my leaving through the front door,* she thought.

Ulrieg, is the way to the front clear?

Almost. Mystique is at her usual place, and Jet appears to be sleeping in a corridor not far away.

Can you see the snake or the monkey?

They seem to be staying close to where you encountered them.

Samara returned to the common room and softly called Gray, who was still perched on the railing. "Come on, Gray. We need to get you out hunting."

It felt good to see the owl conscious, and although he had been fed, he seemed to understand that they needed him, and he always enjoyed his temporary freedom. He spent a moment glaring down at the snake, and Samara wondered if he was about to hunt it. After all, snakes were part of an owl's diet. But he finally flew down to Samara and landed on her outstretched hand.

Quietly, she sidestepped around the corridor Jet was sleeping in and approached Mystique. Callista's words about her suspicious nighttime strolls filled her thoughts, and her heart quickened as she wondered if Mystique would let her through.

The black jaguar shifted out of the dark corner, her eerie yellow eyes studying Samara as she approached.

Samara placed Gray on her shoulder. "Hello, Mystique. I'm just going out to let Gray catch food for the night."

The large cat shifted and sat directly in front of the door, her eyes never leaving Samara and Gray.

When the uncomfortable silence lasted a long time, she asked again, "Do you mind if we pass so he can roam free for a few hours and catch a meal? I'm sure you appreciate those times you can do the same."

Mystique stayed where she was, eventually

beginning to groom herself. Samara didn't know if that meant she could pass or not.

Ulrieg grumbled, *This is taking too long. Try to walk around her and see what happens.*

She'd probably eat me, Samara quipped. *Then that would eliminate one troublesome apprentice.*

I'd step in and fight for you.

I'm not at all feeling comfortable. Samara tried her luck as Ulrieg had suggested.

Mystique lunged to the side. The movement caused Samara to jump several feet away, and she received a smug look from the large cat. It almost looked as though the jaguar was tormenting her on purpose.

Frowning, Samara continued toward the front door then closed it quickly behind her when she felt the breeze from Ulrieg's wings passing through. She wiped her brow, and her arm came away with beads of sweat. Fighting the urge to run down the stairs and hide, she allowed her eyes to focus in the darkness, studying every shadow possible.

When she reached the bottom of the stairs, she raised Gray and propelled him into the air. The owl instantly headed toward the forest.

Ulrieg, I need you to watch for foxes and anyone else out here. We cannot risk being caught tonight. The new captives and possibly Byzarid rely on us.

I'm already scouring the outskirts and the building surroundings.

Despite being shrouded in darkness, Samara sneaked past the windows and headed to the hole. When something moved on the outskirts of the forest, she startled.

Daena crept toward her, Paxton by her side, and Ulrieg landed near the hole not long after, turning visible when he was out of the building's sight.

Quickly, they descended into the underground, Paxton pulling the torch off the wall and leading the way down the tunnel.

Ulrieg paused, cowering against the wall.

"Are you all right?" Samara squatted and placed a hand on his wing. He felt cold.

He groaned and placed a talon on his head. *Something's not right. The power from the orb is different. It's making me feel sick, and my head is throbbing.*

"You can stay here if you like. There should be enough of us to carry some captives out." She placed her other hand on him, injecting some healing powers into him.

Paxton handed the torch to Daena, squatted by Ulrieg's head, and placed his hands on his head, closing his eyes.

Ulrieg relaxed slightly, although his body shook.

"Do you feel better?" A frown creased Paxton's face.

Ulrieg's expression looked tortured. *A little but not really.*

"Then you should stay here. It will probably only become worse the closer you get." Samara caressed his wing, slowly placing it by his side.

No. I'm coming. I'll push through it. You lot go ahead, and I'll follow at my own pace.

Samara didn't like the idea, but they had to make the most of their visit while they were there. If Ulrieg felt like that, she could only imagine what the other dragons were feeling.

Slowly, they pressed forward. When they reached the door, Paxton pulled the key from around his neck, and he and Samara worked together to open the lock. After a soft click, they pushed the door open a few inches, enough for the bright-orange light of the orb to illuminate the catacombs. Paxton placed the torch in the sconce, and Samara peeked through to assess the cave and see if anyone was in it. She blinked, blinded for a moment, unsure whether it was because of the darkness of the corridor or the orb was indeed shining brighter than it had before.

After careful observation, she was confident that no one was in the large cave. She pushed the door open fully, giving the other two access, then closed it most of the way, leaving enough space for Ulrieg to move through later or for them to see the dark crack leading them out of the cave in case they needed to go in a hurry.

They tiptoed into the cave. Uneasiness sat in the pit of Samara's stomach. Not only had something made Ulrieg sick, but it was deathly quiet. There was no moaning or groans of pain. She hoped all the captives were asleep and had been given a reprieve from their torture.

"Is it me, or is this orb glowing brighter than before?" Paxton whispered.

"I was thinking the same thing when we were at the door. Maybe it is glowing brighter if both of us noticed it." The thought filled her with unease as she passed the large, glowing sphere half sunken in the ground.

With the bright light behind her, she noticed a mark on the floor. She shifted toward it, keeping an eye out for any movement. As she narrowed in on the spot, she noticed more marks of different sizes. Squatting, she wiped her fingers over the first one, only to find a long smear trailing her fingers. She blinked in disbelief. "This looks like blood."

Uneasy, she stood and followed Paxton as he pressed forward, following the trail into one of the smaller caves. He paused at the door, and Samara bumped into him then froze.

Daena peered over her shoulder into the room and gasped. "They've taken her heart!"

Paxton moved into the room. His body was rigid as he investigated the black dragon's body, which was the same size as Ulrieg's. His face pale, he nodded at Samara. "The heart is gone. I'd say that's what the trail is from."

Samara pulled back and went to another room. On the table lay a still form of a gray dragon, slightly smaller than Ulrieg. He was also lying on his back, tied down with his heart removed. A tear trickled down her face, and Daena grasped the wall to hold herself steady. There was nothing they could do. Paxton wouldn't be able to heal dead dragons.

Trying to pull herself together, knowing they had to get out of there as soon as possible, Samara went into another room. She breathed a sigh of relief when that one was empty.

Paxton went to a room in the other direction, only to stop short at the door again. All color drained from his face.

When Samara rejoined him, he spoke only loudly enough for her to hear him. "They must have been a family."

Daena went to another room and moved on

when she found it empty. Samara and Paxton went to the third dragon. He was tied down to the table, his teeth bared and his eyes wide with terror. It seemed the hearts had been removed while the dragons were alive.

Samara leaned her head against Paxton's shoulder, and he placed a hand comfortingly on hers. She was starting to lose hope. Even after all this time, there hadn't been any groans of pain or noises to tell them a dragon was still alive.

A distressing cry sounded through her head, and she looked for Ulrieg and wondered if he was in trouble. She couldn't see him, so she searched the remaining rooms. After the third door, she found Ulrieg on one of the tables, hunched over a dragon's body. She rushed to his side to study the dragon underneath him, each step filling her with dread. The dragon was brown and tied by all four legs to the table. She held her breath, hoping he wasn't the dragon it looked like.

CHAPTER FORTY-EIGHT

"Oh, Ulrieg. It's not him."

Ulrieg's front legs were shaking as he cradled the dragon. *No. But it's his sister. I don't know how I'm going to tell him.*

Samara gently pressed his head against her chest, carefully avoiding his horns. "I'm so sorry. No wonder Byzarid was so determined to rescue the dragons that he didn't even wait to tell us."

Ulrieg's breathing was ragged.

"Come on. We have to go before we get caught."

Ulrieg stiffened, and Samara thought she had upset him until he looked at her, his eyes wide. Within his arms, the dragon moved. It was only slightly, but it was enough.

Quickly, Samara started unlocking the cuffs. "Tell the others. Hurry!"

Paxton and Daena entered the room in a matter of moments. Samara pulled the sheet from her quiver pack and spread it on the floor. Without needing instruction, Daena and Paxton lifted the dragon off the table, cradled her in the sheet, and carried her out of the cave.

Samara got Ulrieg to climb onto her back. "At least Byzarid could be out there somewhere. We'll keep looking."

As they closed the door to the orb's room, both sadness and hope filled Samara.

THE END

~~~~~

THANK you for reading Dragon Heart. If you have a few minutes, I'd love for you to leave a review or rating on Amazon. Your feedback helps to spread the word about my books.

YOU CAN FIND the next book here: Dragon Breeze

ACKNOWLEDGMENTS

I'm touched by the enormous support I have received from my immediate family. My husband has been a helpful first reader and, at times, been an excellent motivator, with hints of ideas to help me through the blanks. The support from my three sons has also been overwhelming. They have spent years putting up with my head in the clouds, thinking about the next plot twist or story, along with many hours spent working on my books and keeping in touch with my readers.

A huge thank you to my editor, Susie D., for her editing and writing tips, and my proofreader, Kim H., for picking up the things we missed.

Thank you to all of my readers who have loved my work, and continue to read my stories.

BOOKS BY KATRINA COPE

Pre-Teen Books

The Sanctum Series

JAYDEN'S CYBERMOUNTAIN

SCARLET'S ESCAPE

TAYLOR'S PLIGHT

ERIC & THE BLACK AXES

ADRIANNA'S SURGE

~~~~~

Young Adult Urban Fantasy

Afterlife Series

FLEDGLING

THE TAKING

ANGELIC RETRIBUTION

DIVIDED PATHS

TRUTH HUNTER

Afterlife Novelette

THE GATEKEEPER

~~~~~

Young Adult Urban Paranormal Fantasy

Supernatural Evolvement Series

(Associated with the Afterlife Series)

WITCH'S LEGACY (Prequel)

AALIYAH

~~~~~

Young Adult Norse Mythology Fantasy

Valkyrie Academy Dragon Alliance

MARKED (Prequel)

CHOSEN

VANISHED

SCORNED

INFLICTED

EMPOWERED

AMBUSHED

WARNED

ABDUCTED

BESIEGED

DECEIVED

Thor's Dragon Rider

SAFEGUARD

PURSUIT

ENTRAPMENT

HOODWINKED

RELINQUISHED

SHROUDED

ASSIGNED

ACCOSTED

DESTRUCTION

~~~~~

Young Adult Epic Fantasy

<u>Dragoria: the Lost Dragon Realm</u>

DRAGON MOON

DRAGON HEART

DRAGON BREEZE

Get updates & notifications of giveaways

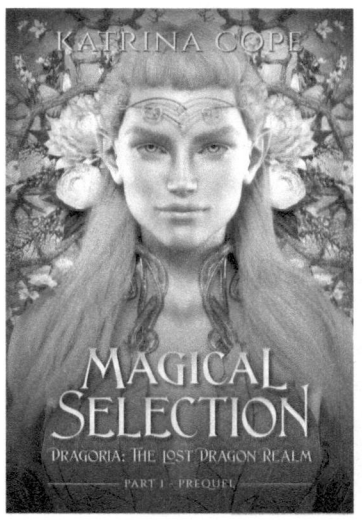

Would you like a FREE ebook?

Click here to get started: FREE copy of Magical Selection

Through this link you can sign up for my newsletter and receive a FREE copy of Magical Selection plus updates about my fantasy books, sales and notification of giveaways.

ABOUT THE AUTHOR

Katrina is an author of several books in epic fantasy, young-adult fantasy, and a middle-grade sci-fi thriller series.

Her series include:

Dragoria: The Lost Dragon Realm - Coming of Age High/Epic fantasy

Valkyrie Academy Dragon Alliance - YA High fantasy

Thor's Dragon Rider - YA High fantasy (Spin-off of Valkyrie Academy Dragon Alliance but can be read separately)

The Afterlife - YA fantasy (contemporary)

The Sanctum Series - Middle-grade Sci-fi thriller

She often talks to creatures of all kinds and has a passion for animals, nature, and travel. She lives in Queensland, Australia, with her husband and has survived teaching her three children how to drive.

Katrina's online home is at www. katrinacopebooks.com

You can connect with Katrina on:

tiktok.com/@katrinacopebooks

facebook.com/Author.Katrina.Cope

instagram.com/katrina_cope_author

bookbub.com/profile/katrina-cope

twitter.com/Katrina_R_Cope

pinterest.com/katrinacope56